Reader's Comments

I found the book to be an excellent way to learn more about the Deaf-World and understand different perspectives around the navigation of relevant issues. Students would benefit from reading this book because it presents issues around Deaf and oral approaches in a compelling and contemporary story format.

Dr. Hayley S. Arnold, CCC-SLP
Associate Professor | Speech-Language Pathologist
Kent State University

This book is wonderfully written, with current terminology and explanations woven into the story. This novel would be a great addition to any new or current ASL student interested in learning more about the Deaf community and their ties to each other. Combined, the four co-authors have worked in the field of Deaf Studies and ASL for decades in a variety of capacities. Their expertise and passion for the Deaf community are felt throughout this book. It is written with the utmost compassion, love and respect that they have for the Deaf Community and ASL.

Kim Bass, MS, NIC
ASL Coordinator and Assistant Professor of Instruction
ASLA Faculty Advisor
The University of Akron

A good read and informative. Shows that deaf people are no different than hearing people.

Brandon Childers,
Cuyahoga Community College student

Signs Are Everywhere is a must read if you are new to the Deaf Community as I am. It is a wonderful insight to the lives of the deaf and hearing impaired. From beginning to the end you are immersed into a world of discovery, adaptation, and the joy of success.

Kenneth Darby,
Cuyahoga Community College student

The book *Signs Are Everywhere* presents a modern insight into Deaf Culture and into the lives of deaf/Deaf individuals. With a multitude of points-of-view, *Signs Are Everywhere* provides invaluable information to aid ASL Interpreting students and parents of deaf children on their journey in the Deaf-World.

Kate Giet,
Kent State University graduate, 2021

From beginning to end this book was absolutely incredible! Coming from a hearing family this was a unique and intimate view into some of the many struggles non-hearing families face. Hearing or not I definitely recommend this spectacularly eye-opening book!

Josiah Hull,
Cuyahoga Community College student

An endearing story giving insight into Deaf culture from the perspective of both hearing, and deaf people. Through a dynamic plot line, and diverse group of characters, the book touches on the challenges of adoption, fame, and immersing yourself in a new community. A must read for ASL students, new parents to a deaf child, or anyone learning about Deaf culture.

Micayla O'Keefe,
Cuyahoga Community College student

SIGNS ARE EVERYWHERE

An Ohio Collaborative Project
Powered by the Deaf and ASL/English
Interpreting Communities

Written by
Stefanie Amiruzzaman, Patricia Bettis-Eddie,
Marsha Moore, Leah Subak

with
Jeanne Dutton

and
Cathy Alznauer, Jimmy Beldon Jr., Vivian King Brown,
Kathy Geething, Lucas Hamilton,
Clara Jean Mosley Hall, Randall Hogue,
Tina J. Perry, Carole Stacker

May 2022

SIGNS ARE EVERYWHERE

ISBN: 978-0-578-26783-8

Dedication

For Deaf, deaf, hard of hearing, DeafBlind, Deaf Plus, CODA, GODA, SODA, and hearing children everywhere.

Contents

PART IV

MULTIPLICATION SIGNS

BIOS

Foreword

Oh, I hate the feather.

I was born October 9, 1950. At roughly three years of age, my parents noticed I was not responding to sound. They took me to a doctor, who labeled me mentally retarded (an outdated term not used anymore). I remember they took me on a train to Washington, DC, to run hearing tests on me. I was frightened because the doctor put a lot of wires on my head. I screamed. After the tests, my parents took me to a museum, where I threw up. I threw up on the train too. I resisted the hearing aid until I did not.

My education consisted of a few schools where my parents were told *not* to allow me to sign. Some other deaf kids and I used homemade signs. There was a lot of speech therapy—oh, I hated the feather. Speech therapy sessions consisted of countless hours of the therapist showing me how a feather would move when the air would explode, like the sounds P, T, and K do this, as opposed to B, D, and G without the puff of air.

I don't know if Kimmie and Ella had speech therapy using the feather method for sound recognition: the book does not focus on that. The book focuses on how they lived as deaf people in the twenty-first century. Things have changed a lot in the seventy plus years since I was found to be deaf.

I love kids with flying hands!

I recall not seeing signing, but possibly homemade signs. There was a woman, another mother of a deaf child whom my mother met, and she told her not to let me sign: it would cause me to lose the ability to use speech. My mother said she had no idea about sign language and had never heard of the Ohio School for the Deaf, but I find that odd. At the Catholic church we attended, the priest advised my parents to send me to St. Rita School for the Deaf, a Catholic school for the deaf in Cincinnati, Ohio. I was told that my parents, or my mother, didn't want to put me there because it was too far away. I wish they would have put me there or at the Ohio School for the Deaf because I love kids with flying hands! So, their decisions led to deficits in communication when I became an adult. Circumstances are so much different today!

So, I had a deaf friend who really was my sister.

Growing up, there were six of us. I had two older sisters and a hearing big brother. There was one hearing sister after me, then another, my youngest sister, Barbara. I just assumed she would be another hearing sister. It was strange because, being older than her, I noticed Barbara was the same as me. I could tell by the way she smiled and looked at me all the time. I noticed that when my mother or sister called her name, Barb didn't turn toward them, like she was ignoring them. I suppose they noticed her speech was different. I believe when she was three years old, they took her to the doctor and found out she was hard of hearing, preparing a hearing aid for her. I remember that I was so happy in all the world. So, I had a deaf friend who really was my sister. She was such a cute and funny little girl.

We became very close and felt a connection. Barb has better hearing than I do. She is hard of hearing and speaks clearly. But our minds and hearts are the same. As we were growing up, we were close and what I called "secret sisters." We had to hide to use homemade signs. My father scolded us not to use our hands but to talk. Why couldn't we just be happy with who we were?

Kimmie and Ella did not have to hide their visual language. The story you will read is fiction, made up, but why can't this kind of experience happen for more deaf children?

So, enjoy the story of a deaf family of today. It is much different now than it was in the not so distant past. I love flying hands!

Cathy Alznauer
February 14, 2022

Preface

If You Are a Student of ASL, What You Are Doing Is Significant!

Students who are studying ASL or the Deaf community (Deaf education, interpreting, rehabilitation, counseling, etc.) will naturally be led to understand issues seen in the Deaf-World. One way to learn is through reading. Students have plenty of textbooks, but this is a different way to tackle this subject, a novel telling the story of a bilingual (ASL/English) American family. Research, theory, and historical events are weaved into the story. We want students to develop a deeper understanding of the Deaf-World. Or you may be reading this book because you are interested in the topic. We are so glad you are joining us!

The Deaf-World: An American Community

The Deaf-World is home to various ethnicities, identities, and persons known as Deaf Plus (with additional disabilities). The Deaf community safeguards the world they have created and has established customs (the Deaf Way). Hearing persons who desire to work in partnership with Deaf communities will experience more success as they begin to understand American Sign Language (ASL) and Deaf culture. In this book, we have chosen to focus on one fictional Deaf family. We could not put every identity found in the Deaf-World in the book. Time, space, and expertise limited us. Perhaps you will add your unique story in the future?

The Invisibility of the Deaf Community

The Deaf community is rich in its language (ASL), culture, and traditions but is often invisible to the general hearing community. Is this situation changing? We hope so. As we were finishing this book, the film *CODA* won the Academy Award for Best Picture of the Year (2022). Perhaps more media exposure will shed light on the Deaf community. Deaf-World culture remains somewhat veiled until one is intentionally introduced to its vibrancy and complexities, mostly through educational opportunities. Education at all levels is key, and students can be introduced to the idea that *deaf ≠ deficit*.

A Collaboration of Many

This project was a collaborative endeavor by interpreting and ASL educators of Ohio. Collectively, the four co-authors brought 43 years of education and 116 years of experience as interpreters and educators. Our wonderful contributors brought 80 years of education and 237 years of work in the field to power this project! We are proud of Ohio as the national "heart of it all," the crossroads of the Deaf community (in historical Akron, where deaf people were employed during World War II, and Cincinnati, where the National Association of the Deaf was born), and the home to four interpreter education programs, two Deaf education programs, and numerous ASL offerings in both high school and post-secondary programs!

Deaf Educational Opportunities Are Important

The majority of deaf children (over 90%) are born to hearing parents, which poses potential disadvantages for acquisition of language(s). American Sign Language, as the foundation of the American (and Anglophone Canadian) signing Deaf community, is often the language of choice. ASL utilizes linguistically researched information that includes nonmanual aspects as well as grammatical features, which vary from spoken languages. Many Deaf Americans identify as bilingual, utilizing ASL and English (written or perhaps spoken). The story represented in this book is an idealized scenario. It is partially based on deaf people we have known who have flourished within the worlds they have created in the communities in which they live. We hope that by seeing a successful deaf family, students will be able to recognize what works, and what does not, and how they might do their part (we hope large or even small) to be agents of change when given the opportunity.

Where Did the Idea for the Book Come From?

The plotline of the book was created from an idea: what if a famous hearing person had a secret deaf baby? This fantastical idea led to the creation of an idealized story where the Deaf and hearing worlds interface, and issues from the Deaf community, culture, and language are interwoven into the story.

How Did the Book Become a Reality?

Through meetings with various stakeholder groups, interpreters, interpreter educators, ASL teachers, Deaf community members, and students, the plot was expanded. The expanded plot then needed to be made into a "real story" by a professional writer. Knowing that none of us were professional writers, we depended on the talents of the creative writer, professor, published author, and doctoral candidate Jeanne Dutton (pen name: J. T. Dutton) to create the story. Jeanne has hearing loss but is not fluent in ASL. We think she did a terrific job of filling in the story and creating multiple thought worlds of the characters.

Cheers to a new way for readers to access theory, research, and historical information!

Happy Reading!

Stefanie Amiruzzaman
Patricia Bettis-Eddie
Marsha Moore
Leah Subak
May 2022

PART I

Addition Signs

1
Signs of Life

Quinn arrived at the barricades right when she had said she would. A blonde girl not that much younger than Quinn was fussing with the badge on Roz's waistband. Two cameras maneuvered into position around Roz: one for profiles, closer than Quinn thought filming ever got, and another a few feet away. The operator of the first hunched so that all Quinn could see of him was a black baseball cap and a plastic receiver of an audio headset. A number of Hollywood-looking people milled beside the more stationary camera, and spectators gathered around the barricades. The commotion prohibited Quinn's attempts to get Roz's attention, though she was tall, every bit as tall as Roz, and Roz was expecting her. A security guard ignored Quinn's request to pass a message to Roz. He said he couldn't interrupt because filming was in progress.

The girl at Roz's waist worked at the badge in a furtive and hurried sort of way, like she was losing daylight hours to get the detail just right. Quinn fiddled with a pair of bracelets on her wrist, a gift Roz's adoptive mother, Viv, had given her as a teenager. A stream of sun cut between two buildings and shimmered around Roz. She glittered almost supernaturally in the late afternoon light, or so it seemed to Quinn, who had forgotten how surprisingly beautiful her caramel features were. Though Roz was wearing ochre slacks and a long-sleeved white blouse, she appeared not to notice the late fall heat wave—or the girl bent beside her or the cameraman shifting angles and zooming in close to her face.

The director asked Roz if she didn't mind running whatever scene they had been working on one more time. He called her "darling" and treated her as if she were more than just a secondary character who appeared in but a few episodes of the series. Roz smiled brightly at him, her eye passing closer to the crowd where Quinn stood. No recognition crossed her face, but she had always been nearsighted and didn't like wearing contacts. The blonde girl finished with the badge and skittered out of the shot. An actor stepped up onto the curb, blocking Quinn's view, and Roz began running lines with him in keeping with the characters they played on the series. When the director called "Cut!" there was applause from every direction, then more darlings and compliments and kissing of cheeks. The insider talk was audible to Quinn, who had moved close to the barricades despite the increasing number of spectators. People closest in were reluctant to cede room to Quinn, but she found her way forward with some light bumping of those on either side of her. She tried again to summon her friend, this time waving but not calling because there had been requests for spectators to remain silent.

The director placed his hand on Roz's back and turned her away from the barricades while the actor Roz had been doing the scene with signed autographs and posed for selfies with the teenage girls next to Quinn. The director talked close to Roz's ear. He walked beside her with a half-limp that Roz seemed to support with the nearness of her body. The crew set up a new scene that involved Roz discussing something with a small boy holding a skateboard. Quinn watched for a few minutes as Roz kneeled to face the boy, behaving the way a caring detective might when addressing a witness in a risky situation.

Rather than approaching the set from another angle, Quinn drifted up the avenue to a crowded coffee shop. The people in line were talking only about the shoot. When she reached the counter, she ordered a latte and carried it carefully to an open stool near a window that faced away from the spectacle. She texted Roz her location. She had expected a commotion surrounding the filming since the series had gathered a huge following. Quinn had expected to be kept waiting but not ignored . . .

She sipped nervously at her coffee, nursing it until the liquid turned cold. A week earlier, she had called Roz and had told her she was coming to town—ostensibly for a conference. Roz had seemed happy and nostalgic about hearing from her and had treated Quinn to lots of gossip. She dished on Hollywood insiders she had recently met, the Emmy her show had been nominated for, and two recent auditions for bigger projects she had been asked to do. The way Roz babbled, you would have thought she hadn't climbed a career ladder but had taken an escalator straight to the top. The absolute naturalness of the proximity of stardom differed from the humility with which more successful people discussed their rise in the form of college performances, community theater, and commercials. Before landing a small role in the Netflix series, Roz had done a soap opera, then some roles off-Broadway, and finally some Broadway shows. She hinted to Quinn that there was talk of a feature film.

"That's all I can tell you." Roz paused, to give the statement mystery.

"Listen, queen of the acting universe—"

"I promised my boyfriend, Kent . . ."

"The married man?" Quinn had heard about Kent from Roz's adoptive mom, Viv. Aunt Viv, as she was called, hadn't paid him compliments.

"He's leaving his wife," Roz said, defending him.

"The other night he took me to a gala and introduced me to this big-name producer—maybe you have heard of him—Henry Westraub?" Roz spoke of the producer as if he were an old friend. Quinn wanted to wag her finger at Roz, a gesture Roz wouldn't have been able to see on the phone. Roz, Roz, Roz—the beautiful dreamer, the girl voted *most likely to succeed* and *best looking* in the high school superlative popularity contest. Why hadn't she won *best all-around* and *life of the party* too? There wasn't a positive category that didn't fit her.

"Are you sure he is a big name?" Quinn pretended not to have heard of Henry Westraub. "You know, some people inflate their importance—especially if they think you don't know better. Be careful, girl . . ."

"Oh no, this guy is legit. He's produced two of the highest grossing films in the past five years. He told me he has a part in mind—tailor-made for me. He said I have the 'it' factor and invited me to his penthouse in Manhattan. I am supposed to see him in New York before you visit next week."

"Are you sure all this guy wants is to give you a part?"

"Are you suggesting I pass this up? Why? Should I be afraid the guy might lure me into his bedroom? I know how to say no."

"Roz—really?! He could *expect* something in exchange for a movie role!"

"Nah—I have 'it,' remember?" Roz said.

"You're being so naïve! What would Viv say if she knew you were meeting some strange man for a movie part? If he came on to you, what would you do?"

Roz claimed to have another call on the line.

Even in the old days, they used to bicker about how far each would go to meet a man. Since the phone call, Quinn had rehearsed how she might talk sense into her friend. It seemed to her that her shock at Roz's behavior was a sign of their losing touch with each other. By now, wouldn't it be too late to say anything since the meeting with the producer had already happened?

Quinn texted Roz the exact address of the coffee shop where she was still waiting two hours after being blown off on the set. There might have been more than one café like it in the area. In high school, Quinn and Roz had had nothing to lose whenever they'd had small arguments, but now, a disagreement could be the reason for ending visits. Quinn kept nervously thinking about the past, about things like their weekend road trip to Nashville after she had gotten her license and the limo Roz's aunt Viv had helped them rent for prom.

The light outside the coffee shop dimmed, and the crowd died down. Quinn moved so that she could see what was going on with the shoot, wondering if she should order a scone so that the workers didn't take offense at her holding a table so long.

Her phone buzzed, but it was nothing—just a text from work. She stared idly at the screen, scrolling through emails and the names of plenary speakers at the conference she had used as an excuse for traveling. Two large trucks rumbled from the side of the street and cars began passing, their headlights sliding along the window glass. Quinn checked the time. The restaurant Roz's aunt Viv had recommended wouldn't hold her dinner reservation for another hour. Quinn called an Uber to take her away from her failed attempt and the fading buzz outside.

She had never wanted to be someone who depended on the good fortune of her best friend for her own success. She stopped trying to contact Roz. She kept the incident of being stood up from her friends and coworkers and avoided talking about the trip with Aunt Viv. Quinn accepted a job transfer to Austin a month later and didn't send Roz a forwarding address, sure now that they had reached the end of what was left of their friendship. Roz had a history of neglecting Quinn for weeks in high school, even avoiding her on social media, and then one day threading her arm through Quinn's in the hallway. She would entertain Quinn with details of a crush or conquest, becoming so animated that Quinn would forget her own crushes and conquests and fully embrace Roz's life. There had been teenage secrets and scandals too, though nothing that had stood in Roz's way on the road to stardom.

Three weeks after the failed reunion in St. Louis, Roz's show won its first Emmy for Outstanding Performance by a Cast in a Drama Series. Quinn read a *People* magazine blurb describing plans for a big feature film that included Roz.

Shortly after that, Quinn opened the door of her apartment to find Roz standing in the hallway wearing a loose gray coat. When she took it off and hung it up on a peg in the hallway, Quinn spied her greatly defined baby bump.

Quinn took her in without a second thought. She attended birthing classes and held Roz's hand during the first breaths of labor. Quinn set a rhythm using a synching technique she had read about in a birthing book. When the right moment came, she packed Roz's bag into her car and drove her to the hospital. A nurse with heavy eyeliner checked them in and showed them to a private room.

"I read once that some actresses get Cesarean sections because they are easier on the body." Quinn had taken on the role of advisor.

"I can't think about this now. I'll go crazy if I do." Roz quoted a line from *Gone with the Wind*: "I'll think about it tomorrow."

In the old days, Roz and Quinn had acted out bits of films whenever ordinary conversation bored them. Roz apparently hadn't seen the controversy surrounding the movie *Gone with the Wind*. Quinn wasn't going to bring it up now—sort of bad timing. The alert on her phone reminded her to call in to work. She left a message that she needed to be out for the day and maybe even the next, coughing in order to sound ill. Roz was working with an adoption agency who was paying her birthing expenses. She planned to give the baby up for adoption within twenty-four hours. Quinn intended to stay with her until it was time to put Roz back on a plane.

A doctor had been in and had told Roz that her labor was taking longer than it should and that the baby was at risk of infection if not delivered soon. Roz clutched Quinn's arm and braced herself for another contraction. Quinn dropped her phone into a chair.

"God is in the room on such occasions," Aunt Viv had preached before they had left for the hospital. Roz, of course, had divulged the story to Viv. Aunt Viv had suggested Roz seek out Quinn for help, knowing no one else would see the situation through like her longtime loyal friend, Quinn.

Quinn pocketed the hopeful thought that some higher being was watching over them. She loved the thought and the woman who had said it. Viv was a treasure among women. Roz had always been Quinn's most sacred friend, the one she feared offending and the one who seemed the most likely to disappear into thin air if she did not keep a careful eye on her. Roz cast a spell that either drew others to her or, in rare instances, repelled them. Whether people loved or hated Roz, opinions could vacillate depending on factors that always seemed beyond Quinn's ability to predict.

When the contraction passed, Quinn wiped the sweat off Roz's forehead. The pressure of another contraction entered Roz's body and lifted her midsection from the gurney. Since Roz had checked into the hospital under the name Rosalind Brown rather than her professional name (Roz Taylor), she had become more like her old, less famous self. The assured sharp-witted officer Roz played on *Metro Police* took a back seat to the confused young woman trying to hide evidence of her misguided affair. Kent had gone back to his wife while

Roz had cut and straightened her magnificent brown curls so no one would recognize her and associate her shame with him.

Each of the professionals who entered the birthing suite offered advice for coping with the labor. They treated their work as if on an assembly line and Roz as another piece of machinery in a day-to-day routine, an ordinary cog fit into place.

My best friend's Netflix series just won an Emmy! Quinn nearly blurted out in order to break through the hospital staff's attitude of treating Roz as basic.

Roz had camouflaged not just her own identity but had also shielded Kent's, never naming him as the baby's father to Quinn—though who else's baby could it be? Roz had explained that a bombshell pregnancy might blow the lid off his marriage and damage *his* career. She hadn't wanted Quinn to tell people at work the reason she needed days off. But what about Roz's reputation? Quinn fumed at the thought of the father skating away while Roz lost her chance at the brass ring. What if the gossips of Roz's industry found out she had given a baby up for adoption? Or learned the truth of her pregnancy many years in the future? What if the baby's father heard that the pregnancy he believed terminated actually wasn't?

A nurse appeared at the door and asked how the two of them were doing.

Roz squirmed with another contraction, but apparently the time was still not close enough to the pushing phase. The ward was replete with hopeful women whose contractions progressed and whose babies came squalling into the world. A woman down the hall screamed like someone had set her on fire.

"I think we are close," Quinn told the nurse, hopeful for the end of this nightmare.

"I'll come back in a few minutes, dears." She bustled away.

Roz weakly attempted to pull her knees toward her chest, sweat causing her newly short hair to stick to her cheeks. Quinn tried to think of a movie quote that fit the moment.

"Life is filled with goodbyes, Eve, a million goodbyes, and it hurts every time." Quinn recited dialogue from *Eve's Bayou*, one of Roz's favorites films. After all, wasn't Roz saying goodbye to the life she knew through the pain of giving birth?

Roz did not respond.

Another contraction came and went. The nurse slid in through the swinging door and asked the same question: "How are you doing, dears?" Roz answered with a distant stare, the room so quiet Quinn heard the fluid drip from Roz's intravenous bag. Quinn was sure her friend was suffering, maybe even undergoing a contraction at that moment. The nurse rolled a small cart with equipment and a box of rubber gloves close to the bed. She performed a quick examination.

She rolled away, seemingly satisfied.

"Eight centimeters dilated, and fifty percent effaced," she announced.

Quinn was puzzled: she couldn't remember what that meant—why had all the information she'd learned in birthing classes just flown out of her memory?

"It means we're in business."

"We're in business?"

The lights in the room flickered.

The nurse rearranged objects in the room and propped Roz's legs up into a set of metal stirrups. A doctor with an umbrella arrived. Before scrubbing up and putting on his gloves and mask, he explained that it had begun to storm outside. The humdrum news shifted Quinn's focus. She and Roz seemed to have passed through a portal into a world where the noisy, stormy bustle of the city street did not exist.

2
Early Warning Signs

A different physician, a young resident in her late twenties, carried Roz's baby to her and shared the news that she was a girl. Roz looked at the squirming baby, so tiny in the doctor's gloved hands. A nurse rearranged Roz on the bed and placed two starched pillows underneath her back to help her sit upright. She listened to the sound of voices in the hall and felt light-headed with the realization that the doctor had given her *her* baby, a person whose life she had just moments before fought into being. She cupped the baby's head in her right hand and, with her left, stroked her fingers, which curled inwards toward her palm, noticing the tiny perfect hands. What did it mean to be a parent? Roz had planned her life so carefully around her career that this was a question she had never asked herself, even from the perspective of a mother intent on giving her child up for adoption.

Delivery had been intense, to put it mildly, not something she wanted to repeat anytime soon. The same nurse who had propped Roz up apologized for the intrusion and gathered the baby from her again. She explained that the little one needed her first set of tests, an Apgar score, which would categorize her strength and vitality. The baby seemed all of a piece to Roz, and there was nothing she feared about letting her go, though her first instinct was to be frightened by her smallness. Quinn tracked the nurse, following her instructions. Roz, in another headspace, closed her eyes and recalled her daughter's slippery, wet warmth and the shape of her tiny head, her features, and her swirls of hair. She thought about her tiny fingers. The moment she and the baby had been together had been so surreal and strange. Roz had heard about women changing their mind about giving their child up for adoption, stories about decisions being reversed out of the blue.

She did have plans . . .

The future had once looked so golden! How thrilling it had been to land job after job in a field where people struggled and waited for the slightest break. Roz was lucky to have enough pull to take months away to do what she needed. She was lucky to have a friend willing to upend her life to see her through her weakest moments: Quinn McAlvery, the quiet white girl from Roz's high school cheerleading squad. Who would have thought Quinn would have been such a rock? Most of the people Roz knew from high school disliked her now, treating her as if she had done something wrong in fleeing Ohio to chase fame. And most of the people Roz knew from New York would sell her secret for whatever minute of power or amount of money it would bring them.

She reflected on her chaotic childhood and what it had taken to accomplish all she had achieved. Roz's memories were way out of focus, but she remembered one particular Halloween, trick-or-treating in the neighborhood where she was born in Cleveland, Ohio. As Roz walked up the steps to a house to get some candy, her biological mother, Belinda, waited below on the sidewalk, maybe to give Roz some independence or maybe because she was having a hard time walking.

The homes in their part of Cleveland were tall and thin with multiple steps leading to each front door. Roz climbed to the porch of a home, believing her mother was waiting down below. Instead, Belinda slumped on the sidewalk, passed out, falling in front of the house where a happy little Roz just landed some candy and put it into the little pumpkin she carried. Roz remembered a lot of commotion—the sound of a smashed bottle, parents reacting by pulling their children out of harm's way. Roz's memory of the night, like practically all the memories she had of Belinda, was fuzzy. Viv had verified the story as the reason Roz had finally been taken away from her biological mother.

Afterward, she remembered living with Belinda's white parents for a time and then with her African American father, Michael Taylor, who was in the military. When he was called up for active duty, Michael contacted Vivian King Brown, a woman his sister knew from church. "Aunt" Viv took Roz in when it looked like Roz's father's only option would be to place Roz in foster care. Roz mumbled a small prayer of thanks for Aunt Viv, who had adopted her and nurtured her into the person she had become.

An orderly pushed Roz to the elevator and then to a room in another part of the hospital. She and Quinn spent the night sleeping and waking each time the baby cried. Toward daylight, Roz lay staring at a small window on one side of the bed that let in only a tiny amount of light. The white walls and the drab art reminded her of the small roadside hotels she had stayed in when she had once traveled the country with a summer theater group, cut off from home and spending most of her days with strangers. The room also brought to mind her long-ago life with Belinda, living in an apartment belonging to one of her transient boyfriends.

Quinn dozed in an armchair. The nurses had placed the baby's bassinet between the window and the bed so it was closer to Roz. The sides of the bassinet were clear so Roz could glance over and see the baby, although she mostly avoided looking in that direction.

The exterior light from the window did not seem to change. The hospital stirred and roused itself. Different members of the staff arrived to take Roz's blood pressure, to ask about the baby's sleep and food intake, to take the baby's vitals, and to ask Roz to sign legal forms. Roz slept between visits, waking at each knock. The door did not seem to stay shut no matter how many times Roz asked Quinn to close it for privacy. Roz's chart should have stated that the baby was to be adopted, yet the name tag on the bassinet read Baby Brown, and the doctors and nurses acted as if Roz would remain the custodial parent forever and answer all their important questions, right up to how the baby was going to vote. They urged Roz to schedule vaccines and to take note of future benchmarks and reflex tests. They wanted her to breastfeed, an act Roz was determined not to do.

When she had been awake for an hour, a nurse came to wheel the baby to the nursery for a weight check and a few more exams. Quinn stretched and rose from her chair. With the baby gone, a chance to get to the cafeteria presented itself.

"I'm starved."

She asked Roz if she wanted anything from the cafeteria.

"No, thank you." Roz rolled over so that her back faced the window.

She gazed at the hospital amenity bag on her bureau, the baby's name jumping out at her again. The name was written on the outside of the bag with a free breast pump on the inside. It was then that Roz was determined to come up with a name. A placeholder until the adoptive parents, whoever they were, chose the name she would carry through life. Roz settled on Elle because Aunt Viv's late husband, Reverend Freddie Lee Brown, had gone by the nicknames FL or L after a fellow pastor had given him the pet names for his initials. Roz decided she liked L and spelled it Elle: it seemed to fit. Of course, Elle's adoptive parents might not like the name, but for now, Roz had something to call her until the moment she had to say goodbye.

Roz had multiple names for people in her life. Quinn was sometimes QuinQuin or Biff, which was shorthand for Best Friend Forever. She called Aunt Vivian, Auntie, Viv, BB (a name that came from mispronouncing *v* for *b*), but mostly her preferred moniker, Aunt Viv (like Aunt Viv from *The Fresh Prince of Bel-Air*). At times, she called her Momma, or Mommy, when she felt an attachment, a specific feeling, more than just a word spoken aloud. Viv was the shape of someone she had always known, a person she could summon with a feeling. Why shouldn't Roz have a private name for Elle to communicate with her after they had parted? Giving the baby the placeholder name of Elle was her private way to honor Aunt Viv; she loved her husband more than life itself.

An orderly in a green uniform rolled in a warmer filled with trays. Roz asked him to leave hers on the table next to the amenity bag. She wasn't hungry. She had sipped a little juice after delivery and had had nothing since: her body was overwhelmed and not ready to take in more. There were so many forms to sign and tests and exams with scores that only doctors and nurses seemed to understand. Roz hadn't felt fully up to the process of thinking about the future, or how she might sustain herself once she walked out of her hospital room. She was grateful that Quinn had assumed control of many of the adoption details: Quinn who until now had hardly seemed able to handle her own life—Where had she been working? An insurance agency? Quinn had answered many of the staff's questions and explained that they would be turning the baby over to the social worker who would then make the arrangements with Elle's new parents. Quinn and Roz knew that Roz had a certain number of days to change her mind about the adoption, but it did not seem likely to happen. Roz was determined to pursue her acting plans but wanted her last hour with Elle to be as quiet as possible.

A different, older nurse than the one who had taken Elle into the nursery wheeled her bassinet back into the room.

"The boss needs to be fed, and I suspect someone in here is the only one who can fill the need!"

The brusqueness and audacity of the nurse's tone startled Roz. Had she missed the order on the chart that stated no breastfeeding? There had been trouble during the night with Elle not latching on to the nipple of a bottle. The nurse emphasized that breastfeeding provided a baby with nutrients and immunities for life. But Roz was working on stopping her milk from coming in so that she could speed her return to acting. Roz planned to get on birth control pills and wear a tight-fitting bra. She had heard those things helped to slow down milk production. Plus she just was not going to nurse the baby, the surest way to prevent breast milk from coming in.

She put her hand on the bassinet and looked down at her daughter fussing and squirming against a sheet with pink bunnies. Roz gave herself permission to really see her daughter—it might be the last time she did. Elle's eyes were drawn to the light from a standing lamp in the corner of the room, and one of her tiny hands seemed to grab in its direction. Quinn appeared just as Roz was about to lift her from the bassinet. She gave the nurse a hard look.

"I'll take over here."

Quinn nudged Roz out of the way. She rocked Elle while Roz shuffled back to her bed and sat down. She began to untie the strings of her hospital gown and search for something else to wear. She was afraid to look in the mirror, afraid of the aftereffects of such a long, physically exhausting night. Quinn, meanwhile, had discovered a second wind while in the cafeteria. She warmed a bottle of formula, cradling Elle against her shoulder as she waited for the light on the heater to signal the liquid had reached the right temperature. Roz observed Quinn's patient and deft management of Elle's needs, envying what appeared to be an instinctive grace under the pressure of an insistent and bawling baby.

"Did you have to take care of your younger brothers and sisters?" Roz couldn't remember.

"Oh yeah." She changed Elle into a pink-flowered gown Roz had asked Quinn to purchase for her in the hospital gift shop. Roz noticed that Elle was wearing a soft pink hat.

"Where is the hat from?"

"They must have given it to her in the nursery."

Quinn removed the bottle from the warmer and shifted the baby into the crook of her arm. Cradling Elle's head, she stroked her mouth with her finger and lowered the milk toward her.

Roz tried to picture baby Elle in the prom gown she would one day wear.

Quinn said, "She's gorgeous, like Mommy."

Roz seemed to recoil.

Quinn paced while she fed the baby. Elle audibly slurped, clearly having gotten the hang of how to eat.

"This is all such new territory. Are we in the Twilight Zone?"

Quinn snickered. The thought of adopting Elle herself was an evanescent thought. If she were to take Elle as her own, Quinn would surely lose Roz's friendship. That could not be.

Roz slipped into a dress that draped fashionably over her swollen abdomen.

As Roz was putting on a pair of nude pumps she had purchased in New York before she had gotten pregnant, a knock on the outside of the door caused Quinn to accidentally pull the nipple from the baby's mouth. The baby reacted with noisy frustration, clearly upset at another interruption. Quinn patted Elle on the back. Someone knocked again, and Roz limped over to answer the door, her swollen feet chaffing in her pretty shoes. A woman who seemed to be part of the hospital staff and not from an adoption agency, whom they had been expecting, asked if she might come in. She was wearing a lab coat with a hospital badge.

"Are you a social worker?" Roz wondered what was keeping the adoption agency people.

The woman looked from Roz to Quinn as if deciding which was the parent.

"The father is not in the picture," Roz answered the unspoken question. "My friend Quinn here has power of attorney, and you can speak freely in front of both of us."

The woman held a file folder close to her chest.

"I am an audiologist."

Quinn settled into a chair, her attention on the baby rather than yet another staff person. Elle gulped with gusto. Quinn felt relieved that Roz was depending on her, needing her just like in the old days. The woman explained that she had been in the nursery earlier testing Elle's hearing.

"And?" Roz taunted.

"Your baby did not pass the hearing screening test," the woman answered in a small, embarrassed voice. "We think you should stay in the hospital one more day so that we can get a second test scheduled. The social worker needs to clear it. She will be in touch with you soon."

Roz waved her hand and thanked her for the information. When the door was once again shut, she opened her cosmetic case to start touching up her face. Quinn looked at Roz, stunned. Surely Roz was feeling it too. Quinn knew Roz so well and had witnessed the shine in her eyes dulling hour by hour through the pregnancy, birth, and delivery sojourn.

"I-I'll think about this tomorrow," Roz whispered as if she were alone. In anticipation of the arrival of the adoption agency representative, she checked the status of her makeup.

3
Signs of Hope

Roz's adoptive mother, or Viv as she was called by many, had been a law intern for Supreme Court Justice Thurgood Marshall once upon a time and knew some of the legal implications of Elle's hearing loss and adoption issues. Quinn called her because the agency that Roz had used to arrange the transfer of custody had informed her that the potential adoptive parents had backed out after learning of Elle being deaf. The second and third consultations after Elle's initial screening had confirmed the first audiologist's assessment. Now the agency itself was cancelling their agreement to secure an anonymous adoption, citing a policy that released them from an obligation of placing a child with special needs. Quinn arranged for a social worker to find a foster family to take temporary custody of Elle while she hurriedly began to search for other options. She really needed Viv in the worst way, not wanting to walk this winding road alone. Roz was next to worthless after giving birth, giving up an infant, and now being given counsel about the deaf baby she gave up. At this point, Roz had all but emotionally checked out.

Quinn listened distractedly as Viv, always talkative, walked Quinn through a landmark 1982 supreme court case that she had assisted Justice Thurgood Marshall with as one of his law clerks. The case was called Hendrick Hudson Central School District vs. Rowley and concerned the education of a deaf child, Amy June Rowley, who was denied an interpreter to provide needed linguistic services as she pursued a public school education. Viv considered the case to be one of the most important and influential she had ever worked on in her nearly four decades of practicing law. Six of the nine justices had ruled that the school had had the right to deny sign language services, a violation of the basic human right to communicate.* Quinn was unsure how the case connected to Roz's situation, but she was glad Viv was taking time out of her day to speak with her. Her friend's mother was a sharp and competent lawyer, well known in the Columbus community where she had raised Roz.

To reach Viv, Quinn had navigated a receptionist and a secretary before leaving a message for her, only to receive a return call hours later when Quinn had her hands full. Viv apologized for the delay. She was in the throes of a huge civil rights case. She informed Quinn that she was not an expert in adoption law or disability rights but believed that a child with Elle's needs would be better off with caregivers who were prepared to make difficult communication decisions. She assured Quinn that although the adoption agency had backed out, given Elle's situation, their change of heart was perhaps a good thing.

Quinn was talking to Viv outside her former place of work, carrying a box of photographs and other odds and ends, her phone pinched between her ear and shoulder. She had not been able to gather her things from her office before she and Roz had left for the hospital but had given her boss her two weeks' notice.

* Justice Marshall, charged with writing a dissent, famously argued that deaf children required interpreting services as an accommodation to create equity in the classroom. Marshall believed that in order to provide deaf children with fair learning opportunities, schools needed to provide access to communication through a language they could follow. To do so, they needed to hire sign language interpreters (Oyez, "Board of Education").

"An adoption agency wouldn't take Baby Girl's language needs into consideration." Viv's voice sounded tinny and far away.

She asked Quinn for more details about Roz's state of mind, and Quinn filled her in on the last few days of arranging Elle's foster placement and their meetings with the two audiologists. They'd sat in a number of waiting rooms, been through some difficult consultations, and learned the unpromising results of a number of time-consuming tests. Though Roz's patience was worn thin, Quinn assured Viv that she mostly was okay and that Elle was a good baby, docile and beautiful, and unaware of the turmoil swirling around her.

The news seemed to cheer Viv, whose voice always had a singsong happiness to it.

"How are you?" Viv sang. "What a nice thing you are doing for my girls."

"It's crazy, but I feel Roz is expecting me to make everything all right."

"I have some connections at Gallaudet University, which is in DC. So don't let the possibility of Elle being deaf scare you." Gallaudet University, Quinn learned from letting Viv ramble further, was the world's only higher educational institution for deaf students.

Quinn placed her box full of office supplies on the ground and pressed her key fob to open her car while Viv spun a tale about someone she knew at Gallaudet. When she was clerking for Marshall back in the day, she met a deaf man named Charles Stacker, who was from a prominent African American family in Northwest DC. Chas, as she called him, showed Viv how to play chess. He used their chess matches as a first step toward teaching her some Deaf culture information and the basics of American Sign Language (ASL),* skills she would

* American Sign Language (ASL) is a visual language processed through the eyes. Handshape, placement, and movement of the hands, as well as facial expressions

need to help Thurgood Marshall on the Rowley case. His teaching techniques and information clearly made an impression. Quinn had only known her friend's adoptive mother as a single widow. Clearly, Viv had once had a life before she had met her late husband.

Quinn interrupted Viv to tell her that she and Roz were consulting with a new pediatric audiologist, a hearing specialist, later in the afternoon.

"Oh good. Oh good." Viv halted her meanderings. "Please call me after. If I don't pick up, text me on my cell phone right away." Quinn wondered why she was reading out her number but decided to write it down on the inside of her arm in case the number was different from the one she had in her phone.

They said their goodbyes, and Quinn loaded the box into her car, making room for it among some new pots and pans she had purchased. Roz had paid for the new cookware along with Quinn's rent and a down payment on a place in Chicago. She had invited Quinn to move with her after they settled Elle's affairs, and Quinn had seized the opportunity because being Roz's personal assistant was much more glamorous than working as a claims adjustor. But already she doubted if she could serve all of Roz's needs. Would the job include becoming a nanny? Would she need to make decisions about Elle's hearing needs? She knew nothing about the Deaf community. Good thing Viv seemed to know a thing or two.

When Quinn was in college, a deaf man once approached her while she and her friends were doing homework in a McDonald's. He handed them a little flag and a card with

---

and body movements, all play important roles in conveying information. ASL is not universal: countries have their own signed languages, and regional dialects exist. ASL is a language with linguistically studied rules of grammar and syntax. It is a living language and changes over time. ASL is signed predominantly in the United States and Anglophone Canada. The language is taught in many high schools, colleges, and universities in fulfillment of modern and/or foreign language academic degree requirements across the United States (National Association of the Deaf, "American Sign Language").

sign language instructions printed on both sides. One of her friends spelled out words asking him what he wanted while he leaned over the table and tried speaking to them. In the end, because no one in the group could figure out what he was asking, the girl who started the conversation gave him money. The memory was so uncomfortable, it returned to Quinn as she sat in the office of the pediatric specialist later that afternoon. A restless little girl in the waiting room clung to her mother's knee and tried to ask her for something with words that were inarticulate. Her head was shaved on one side, and she had what appeared to be a hearing aid attached behind her ear. Quinn remembered that the man in McDonald's had worn some kind of device. The device looked strange: there was a circular portion that seemed to somehow be attached behind the ear, not like a hearing aid exactly.

Roz peered up from her phone and frowned at the loud squawking the little girl was making.

Quinn thought it might be a good idea to get the speech and hearing specialist to discuss sign language as an early communication option for baby Elle. What was the answer? Would Elle grow up to be like the little girl in the waiting room? None of the procession of professionals they had spoken to had mentioned how sign language fit with the adoption plans that Roz was forming, but a few had mentioned hearing devices. Quinn didn't know how to bring sign language into a conversation with a doctor, or whether it even made sense to discuss the issue with a baby so young.

Roz silently scrolled through her social media while Quinn carried an insurance form back to the desk, probably the five hundredth she had completed that week. A children's television show was airing on a set in the corner. Its bright flashing colors captured the attention of the girl with the hearing device.

"Aunt Viv sent me something," Roz said when Quinn returned to her seat. Roz opened an attachment on one of her emails.

"When I spoke with her earlier today, she said she might send us some information on American Sign Language." Quinn sounded hopeful.

"Viv sort of has a bias toward what she thinks should happen." Roz's tone was snarky.

"We can take it slow. You don't need to be pressured," Quinn reassured her. After all, she did not want to be too confrontational toward Roz.

"How did I end up with a deaf baby anyway?" Roz pushed their conversation into a place they had only tiptoed around.

Quinn had asked some of the experts this same question in and out of Roz's hearing. They had listed everything from family heredity to the baby's health in the womb. One clinical assistant who had struck Quinn as the most honest had said that sometimes nobody ever knows why a child has a hearing loss, that the condition might be like eye color or a personality trait, just the genetic hand of cards Elle was dealt. There could be any number of reasons why Elle didn't hear.

"In a few days, all of this will be behind us, and Elle will be in her new home." Quinn made an effort to embrace the baby's future.

Tears rimmed Roz's big hazel brown eyes.

"The social worker said that everyone is doing their best to find her a good family. People have fallen in love with her already. She's such a good baby."

Roz faced her phone in Quinn's direction and showed her a photo of a man with dark wavy hair. Quinn was surprised at what seemed to be Roz engaging in their age-old habit of scoping out men's looks. She had picked a handsome one.

"Who is that?"

"His name is Nyle DiMarco." Roz shrugged. "According to this article Aunt Viv sent, he was born deaf. He believes parents should teach deaf babies a way to communicate right from birth to avoid what he is calling language deprivation."

Quinn took Roz's phone and scanned the article to see if it said more about how to start a conversation about sign language with a specialist. Also, Nyle DiMarco rated a ten out of ten in her mind, but she did not say so to Roz.

"Viv says she has been researching adoption. She says there may be someone in the Deaf or Deaf language community who is looking to adopt a deaf baby rather than a hearing one."

"Someone would actually want a deaf baby?" Quinn couldn't hide her surprise. She suddenly realized how she sounded. Awful.

Roz took her phone back.

"It's great you are so far along in processing the situation, Roz. You can trust Aunt Viv with your life. I think you should consider whatever she tells you. She is the most levelheaded woman we know, and she loves you more than life itself."

Roz maintained her silence.

"You had me at hello," Quinn quoted Renée Zellweger in *Jerry Maguire*.

Roz stared at Quinn in such a way that Quinn feared she might fire her from her job as personal assistant before she'd had a chance to prove herself.

"I'm done trying for an anonymous adoption through an agency. It's too much. I am putting the situation in the hands of Aunt Viv." Roz's stare lingered a second more and then she returned to looking at her phone.

"Okay." Quinn's throat grew tight.

"All we have to decide is what to do with the time that is given to us," Roz quoted Gandalf from *The Fellowship of the Ring*.

Quinn felt a surge of relief—and gratitude for movie quotes.

If Viv arranged the adoption, that meant that the new adoptive parents, whoever they might be, would likely learn that Roz Taylor, the rising actor, was the baby's mother. At least such an arrangement meant not abandoning Elle to the state. Quinn had not realized how much the possibility had been weighing on her and how guilty it made her feel.

She went back to watching the children's television show on the screen in the waiting room. A small boy in overalls also had a hearing device attached behind his ear. He joined the little girl, and they formed an impromptu club of future Deaf community members. A set of Muppet characters were dancing on the screen, keeping time to the happy music. Both children began moving too, imitating the Muppet who wagged his head from side to side. The boy gestured, pointed to the screen, and smiled at the girl. They communicated by vision and laughed with abandon. They visually tracked the rhythm of the characters on the screen, unaware of the legacy that nature had bestowed on them.

4

Equal Sign

After God took Viv's beloved husband, she thought long and hard about how to keep going. Saying a permanent good-bye to a man who was the most God-fearing and wonderful person she had ever known broke her for a while. A preacher from a long line of faith leaders, Reverend F. L. Brown had lived by the biblical verse Ephesians 5:25: "Husbands, love your wives, just as Christ loved the church." After he was gone, Viv kept spiritual options open. Being wracked with grief, she hoped to meet with him again soon in heaven, if God willed it.

A distraction from her pain came in the form of a young man from church who desperately needed help raising his daughter. As she had done so many times before, Viv didn't deny her "children" access to her home or her heart. She saw something in this little girl and didn't hesitate to spend time nurturing her because it had been her dream to raise a child in the days before she lost her beloved husband. She eventually made the gesture legal by adopting her blessed Rosalind. Every school lunch she packed, every dance performance she attended, all the playmates of Roz's that dashed in and out of her house blessed the years that followed in new ways. When Roz headed to NYC for her off-Broadway work, Viv missed her adopted daughter and her deceased husband. Even though Roz called once a week as she was becoming well known and important to everybody, it wasn't until she became pregnant that Viv felt the joy of a new call to action.

She placed some of the heavy lifting of her current civil rights case in the hands of her partners and flew to Austin. Rather than getting anyone to pick her up at the airport, she used the Uber app Roz had shown her on her last visit. A nice young man with what the young people were calling a "man bun" and sleeve tattoos pulled up in an SUV. He shut off the engine and helped her lift her belongings into the back. She noticed he had a guitar, and that led to a conversation about his band and the music he liked on the way to her hotel. Viv also noticed that he was wearing a pair of hearing aids. What a wonderful coincidence! All the bright sunshine in Austin also seemed to be part of God's plan. In Columbus, the rain had slowed the traffic down to a crawl, but here in Austin at eleven in the morning, the roads were big and open and the sky was high and bright blue.

A deaf baby! Could it really be? Before leaving for Austin, she had contacted her old friend Charles "Chas" Stacker, the person she'd told Quinn about, the fellow who had taught her chess and ASL. She hoped Roz wouldn't mind having one more person in on her secret. Chas had a lot of knowledge about communication issues for deaf children, having once been a deaf child himself and also because of his academic work at Gallaudet University. He was such a well-respected leader, Vivian feared that he might not remember her or their talks more than thirty years earlier. Chas proved at once to be social and kind and willing to be a resource for her. She mentioned the Rowley case, and suddenly, he remembered everything about Viv. Then they were reliving their mutual disappointment in the final ruling.* Chas had married and

* The Rowley parents wanted their daughter to stay in public school, even though Amy could only understand about 60% of the communication in that context. The lower court's rulings were in support of the provision of an interpreter, then an appeals court ruled against providing the service, and finally the supreme court

fathered two children, one who was deaf and one who was hearing, since they last spoke. His marriage had also ended, a fact he didn't dwell on. Viv told him about losing her beloved husband.

She hadn't told Quinn or Roz that she planned to tap into her Deaf community network for fear that Roz might not want new adoptive parents aware of her identity. But a more intimate, open adoption arrangement would make it easier for Roz and Viv to stay in touch with Elle and watch her grow. After all, this was Viv's first grandbaby. No one would have to miss the first steps or stories from the early days of school.

Chas could be trusted to keep secret what he knew of Roz's situation and to a find a family who would also be discreet. Deaf children should have access to linguistic care,* and Viv could make sure that happened. Viv would never have learned about the life of deaf children if not for Chas's friendship. Viv felt the hand of God guiding her path.

Chas's parents had discovered that he was deaf in a much different way than Roz had learned about Elle's hearing loss through a universal newborn hearing screening. After Charles's

---

upheld the ruling that favored withholding additional support. When all of the evidence had been weighed, the justices determined that Amy had an equal opportunity to education without the provision of an interpreter mostly due to her high level of achievement and the fact that she was an honors student. Since her grades were good, even with understanding little more than half of the spoken language around her, Amy's family was not able to request more services, and the school denied the request for an interpreter (Traynor, "Breaking the Legal Sound Barrier").

* Over one million profoundly deaf individuals live in the U.S. People with severe hearing loss make up four times that number. Per four million babies born in the United States each year, two to three tenths of a percent have a hearing loss, which comes to between eight and twelve thousand every year, not including children who become deaf or hard of hearing due to bacterial meningitis, high fever, ototoxic medications, and other causes (Dallas Hearing Foundation, "Facts"). A fortunate few have clear access to language early enough that their educational progress isn't impacted. Others rely on what they can understand through hearing aids or surgically inserted cochlear implants. Some experience language deprivation and social isolation, not just when they are young; they may carry residual effects for their entire lives (Hall, "What you don't know can hurt you").

pediatrician noted that he was not developing language by eighteen months, he referred the parents to consult an audiologist, who evaluated his hearing and recommended hearing aids rather than acquisition of ASL. After Chas's language did not progress in school, another set of professionals diagnosed him as an oral failure.

Viv had been horrified to learn that one of the smartest and most confident people she knew—a full professor at Gallaudet—had struggled with his education and had almost not graduated high school.

His mother was the only one in his family who could fingerspell, a time-consuming way to communicate, while the rest of his family members and extended family did not sign at all.

Not having a way to communicate led to an intense loneliness through Chas's adolescence. He often watched television and spent a lot of time in his room. He couldn't join in family conversations, and so, unlike his siblings, he didn't catch up with his parents at the dinner table. He chose to eat his meals in front of the television set on a TV tray. The family purchased a closed-captioning device to add words to some programs. The device worked in a hit-or-miss manner, which frustrated Chas, but it was better than nothing. Unlike his siblings, Chas did not have best friends who explored the neighborhood with him.

At age ten, the experts made a new recommendation: updated hearing aids. Chas could detect more sound, but the aids did not reconstruct hearing in the way typical hearing people process sound, and he felt tortured by the speech therapy that followed.* Once he transferred to a deaf school and began making deaf friends who used ASL to communicate, his life transformed for the better.

* Not every deaf person who wears hearing aids or other assistive listening devices is able to process speech with clarity equal to that of a typical hearing person. Earlier technological devices were not as sophisticated as those available today. Benefits from hearing aids vary widely. (ASHA, "Degree of Hearing Loss.")

Viv's driver pulled up in front of the hotel. He waited with her for a bellhop to provide a trolley for her luggage.

"How long have you worn hearing aids?" She indulged her impulse to nosiness.

"A year." He pocketed the fare money and ten-dollar tip she handed him. "I take them out driving around town sometimes because they itch."

"Really?" Viv laughed when he added that they itched like the blazes.

She reached into her suitcase and removed a tin of cookies. Viv had baked them at home and had been planning to give them to Roz and Quinn. But Roz would likely be dieting, and it was not every day she met such a nice young man so willing to be of help.

5
The High Sign

Roz was in the kitchen of Quinn's extended-stay apartment, preparing her first homemade meal since Elle's birth. Quinn's cooking didn't count. She emptied packages, added butter, and sometimes included a vegetable, more often than not from a bag in the freezer. Roz had sent her out to buy fresh garlic and seasoning salt she could stir into her greens, ingredients Aunt Viv included in many of her soul food recipes. After she started the gravy, she tried to locate Viv, who wasn't answering her cell or the landline at her house in Ohio. She often worked late and didn't always remember to charge her devices. She lived in a different world, less tied to technology. It was never just a matter of Roz doing some scrolling on social media to know what Viv was up to. Sometimes she had to try Viv's God network, tracking down a church friend and asking if they had seen her recently, then interrupting her in Bible study or while volunteering at the food pantry. Roz wanted to share her conflicted feelings about Elle with her momma, the one person who always listened. Each day brought new decisions. Even if Roz gave up her high-profile life, she didn't feel prepared to care for all of Elle's needs. Yet how could she let a daughter of hers go into the foster care system after her own messy childhood?

Aunt Viv was perceptive, wickedly smart, and the type of person who could peer into a person's soul and help them see through the clouds of indecision to a better solution. She was like a razor blade, cutting through self-rationalization to find inner truths. Roz's favorite thing about Aunt Viv was that she took it upon herself to be present with people no matter what else she had on her plate. Even though she was tied to a big civil rights case in Columbus and hadn't been able to leave home to be with Roz during her labor, she had somehow found the energy to soothe Roz's hurts the last few days and send her the biggest arrangement of flowers she had ever seen. What was next? Cookies?

Roz's biggest fear was that Quinn had stumbled on a truth she wasn't ready to admit. What if there were no families out there willing to adopt her little girl? What would Roz do? She had imagined that she would already be back working out with a personal trainer, conferring with her agent, and reading scripts. Not only did Roz feel unprepared physically to resume her old life, but her emotions also swung from one extreme to another.

She reduced the heat on her pork chops. A little fat and protein might do her soul good, even if she risked padding her figure.

She knew Viv had been conferring with Quinn, speaking to whichever of the two of them answered their phone. Perhaps Viv had been discussing things with Quinn in private. Maybe Viv thought she was acting like Belinda, selfishly bringing a child into the world and then not taking responsibility. After Roz became pregnant, she was surprised how quickly Viv embraced her choices, relieved that Roz was going through with the pregnancy. Yet, what if, unbeknownst to Roz, Viv had lost faith in her? Was it a statement of Viv's parenting that Roz did not feel ready to mother Elle in the way Viv had parented her? Roz had learned love from the best, had been schooled by a great master. Yet Roz could not see herself sacrificing the way Viv had or giving up the idea of marriage and a family with another man to parent a child alone, and a deaf child at that.

Roz was finishing the gravy when the doorbell rang. She did not know anyone besides Quinn in Austin and so feared one of the tabloids had tracked her down. What if a pap (paparazzo) was standing behind the door with a camera? Was it possible that Quinn had somehow lost her key, or was carrying so many groceries she couldn't open the lock?

Roz slid the saucepan with the gravy to an unused burner and rubbed her hands on her apron, an item she had brought with her to Texas because she wanted to blow off her diet while she was pregnant. Then, it had been okay to eat heavy meals, and she had enjoyed her vacation away from carrot juice. Now, she had to consider her weight gain. Would the camera add ten pounds, or were ten there already and it would look more like twenty? Unlike her apartment in New York, there was no intercom/camera system to tell her who was outside and who might snap a photo of her newer, rounder self. She shut off all the burners and went into the vestibule. Perhaps she should just pretend no one was home. She checked herself in the mirror and saw a little less exhaustion in her eyes than she expected and a little more of the old Roz. The apron was perhaps hiding what was left of her baby belly. Anyone seeing her now might think that she was just tired.

She prepared herself to smile down the person on the other side of the door, give them the old rather than the new, fragile Roz. When the door swung wide, she practically did not recognize Aunt Viv, being so surprised to see her. But then her heart flooded with joy and her face relaxed. She dove into Viv's open arms, nearly toppling her tiny momma. Roz had never been so glad to see anyone.

"Aren't you going to invite me in, my baby?"

Roz lifted and carried in the satchel Viv had brought with her.

"I didn't know you were coming." Roz's first thought was that she had not prepared enough food for her mom and Quinn both.

"Don't you worry. It was a surprise."

"But why are you here? Don't you need to be working on that important civil rights case?"

"Oh, baby. You think I could wait through all that to be with you? I love you more than tongue can tell!"

"LYMTTCT too, Mommy!"

Roz had forgotten how it felt to say these words and feel the sentiment in return. She showed Viv to one of the stools at the breakfast bar and prepared her greens without the extra garlic Quinn had gone to fetch. When she had a second, she texted Quinn to tell her that Viv had surprised them and asked her if she didn't mind waiting to come home, hoping Quinn didn't feel kicked to the curb.

Viv, never one to sit more than three seconds, asked what she could do. Roz made her an impromptu apron from a towel and put her on seasoning the gravy. They sat down to a purely good mother-daughter meal together, the first they had had in years, what with civil rights cases, auditions, film sets, and babies. Roz forgot that Viv always started with the blessing and started to fill her plate.

"Hold on, baby. Got to give thanks!"

Viv thanked God for their always togetherness and asked Him to watch over them in the days ahead, especially tiny baby Elle. They ate, talked, and laughed so hard, they had to dab the tears from their eyes with their napkins. After they had stuffed themselves, they had a chance to get serious. Roz confessed, for the first time since she had held Elle in the hospital, how beautiful she had found her daughter, how unequal she felt to the task of raising her, and how she didn't believe that she was ready for all that would be required. She imagined that as the years passed by, she might even regret giving Elle up.

Or, if she kept Elle, she might be offered other roles that she wouldn't be able to pursue. And what if any other children she had were also deaf?

"That's a lot of 'what-ifs' to carry." Viv chuckled. "You are doing a beautiful thing in helping another woman have a chance to love and care for a baby, a woman who would cook Baby's favorite foods and drive her to dance classes."

"But she's deaf."

"I know. Isn't that wonderful?"

"Is there such a person?"

"Yes, and she's looking for us too."

Roz dried the dishes as Viv washed them. She imagined her daughter full-grown, helping her with small chores. She reached over to the soapy sink and clasped her magical mother's hand.

PART II

Subtraction Signs

6

Can It Be a Sign?

Eliza Jean-Baptiste was writing an article about ASL when her videophone (VP)* light flashed with an incoming call from a person named Charles Stacker. Eliza took her job as an interpreter seriously and often interacted with deaf individuals while drafting stories for the local Danville paper. The VP ringing triggered the thought that someone deaf was calling, and though she didn't recognize the name, it may be someone trying to reach her husband, Paul. As soon as the call came through, she signed a greeting to an older, academic-looking African American gentleman on the TV that was connected to the VP. He greeted her with a warm hello and asked her if she was surprised to get a call from him. He mentioned that he was Paul's former professor from Gallaudet. He explained that it was through one of her academic articles about adopting a deaf child from another country that he had tracked her down. He fondly remembered that Paul had been one of his star students at Gally—a nickname affectionately applied to Gallaudet University.

* Videophones and VP apps allow for local and long-distance communication when both people use ASL. The Video Relay Service (VRS) makes it possible for individuals who are deaf/hard of hearing to speak with non-ASL users who generally can hear (Sorenson, "About Us").

"Oh yes, I remember Paul mentioned you and called you Dr. Stacker."*[1]

"Right, but students know me by my sign name."**[2] Chas showed her the sign that represented his name—a *C* handshape moving from the forehead to the chin.

Eliza briefly paused to listen for rhythmic breathing through the baby monitor, a good sign that her daughter, Kimmie, was still in her bed napping. It had taken nearly an hour to get her down that afternoon, and a Kimmie without naps meant an Eliza without patience for the rest of the day. Perhaps recognizing that Eliza had her hands full, Chas cut to the chase, signing so quickly she struggled to follow. He said that he knew of a woman, an old friend of his, who was looking to place a deaf child in a family with other deaf members.

"Would you be willing to meet this person?"[3]

Eliza's heart raced. She and Paul, unbeknownst to either of their own families, had begun trying to have a second child but had not been able to conceive. The same heartbreaking problem had slowed them down prior to the adoption of their daughter, Kimmie. There had been countless visits to the doctor for Eliza's infertility treatments. Eliza had taken clomiphene, which had not worked, followed by injectable hormones to stimulate ovulation. Both procedures had proved to be a bust. Paul and Eliza had lived with near-monthly dashed

---

* ASL Gloss is a notational system used to transcribe ASL. ASL has no written form, and glossing does not attempt to be an official linguistic substitute as such (American Sign Language Teachers Association, "Definition"). The first two translations utilizing ASL glossing conventions are described here. For an explanation of conventions used in these glosses, see the appendix.

Gloss #1: OH-I-SEE #YES, ns-PAUL MENTION/STORY PRO-2 (you). SELF-3 (Paul) [INJECT/ADD NAME WHAT] RhQ #DR fs-Stacker.

Gloss #2: TRUE++. UNDERSTAND++ STUDENTS PRO-3-pl (they) x-LOOK-AT-y (me), [NAME/CALL WHAT] RhQ ns-Charles (C hs forehead to chin).

Subsequent glossed translations appear in an alternate resource. For more information and inquiries, see www.neoaccess.org or email neoaccessllc@gmail.com

hopes. They recently discussed trying to adopt again through the agency they had used the first time. That meant traveling to China for at least a month, but, for the time being, Paul's work schedule wouldn't permit a leave of absence. Unsure what to say to Chas without going into all of their personal details, Eliza told him that she would share his question with Paul when he returned from work. She tried to project an all-business attitude, yet, inside, she was trembling with the sense that a remarkable thing had just occurred.

Chas had been Paul's professor for not only history classes, but also for a class on the U.S. Civil Rights Movement and its impacts on the Deaf-World. Eliza had also been a student at Gallaudet, but she had never taken a course with him. In their brief VP call, she noticed he seemed friendly and easy-going, with graying hair, slender hands, and a turtleneck that gave him an academic aura. Paul had only good things to say about him when he returned from work. When Eliza explained why he had called, Paul's dark eyebrows raised up toward his hairline. They discussed what they should say. They needed to know how serious Chas's proposal was so as not to get their hopes up or leap in. They talked the matter through in the living room, with Kimmie running in and out waving assorted dolls in the air.

Eliza had fallen in love with her husband when he was a handsome student in a linguistics class, he a senior and she a first-year graduate student at Gallaudet. After they married, the two of them left the DC area and settled in Kentucky, losing face-to-face contact with many of their Gallaudet friends and acquaintances, even Chas, whom Paul had so admired. However, people did keep in touch by sharing social media posts. Paul worked for the School for the Deaf in Louisville as a psychologist. Eliza interpreted part-time, wrote articles, and stayed home caring for Kimmie rather than sending her to day care. They had a nice balance to their family and a lovely life together. Why would they want to complicate it with another child? And yet Eliza couldn't stop herself from imagining taking Chas up on the offer. She knew how rarely an opportunity like this came along.

Paul rolled an extra chair over to the VP so they could sit side by side to make the video call. To have access to the telephone through the Video Relay Service was a wonderful benefit of technology. Within his lifetime, the unprecedented opportunity to be able to dial a number and have an interpreter appear on the video screen for Paul to make a call to whomever he wanted had become reality. However, no interpreter was needed for this VP-to-VP call.

Chas answered their call right away. After they exchanged warm greetings, Chas excitedly explained about the possibility of Eliza and Paul expanding their family, that is, if they wanted to. Their conversation blended into reminiscence and nostalgia about Paul's and Eliza's time at Gallaudet. Eliza and Paul had not settled whether they wanted a second deaf baby or a hearing child or whether they wanted to adopt or keep trying to conceive on their own, but with all their memories of Gallaudet flooding back, it was easy to imagine their lives transformed by the child Chas was telling them about. Paul touched Eliza's arm. She turned to him and saw her own excitement reflected in his eyes. Chas did not wait for one of them to tell him what their shared look meant. He told them to expect a call followed by a visit from an old friend, a delightful and sharp Ohio attorney named Vivian King Brown.

7
Just Sign This

Vivian had just handed a letter off to her assistant when a message popped up on her MacBook with Chas's phone number flashing across the screen. She clicked on the message and then saw Chas's image appear. There he was, her old friend right on her computer. She tentatively signed toward the video camera, using whatever that program was, just glad her assistant had recently taught her how to use it.

"I have good news for you,"[4] he signed in English word order for Viv.

Viv's slow signing was at optimum effort, and Chas understood she was trying her best. Chas slowed his signing for her and reported the news about the Jean-Baptiste family. Vivian whooped with joy, startling her assistant, who could hear her through the open office door. Viv had realized shortly after her promise to Roz that finding Elle a home presented some challenges and that she played a dual role in the process, first as a grandparent who had protective feelings toward her grandbaby, but subsequently as a lawyer who needed to carefully arrange custody details. She needed to wear different hats and perhaps dig in harder and be more relentless than usual.

While she was in Austin, she had a chance to meet Elle. The foster home where she was staying had several children. Her foster mother had tucked her into a playpen in a room with other cribs and toys, not an ideal setting. When Vivian first laid eyes on Elle, she was on her tummy, trying with all her might to roll onto her back. She radiated her mother's determination and vivaciousness. Her eyes sparkled as she took in the world, and she smiled a wide drooly smile as Vivian lifted her into her arms. Though there were no blood ties, Viv swore she also saw late husband's calm intelligence in baby Elle's expression.

Chas shared information about the Jean-Baptiste family, including that they already had one deaf child, a little girl they had adopted from China. Though they had not yet begun the process of looking to adopt another, he sensed they were hoping to soon.

"Oh, what joy!"[5]

Chas complimented her on all the ASL she had learned since they last spoke.

"I have been taking classes, and I sign with some deaf people at our church."[6] She warmed at the thought that he had noticed.

Chas provided her with the Jean-Baptiste family's address and phone number. For six days, she worked tirelessly on her caseload so that by the end of the week, she could drive her old Honda Civic to Danville, Kentucky. She was delayed on the highway and arrived later in the day than Eliza Jean-Baptiste expected. When Eliza settled them down for a cup of tea in the kitchen, Kimmie, who was two, ran up to Viv with a teddy bear and set the bear on Viv's lap.

"Oh, what a surprise. What's this?"[7] Viv laughed, remembering to sign to Kimmie.

Eliza noticed that Viv did not understand toddler sign language and explained that Kimmie meant to share the bear with her new baby sister. Viv could see that the little girl in front of her wanted to know where this sister was. Viv couldn't understand everything that Kimmie was signing, but, thanks to Eliza and her own ASL studies, she could respond with a sign for bear and for thank you. She told Kimmie that the bear would be cherished.

"I am so sorry. We did not mean to let her know about your granddaughter so soon. She pays attention to what we are saying and is very advanced in her language development. We thought we had better tell her what was going on."[8]

With typical toddler stubbornness, after discovering Viv could sign, Kimmie peppered her with more questions about her sister.

Viv was delighted with Kimmie's enthusiasm and saw the gift of the bear as a good sign. Kimmie kept up a steady stream of questions, which were so exuberantly expressed, Viv told Eliza she thought her daughter had a future career on the stage ahead of her. She was happy to learn that Eliza worked as a sign language interpreter and that Kimmie's father, Paul, had been born deaf and signed ASL. The use of ASL rather than spoken language rendered their house less cluttered with noise, but not silent, mostly due to the energy of a rambunctious toddler with a big heart.

The family also seemed to possess all of the baby paraphernalia they might need if they were to adopt another deaf baby. Viv had made a sort of checklist for what would be appropriate. Having a deaf baby is not all that much different than having a hearing one, but there were some visually related enhancements that Paul needed (and Eliza didn't, but certainly could use too), including a video baby monitor with a flashing light. Viv went through the list with Eliza, and Eliza showed Viv how the visual monitor they already owned worked, confessing that it was helpful to her too since the flashing light once woke her when Kimmie had climbed out of the crib. She showed Viv other supplies: a flashing light system throughout the house and the various devices they used for face-to-face calls. In addition to these technologies, Viv noted that their house had lots of books and toys, the kinds of things that stimulate language and cognition in children and that Viv herself had made sure to have on hand when she had adopted Roz.

Viv was so pleased with the Jean-Baptiste family, she prayed words of gratitude as soon as she got back in her Civic for her drive back to Ohio. Finding a family who already signed ASL was nothing short of His doing, and, of course, Chas's too. She had been in contact with and had read the files of several loving families sent through a social worker, but none seemed as equipped as the Jean-Baptiste family to raise Elle.

She still had a lot of work to do. There were a number of regulations to unravel in the adoption process and forms to fill out before the state would transfer custody. Once the family signaled that they were interested in taking custody, she worked diligently to unravel the codes and policies that were unfamiliar to her, eagerly awaiting the day she could tell Roz that Elle was going to the adoptive parents they had prayed for.

8

Sign on the Dotted Line

When Viv met the family on the first visit, she made Eliza feel at ease, despite coming to them on what amounted to a legal errand. Eliza had greeted her at the door, shown her to the kitchen, and put a kettle on the stove. Over tea, she learned that Viv was the baby's grandmother and that the mother, her adopted daughter, was an actress whose name Eliza had heard and who was now busy filming a new project in Chicago. This new wrinkle surprised Eliza. Paul had needed to get in to work and couldn't be at home for Viv's visit, so Eliza had agreed to gather details on what was being proposed. She wondered what he would think about adopting the daughter of one of the most beautiful women on television.

Hearing people sometimes found Eliza's family odd, signing ASL most of the time. Eliza's own family had discouraged her marriage to a deaf man and had been unhappy that she had chosen to adopt a deaf child instead of a hearing one, an act they implied was selfish since they did not sign ASL. Kimmie's energy could be overwhelming, but Viv was completely at home as she sat at their table, holding her teacup with a ladylike crook of her wrist and talking to Eliza with a voice tinged with a southern childhood. Viv acted exactly as if she were visiting family, saying pleasant things about her drive and taking an interest in what Eliza had to say about herself. Then Kimmie raced in with her Bear-Bear and spilled the beans. Yes, they wanted to adopt Vivian King Brown's grandbaby. Could they? Once the wheels started turning, there seemed to be no way to stop the process, and in Eliza's mind, no reason to since the bolt from the blue aligned with all of the couple's greatest hopes.

Viv stayed in touch with Eliza and talked the couple through dispatches she received from the magistrate's office in Cook County in the Chicagoland area. Roz had moved there to film her series. Baby Elle stayed in Austin with her foster family while Viv finalized the details of the open adoption, making sure of the reciprocity of paperwork across state lines.

To take her mind off her nervous anticipation of the day Elle would come to live with them, Eliza began preparing their household. She purchased a new highchair. She re-baby-proofed the corners of the living room fireplace. The photos Viv sent were of a tiny, pretty multiracial child with the most darling dimple. She seemed to beam as if the whole world was a delight.

Eliza and Paul transitioned Kimmie to a big-girl bed and bought new linens for her old crib, reorganizing the nursery so that it could accommodate their two little girls from different parts of the world. Eliza imagined the girls discovering their sisterhood in the days ahead. Would they grow to love one another the way girls should?

The legal wheels turned slowly, and there were days that Eliza feared they had accepted Viv's offer too hastily and were too occupied with their one child to be in a position to take on another. The twos for Kimmie were a rough stage. Eliza struggled to handle Kimmie's potty training accidents and temper tantrums. A few of Eliza's friends from Gallaudet had adopted deaf infants and toddlers, and when she found time, Eliza conferred with them about what kinds of challenges she could expect when a second child lived under their roof. Elle had recently turned six months old, and Kimmie was two and a half. Because they were only two years apart, potty training chaos could mean two children with toilet accidents at once, a juggling process Eliza wasn't sure any person could manage without losing their mind. But Eliza knew these opportunities did not come along very often. And what a weird coincidence that she had watched the show Roz was in, seeing her as a talented actor and drop-dead gorgeous too. If Elle favored her, she was sure to be a knockout. Viv being a mother to Roz had to have been a wonderful experience, and Eliza was excited at the prospect of Viv acting as Elle's sometime grandmother. Eliza would take what she could get of a part-time grandma Viv.

With all the changes swirling around her, Eliza temporarily forgot what she knew in her heart to be true, expanding their family constellation with a little girl who was deaf had happened naturally.* It was the life she knew, but the journey was to continue on an even deeper level. No matter how imperfect the housekeeping compared to pre-kid days, being able to provide an environment where visual language was accessible within their walls was an endeavor she gladly accepted. The family could offer Elle a language she could acquire at once.

The day came when the engine of paperwork finally ground to a halt, and a woman named Angela Orlando, a clerk in the family court of Cook County in the Chicago area, called Eliza and Paul and told them that Elle was officially theirs. Eliza pinched herself.

A day later, Paul fit the new car seat into the back of their Subaru next to Kimmie's. Eliza packed a picnic lunch, and the

---

* Children who acquire ASL at the hands of deaf or hearing persons may develop language equal to hearing children who have hearing parents. Generationally deaf families have the same fully functioning linguistic proficiency as families who use spoken language and pass a visual language on to the next generation (Bailes et al., "Language and Literacy Acquisition"). If all members of a community used signed language, then deaf individuals would have less disadvantages in relation to the hearing world and might, in fact, be bilingually advantaged (Groce, *Everyone Here Spoke Sign Language*).

three of them started their long drive to Austin to pick up their daughter and start a new chapter of their lives.

9
Signs of Discontent

Quinn did not start off her career thinking she might one day be a successful celebrity assistant and sometime publicist, but moving with Roz to Chicago and then later to Southern California led to her taking on more and more work handling media. Since Roz had transferred custody of Elle to the Jean-Baptiste family, she had invested *her* energies in her Netflix series, which had gone on to win critical acclaim two years running. In its third season, the show relocated its sets to the West Coast. Roz's stardom ascended to such an extent that studios like Sony Pictures solicited her for parts in feature films. Movie moguls sent dozens of scripts for her to read. Quinn sifted through the offers and acted as an intermediary with studio representatives. The high-profile negotiating boosted Quinn's confidence almost as much as being an insurance claim adjuster in Austin had once seemed to erode it. These days, Quinn attracted much more attention than she had before. She discovered the power of having eyes on her and was relieved that Roz trusted her as an assistant, publicist, and friend.

It helped that she had grown into her height and that she shared Roz's exercise, diet, and beauty regimens. She and Roz bonded over trips to the spa and workouts they sandwiched into the chaos of their mutually busy schedules. One day after a Pilates class, Quinn brought up the subject of Elle, a topic she had not discussed with Roz in the two years since Roz had signed the last of the adoption papers. A mother and her teenage daughter shared the locker room with them, and they could overhear their argument about a lost Apple watch. Was it Quinn's imagination that when they encountered private family moments, Roz became unusually quiet and attentive?

When Roz spoke of her daughter, she mostly called her Elle, even though Viv had told Quinn that the adoptive family had renamed her Ella, in honor of an ASL poet, Ella Mae Lentz. Quinn, considering understanding who this poet was as part of things she should know, had Googled Lentz. She found five or six YouTube videos and watched one. Lentz performed in ASL, reciting a poem that seemed beautifully executed, almost like theater. Quinn couldn't understand what she was saying. There were no captions, yet the motions of Lentz's hands and body mesmerized her.

"I want to see Ella." Roz led the way toward the club's café.

At first, because she had not used the name Elle as she usually did, Quinn thought Roz meant the poet she had just been thinking about who actually lived on the West Coast. Seeing Lentz perform publicly seemed to Quinn a potentially intriguing idea. She adored cultural events and, since moving to Los Angeles, had attended as many as she could, sometimes with Roz, and sometimes with whomever she was dating. But of course, Roz hadn't meant the poet.

The "Ella" Roz wanted to see was Elle. Viv's legal filings of an open adoption permitted them to reinitiate contact anytime they wanted. But Roz had not previously given Quinn any indication that she was even considering the idea. To Quinn, the risk of exposure seemed great, and getting involved with all-too-recent emotional turmoil, which might need to be publicly explained, seemed pretty darned risky. She didn't hesitate to argue against the plan.

"Why not just ask Viv to forward more pictures."

"I want to talk to her. I want to hear my baby's voice and get to know her. I am still not ready to be a mother, but I want to see her."

A hostess offered them a table in a pretty spot near the window but close to another party of women. They had chosen a time of day when things were quiet in the café, and only a few people were milling in and out, yet Quinn was well aware that gossip columnists often lurked in places like this one, hoping they might discover some juicy Hollywood secrets.

"We'd like to sit over there." Quinn pointed to a booth in a section that appeared as if it might be closed.

The hostess complied with her request.

Over a meal and a bubbly mimosa, Quinn offered to make the flight arrangements and set up a schedule with the Jean-Baptiste family if Roz agreed to meet Viv there. She expected that it would be a fragile gathering and her friend might need her mother's emotional support. Viv could also act as a sort of cover, a reason for making a visit to a child who was a stranger.

"I only need an hour, but okay."

Quinn had her doubts about Roz's ability to keep the visit short, but rather than challenging the woman she depended on for her great California life and career, she went about making arrangements.

A few days later, they boarded a plane to Louisville, Roz barely managing to semi-hide herself on a commercial flight under a pair of sunglasses and a Hermes scarf. They met Viv outside of baggage claim, rented a car, and decamped for their suite at the Hotel Ivy. In their rooms overlooking the Ohio River, Viv, concerned about Roz's recent weight loss, ordered them a meal from one of her favorite Louisville restaurants, a place called Shirley Mae's Café. Viv always made a point to search out the best home-cooked meals in any given city because she did not have to worry about putting on weight, she was so tiny. Viv was always trying to fatten Roz up, thinking she was much too thin and needed a little meat on her bones.

The next morning, they set out for the Jean-Baptiste family home in the suburb of Danville. Viv, who looked and seemed as energetic as ever, insisted on driving. On the road, she talked about what they might expect when they arrived. Eliza Jean-Baptiste, Ella's adoptive mother, was the only hearing member of the family. The girls signed ASL.

The neighborhood where the Jean-Baptiste family lived resembled the part of Columbus where Quinn was from. The wide streets brought back memories of shady rides on her bicycle and neighborhood kickball games. Roz, sitting in the back seat, complained about all the stop signs. Each midcentury two-story home seemed to have a different scented wreath on its front door. A great big elm shaded the family's lawn. A wide porch stretched across the front of the house. They parked on the street instead of in the driveway, and Viv led the way up the steps to a comfy porch with wicker furniture and pressed the buzzer on the door. Instead of a chime or hum, a bulb flashed directly above them. Viv explained that Paul Jean-Baptiste needed to be visually alerted to environmental sounds. He depended on the flashing lights as a way to know when people were at the door, when the phone was ringing, or when the baby monitor was registering sound in his daughters' bedroom.

"He's deaf?" Roz asked Quinn.

A woman about Quinn's age with a long light-brown braid and very blue eyes opened the door.

"Oh, come in, please! Do come in!"

A stunned smile crossed her face. Quinn was amused. Roz had that effect on people. Sometimes Quinn still felt like she had accidentally walked onto the pages of *People* magazine.

Aunt Viv hugged the woman and introduced Quinn and Roz to "her Eliza." Eliza behaved almost as nervously in

Quinn's presence as she did in Roz's. Two little girls, one four and a half and the other two and a half, rushed into the foyer. The older one with streaming shoulder-length black hair had the faint tinge of orange popsicle around her mouth, the younger was an identical copy of the Roz Quinn had seen in baby pictures. Eliza laughed an apology. She placed a hand on each girls' head to slow their dual rambunctiousness. She introduced the oldest as Kimmie, and the youngest as Ella, signing with one hand as she spoke their names. Roz beamed at her beautiful daughter, who, in her pink T-shirt and jeans, had a rugged, happy quality that invited nods of pleasure from all the adults—Viv, Quinn, Eliza, and Eliza's husband, Paul, a slender man with olive skin and thick dark-brown hair who joined them. The two little girls' hands began flying into motion, both of them signing at once. Eliza politely, but with some embarrassment, interpreted what they were saying.

"Yes, yes." Eliza signed and spoke. "These are the special visitors we talked about yesterday. The lady in the middle is very pretty and is an important person."[9]

Ella signed something in return, and Eliza blushed and shook her head.

"Yes, I see a bag, and I think there are presents. But it is not nice to ask the lady for presents. Don't ask about presents. Wait until she offers you one."[10]

Viv laughed a big, infectious, warm-hearted laugh.

"Just like her sister."[11]

Quinn naturally joined in on the laughter, which relieved some of the awkwardness she had been feeling in not understanding what the little girls were saying. Eliza, Paul, Viv, and the girls all were signing ASL. Quinn gathered that the sisters had not moved on from the question of presents and their parents were chastising them for being impolite, though not forcefully.

Viv hugged each girl, who signed in her direction wearing serious but pleased expressions as if they were hoping to impress her with what they were saying. Quinn was surprised at the discomfort she felt at not understanding what was being said. Not only did she not know what the girls or their parents or Viv were discussing, but because their hands slapped together from time to time and they sometimes made sounds, she felt anxious about what to do with her own hands.

Roz's eyes were very bright as if she were seeing something in the scene she, too, had not expected. Roz handed her gift bag to Quinn while she squatted down to speak to Ella.

"Aren't you a beautiful little thing." She held out her arms to invite a hug.

Ella slipped behind her sister. Quinn nervously fiddled with the collar of her shirt. Was this the reunion Roz had been hoping for?

10

I Didn't Sign Up for This

Eliza signed and spoke as she began to lead her guests toward the living room. For the first time in weeks, their house was without the usual dolls and Lego bricks scattered over the floor and dust on the bookshelves. She and Paul had spent most of the morning cleaning the downstairs and scrubbing the kitchen. Roz's intention to see her daughter had only been sprung on them a few days earlier, but no one had called to tell them what time of day their visitors might arrive. Eliza had rushed to get what she could done and prepare snacks from what they had in the house because there was no time to get to the store. When the doorbell rang, Eliza had just finished showering. Her braid was still damp and humid against her neck.

"We are thrilled and honored—" she began to say and sign but stopped before she finished her sentence.

The surreal feeling of inviting Roz Taylor into her house flustered her. She expected she might feel small and ordinary in front of Roz, but the sensation went much deeper. Eliza had dressed in her best blue cotton summer dress, and yet it was Roz in a casual silk jumpsuit with rose gold pendant earrings who seemed to set the tone of the visit. Even if she could afford the clothes of a movie star, Eliza wouldn't have been able to wear them in her child-centered home, not without one of the two girls smearing her with paint or spaghetti sauce.

Roz's friend—Lynn, was it?—was equally well dressed, though somehow more professionally, as if the visit represented a normal form of business for her. Eliza hoped Paul had instructed the girls to wash their hands. In the chaos of preparing, she had forgotten, and any sort of stain could be traveling on their palms, waiting to make its mark. Paul touched Eliza on the back, his quiet way of getting her attention. He asked if he should bring out the crackers and cheese platter she had thrown together. She signed a thank you.

"What a great day this is!"[12] She managed to say and sign when she turned to her guests.

Roz flashed her a gorgeous smile. "We finally meet!"

Eliza blithered nonsense for the next few minutes while her hands seemed to circle without direction. She kept up the small, empty talk as they entered the living room. Paul, Viv, and Eliza crowded onto the couch together with their backs to the window, and Roz and Quinn settled into the two stuffed chairs on the opposite side of the room, where they had to squint at the sun coming through the glass. Paul had set the Ritz Crackers and cheese slices on the coffee table, but nobody touched them, not even the girls. Quinn squirmed for a minute, drawing all of their attention. She removed a Polly Pocket figure that must have gotten wedged under a seat cushion.

Paul laughed and disappeared, returning with a third chair, which he set up for himself near the fireplace in order to give Viv and Eliza more room. Eliza wracked her brain trying to think of things to say, afraid that if she stopped talking, her worst fear, that Roz had come to pass judgment on her, might be realized. She was terrified that Roz would look upon her small, mostly tidy (except for the Polly Pocket) house as a reason for deciding that she and Paul were unfit parents. Ever since Lynn? Quinn? had contacted her to arrange the visit, Eliza had been in a state of panic about what Roz's sudden desire to be in touch meant. She was afraid that Roz had an interest in confessing to being Ella's birth mother, information Eliza felt Ella should know one day, but was far too young to understand at age two and a half, and which would likely confuse her. There were just too many twists and turns in the story.

When Viv had arranged Ella's open adoption, she had been very straightforward about the clause that allowed Roz to be involved in her daughter's life. Nonetheless, over the last two years, there had been no word from Roz, only Viv's occasional visits and phone calls. Eliza had stopped believing that Roz cared to know Ella. Dear Viv, as a surrogate grandmother to Ella, and by default to Kimmie, encompassed the totality of Roz's maternal investment. Roz appeared regularly on their television, but not in their lives like Viv. Her face peered out from magazine covers in the supermarket. Sitting in their living room with her legs crossed neatly at the ankle, Eliza had a hard time looking at her or thinking of her as anything but an image. Her eyes were drawn to Quinn, who appeared to be Roz's agent or personal assistant. Quinn had the same proud, self-assured quality as Roz, but her softer demeanor made Eliza's efforts to break the ice feel less like drowning.

"Those are lovely earrings."[13]

Quinn touched the hoops in her lobes and smiled.

Eliza grappled for what to say next. Thankfully, Viv cleared her throat.

"I am sure we all agree that it is a good day indeed to be in each other's presence! Perhaps naming each person is not really necessary again. In fact, I believe it would be redundant. But protocol rules. I will once again lead the legal introductions of this beloved congregation. After all, I am the only one who knows all gathered here!"[14]

Viv had been Mrs. Freddie Lee Brown, later known as Mrs. Vivian King Brown, Esquire, when she had first come to their house. Then later she had become Vivian, which had morphed into Auntie, Aunt Viv, or V at the side of the mouth in ASL to the girls. She spoke about each person in the room with courtroom decorum, calling each of them Mr. or Ms. and Miss Ella and Miss Kimmie. Viv accompanied her spoken English with corresponding ASL. She acknowledged the competing interests of everyone in the room and managed to relieve Eliza's tension. For Eliza, legal boundaries sometimes felt easier to negotiate than emotional ones.

Viv's simultaneous communication (SimCom)* was surprisingly understandable. Not many people who aren't experienced signers can do it well, as if being skilled at SimCom were a good thing. Viv did not want to leave Roz and Quinn out of the communication loop.

"I am so glad we are all able to start our life together, as a new kind of truly modern family!"[15] Viv made them feel a communal bond in their relation to Ella.

Eliza signed the word "family" to Paul as a kind of echo. She had become very close to Viv in the last two years, as had Paul and the girls. Paul would forgive Viv anything, even SimCom.** The girls watched Viv address the group, avoiding their usual habit of interrupting with questions. They lay on the carpet spectating, flitting their eyes toward Roz when they thought she wasn't looking at them. When Eliza and Paul

---

* Using two languages at the same time can potentially rob each of its expressiveness. English and French cannot be spoken simultaneously, but SimCom can be attempted with ASL and spoken English. Physically, SimCom can occur since one form of language is communicated verbally and the other manually and visually instead of being produced via the same spoken modality. Grammatical differences, subtle meanings, and other information may be omitted. When attempting SimCom, a speaker has to sideline one language's grammar and syntax to accommodate the delivery of the other language. The language that usually gets impacted is ASL rather than spoken English. Reasons include the nonmanual markers of ASL (facial grammar) may be decreased, inappropriate, or omitted, making communication incomplete. Many Deaf community members are acclimated to deciphering spoken language from an unequal position (Johnson, Erting, Liddell, "Unlocking the Curriculum").

** Some deaf people consider SimCom a form of discrimination, even audism (Lapiak, "Simultaneous communication").

had been cleaning the house and the girls had asked who was coming, Eliza had told them that Viv was bringing her important daughter, Rosalind Taylor. Kimmie, because she was older, had expressed a great deal of excitement about having an important person visit. She had wanted to know if it would be possible for Roz to introduce her to Wonder Woman, her very favorite superhero.

Eliza had skirted the issue of Roz's biological relationship to Ella in her preparatory conversations with the girls. Viv, with some dexterity, reinforced the potential need for honoring custody arrangements in legal terms in ways that also prevented the girls from following. Eliza and Paul were planning to discuss Ella's adoption in more detail with her at around seven or eight, the same age they planned to have their conversation with Kimmie, who was getting much closer to a time when she might have questions. Both girls understood the basics. They knew that they were chosen children. They had not yet asked who their birthparents were or begun to understand that having no blood ties to their parents was mildly unusual.

Some of the girls' attraction to Roz Taylor was still connected to the discussion of gifts at the door. Viv never arrived without one. But Viv never seemed to notice when they were rude or impatient. Eliza and Paul raised them to be generally pretty good about manners, but when anticipation got the better of them, they slipped like most children their age.

They were good at reading subtle social cues, and before the group reached the living room, Eliza could see that they had figured out that Roz and Quinn did not understand ASL. As the adult talk drew long, the girls openly discussed each woman. They signed to each other about Roz's pretty hair and her shoes, perhaps knowing that Eliza would temporarily ignore the transgression. Despite their actions being naughty, Eliza felt pride in how easily they were developing communication subtleties like figuring out hearing status. Eliza had heard stories in the Deaf community about young deaf children and kids with deaf parents being able to tell who was deaf and who was hearing in a room, but now she was seeing it in action. They were both very perceptive girls; of course, Kimmie was much more sophisticated, with Ella coming up behind.

"I think I notice some babies who are ready to get beyond the news of the day."[16] Viv chuckled when their conversation got stale to a point where more than just Eliza was noticing it.

Viv lowered her hands and rested them in her lap.

What an undertaking her SimCom had been for the twenty minutes she had been speaking! And she had done it without being a student in a full-time ASL program, just from the classes she had taken, her semi-regular practice with a tutor, and some church conversations. Eliza should have tried to hire interpreters to spare either herself or Viv the duty of interpreting for the group.[*] But there had been so little time. Plus, an interpreter who recognized Roz Taylor posed another threat that Eliza needed to keep in mind. None of them could afford to risk leaking the information that Roz was Ella's birth parent. The story might break in the future, but while Ella was young, it suited Eliza to have Ella and Roz's relationship kept private. If the cat got out of the bag, it would be easier for Roz to reclaim custody, a thought that made Eliza shudder. Eliza took advantage of Viv's pause to scuttle the girls out of the room and bring out a homemade book she and they had finished earlier that morning.

Kimmie gave the book to Roz and explained that it was a gift to her for being so pretty and important and for being Viv's daughter. Eliza interpreted her exact words. The girls

---

* Co-interpreters, while they are team interpreting, usually share the cognitive, linguistic, and cultural loads of roughly twenty- to thirty-minute segments (Acutrans19, "How to Ensure").

had drawn pictures, and Eliza had written captions to tell the story of their family.

"It isn't very much," Eliza said, knowing in her heart it was everything. "But we thought you might enjoy it."[17]

The girls danced around Roz, excited for her to look at the pages and admire their drawings. Eliza had included some of Kimmie's alongside Ella's scribbles because they were a bit more sophisticated. She had picked drawings of Kimmie's that were related to Ella or the whole family. In most of the pictures, the Jean-Baptiste family members were holding hands. Kimmie liked to draw hearts around the borders. She also loved drawing Eliza's hair loose and flowing, although she almost never wore it that way. Eliza understood this detail as Kimmie wishing that her mother looked more like a princess.

Roz expressed delight in each picture, her eyes gleaming as she turned the pages. When she was finished looking, she pressed the book to her heart and told the girls it was now her most treasured possession, a comment that Viv quickly interpreted so that they fully understood the success of their gesture. Viv then presented each of the girls with a gift, a gardening play set that included a plastic hand rake, a shovel, and a quilted carrier, something that would be fun to take outside when Eliza had weeding to do, but also a toy they could take to the beach for building sandcastles on their next vacation to the coast or a lake. Viv was always so thoughtful. Paul thanked her for her generosity. He nudged the girls forward to also sign their gratitude.

"We have not come empty-handed either." Roz looked to Quinn.

Quinn reached down to the side of her chair for the Tiffany bag that rested there. It was the same bag the girls had spotted when Roz had come through the door.

"First of all—" Roz took the bag from Quinn and removed an envelope from the inside. "I am establishing a trust in Ella's name for her college education." She handed the envelope to Eliza, who, shocked at the enormity of what she was holding, fidgeted with it. Her tongue temporarily refused to leave the floor of her mouth.

"The college fund will be taken care of by my financial advisors."

"But you didn't have to—"[18] Eliza mumbled.

"Nonsense." Roz waved her hand. "I am more jazzed by this next gift. I helped design it myself and had it custom made."

All of a sudden, Eliza realized that no one was interpreting for Paul, Kimmie, and Ella. She quickly recapped what had just been said. Paul frowned. Oh boy, she would hear about it later.

Eliza tried to do better and just decided to SimCom. She suspected that the Tiffany bag held an actual Tiffany piece, which, in addition to an entire college education, amounted to a severe imbalance in gift-giving for the day, something that, with her midwestern roots, she couldn't quite accept. When Eliza had first seen the bag, she had thought it amazing enough that it must have happened to be the first bag Roz had on hand.

"When I was filming my recent Netflix series, I went to see one of my favorite jewelers, a master jeweler named Michael Alznauer.* Maybe you have heard of him?"

Eliza shook her head. Why would she know a jeweler at Tiffany's?

Paul had purchased their wedding rings at a Kay Jewelers in the mall in Louisville, and here, on the dressiest occasion of her life, she wasn't even wearing it. She spent so much time painting with the girls or cooking, she almost never wore her ring anymore. Roz removed a white gold heart-shaped locket from a Tiffany blue box and displayed the dazzling item on her

* Michael Alznauer is actually a deaf jeweler who lives in Chicago with his wife, Cathy.

palm, shifting her position so they could all see. There were places for two pictures, one on each side of the locket. On one side, a photo of Roz faced a picture of Eliza's family on the other. Eliza recognized the family portrait in the locket as one Viv had taken. On the outside, an artist had engraved the letters EB to symbolize Elle Brown and EJB for Ella Jean-Baptiste. The letters were etched in an exquisite filigree pattern interspersed with tiny diamonds. It was a delicate, lovely piece of jewelry that must have cost nearly as much as Eliza's family car.

Because neither Viv nor Eliza interpreted Roz's words into ASL, neither Paul nor the girls understood who the gift was for or seemed to notice the initials. They did, however, sense its value. The girls stood close to Roz, and Kimmie boldly reached out and touched the chain. Paul had followed the verbal conversation well enough to get the gist of Roz's words. He rose from his chair and gently drew the girls back to a safe distance. Eliza recognized the crease in between his eyebrows as an expression of amazement.

"It's truly beautiful." Eliza took the locket from Roz and gently placed it in its box. She made sure to SimCom so that her family would understand. "We'll put it away for now so Ella doesn't lose it or yank it off."[19]

Recently, Ella had tossed one of her My Little Pony figures in the toilet.

Eliza wondered what questions Kimmie and Ella might ask later about what had happened that day. After Roz, Quinn, and Viv had gone, Eliza caught her family up on what had been missed in the spoken conversation. Paul and Kimmie seemed intrigued, but Ella went back and forth between watching the conversation and playing with her new shovel. Paul and Eliza agreed that the locket should be hidden in a drawer where it would be safe. Eliza was relieved to put it away so that she could forget about it for a while.

11
Minus Sign

Viv let Quinn drive back to the hotel. She was tuckered from all the legalese she'd had to engage in. The shear craziness of putting so many people together in one room to talk out their relationship to a child they each loved so passionately had drained Viv body and soul. She prayed as they reached the highway that Roz's new interest in Ella wasn't all talk and that she would do more than just shower her with gifts. She thought that Ella was thriving in her current situation and was the happiest of little girls as a member of the Jean-Baptiste family.

Her own girls—Roz and Quinn—discussed how remarkable Ella was as they drove north to the Hotel Ivy. Quinn remarked that Ella was a dead ringer for Roz when she was little and pretty darn smart for two, her hearing difference just about the only divergence between her and her biological momma.

Viv loved thinking back to that time when her baby girl, Roz, was not much older than Eliza's oldest, Kimmie. She adored those times she helped Roz paint pictures and read her first words. After they started high school, Quinn spent every Wednesday at their house, adding to Viv's blessings. She helped Quinn bake chocolate cakes to take home and paid for the girls to go off and get their hair done. And look who they had grown up to be. Who wouldn't be proud of two successful twenty-eight-year-olds, one who had the best organizational brains Viv had ever encountered, and the other famous in nearly every household in the country?

Quinn interrupted Viv's reminiscence in the passenger seat to ask when she thought the Jean-Baptiste couple were going to start teaching Ella to speak. The question surprised Viv. She assumed it stemmed from a conversation Quinn and Roz had had while Viv had been extending her goodbyes on the Jean-Baptiste's porch. It had taken Viv nearly ten extra minutes to leave because, at the last minute, Paul had signed that her friend Chas Stacker was coming to town for a conference. Viv had taken an immediate interest in forming plans to drop in at the same time. Wouldn't it be wonderful to see him again?

"Eliza told me that the process of Ella's spoken language development will happen naturally. Paul and Eliza will do hands-on activities and expose the girls to a lot of books, reading, and life experiences, and then slowly, once the girls follow the syntax, they will add spoken English."

The girls had speech therapy, which was included with Kimmie's kindergarten curriculum and the early intervention program for Ella. Eliza had told Viv that the girls were developing language in a natural way. Spoken English was not natural to them, so they used ASL. Also, they generally did not spontaneously use spoken language at home. They were on track in their speech programs at school, and there was nothing to worry about.

Roz piped up from the back seat to ask when and where Viv herself had learned ASL.

"Do you think your momma is too old to learn something new?" Viv shifted around in her seat to look at Roz while she spoke to her. Her daughter was spread out in the back, leaning as glamorously and wistfully as if she were on a velvet couch. The headlights of the car behind them gleamed through the window behind her.

"You are the smartest woman I know, Mommy."

Viv slackened her seat belt, reached back, and slapped her daughter on the thigh.

"Stop that now. *The* Ohio State University offers American Sign Language classes that I have been taking. My deaf friends at church told me about the OSU classes. And before I met L, when I was a law clerk in Washington, I took some classes at Gallaudet. I didn't use ASL very often when you were young, but I learned it."

The class that Viv was currently taking at OSU required her to interact with the Deaf community. She'd recently met a number of new people. She had also watched ASL videos on YouTube and had attended Deaf events. Since Ella's birth, Viv had worked hard to become someone her granddaughter could feel comfortable with, someone she could confide in using her own words. There was a big question mark as to Viv and Roz's connections to Ella with the open adoption options—all still to be seen . . .

Viv was excited to learn that Chas, who also continued to help her ASL along in their regular VP chats, was planning to be in Kentucky. Chas was very fond of the Jean-Baptiste family and believed that the decision to place Ella with them was spot-on. He thought Ella was astonishingly lucky to be in a signing environment from such a young age with parents who took a deaf child's language and communication needs seriously.

Every time Viv visited the Jean-Baptistes, she basked in the love and joy the family radiated. Every hug she received lifted a layer of discomfort she sometimes felt about Roz not raising Ella herself. Viv felt guilty thinking that Roz likely would not have provided Ella with the depth of community the Jean-Baptiste family had provided her with. It was doubtful that Ella's language progress would have developed to the point where, at two and a half, she was communicating better with the adults in her life than most hearing children did with theirs. Roz was an extraordinarily loving woman, but she had also been tentative and ambivalent about Ella's loss of hearing, and perhaps only saw the ways Ella might hold her back rather than the ways she might make her grow. Viv remembered her teacher at OSU, Marla Berkowitz, discussing the concept of "deaf gain." Marla emphasized that the focus should not be on the hearing *loss*, but on the benefits the Deaf community adds to our culture, or deaf *gain.*[*]

Though Viv was sure that Roz would have eventually adapted to a parenting role, the road might have been long and difficult, and she would perhaps have had to abandon her astonishing career. Ella benefited from family members who embraced who she was as part of their mutual identity and who provided her with an immediate sense of belonging. Viv remembered the communication horror stories Chas had told her about being a deaf child living among non-deaf people. Viv believed that Eliza and Paul made each of their girls feel loved, natural, and confident rather than outsiders in a hearing world.

Viv hoped Roz understood that Ella was one beyond-lucky little girl.[**] As they crossed the bridge into Louisville, Quinn pointed to the barely visible moon out of the car window just

* Bauman and Murray, *Deaf Gain.*

** Some deaf children in America live with language deprivation along with significant delays in language exposure and education (LEAD-K, "What is Language Deprivation?"). Hearing parents may rely on advice from doctors and audiologists about assistive listening devices such as cochlear implants or hearing aids rather than focusing on bilingual language development of ASL and English. Once deaf children receive assistive listening devices, they often are exposed to spoken English exclusively, which impacts language deprivation in the Deaf community. Some American deaf children have access to services that children in some other countries do not. Enhanced access often relates to legislative initiatives. However, countries like South Africa provide numerous educational outlets and community programs for integrating deaf people that the United States does not. The struggle for equal communication rights and access remains ongoing and complex in nations around the world.

to their left. After dinner and getting settled at the hotel, they went out to their balcony to admire the view before going to bed. The moon looked as full and as glossy as a spotlight hovering over the skyline. Inhaling the soft night air, Viv placed her arms around Roz and Quinn. She wished that Roz might one day learn to feel more comfortable with the Jean-Baptiste family. Viv and Quinn, of course, did not have a biological bond to Ella, and Viv sensed Roz was still mourning the child she would not raise. Viv dared not underestimate the expanse of feelings—they ran deep and wide. Perhaps each of them would find something meaningful in the space that held what they believed they weren't given.

12

Sign Off

Paul was home with the girls the day the audiologist from the Early Intervention and Hearing Detection (EIHD) office arrived to do Ella's three-year-old screening.* Eliza left early in the morning for an interpreting gig across the state. Paul, pulling himself away from his huddle with the girls on the couch in front of *Sesame Street*, greeted the dark-haired woman in her mid-thirties who had buzzed the ringer and sent the doorbell light flashing. Taking a moment to realize that she did not follow his sign language, he motioned her inside. She fingerspelled her name, Robyn with a *y*. Paul took several minutes, while the girls were tearing around the inside of the house doing who knows what (they always seemed to be a little wilder when they were home with just Dad), to communicate to Robyn that they should reschedule the visit due to communication issues. Or, if she could do it on the spot, arrange for a video remote interpreter (VRI), someone who could provide interpreting services via a remote device.

After forty-five minutes, Robyn, sitting on the chair in front of the fireplace, managed to get in touch with an agency

* Early intervention (EI) services are required for infants/toddlers who are born deaf or hard of hearing, and each state has an early intervention system. EI services are provided for free or at low cost and ideally should be individualized based on the needs of the child and family. Services are designed to benefit each child's development physically, cognitively, communicatively, socially, or in the emotional and adaptive areas (NAD, "Early Intervention Services").

to secure an interpreter via the VRI system on her iPad. Paul spent the time preparing the girls' lunch and putting Ella down for a nap. Kimmie had recently declared herself "too old" for naps, so Paul convinced her to look at picture books on her bed while he talked with Robyn. The purpose of Robyn's visit was to discuss Ella's long-term hearing needs and set up some spoken language early intervention. It was standard for EIHD to check in at this time of a child's life and begin suggesting plans. Still, Paul hated the pushy bureaucracy of it all.

Through the VRI system, Robyn communicated to Paul that the depth of Ella's hearing loss indicated that she was a good candidate for cochlear implants. She tried to persuade Paul to discuss scheduling surgery right away. Robyn explained the importance of an earlier time frame of implantation: it was better for speech and language development. Paul explained that he and his wife were not interested in having their daughters implanted while they were still learning ASL as their first language. This was a stance he knew was controversial with some hearing professionals but one which he and Eliza had talked over and were in full agreement about.

Through the on-screen interpreter, Robyn asked Paul to clarify what he had just told her, so he repeated himself, slowing his signing down to a nearly sarcastic speed, making the interpreter on the other side of the screen seem to smirk. Robyn appeared to be at a loss as to what to do next.

Surely, Paul wondered, *other parents of deaf children must have reservations about implants.*

Paul had once been fitted for an implant after hearing aids had not worked, and the experience had been traumatizing. Implants and hearing aids sometimes place a child in a kind of purgatory between the hearing and Deaf-Worlds. Some hearing people think the devices are a cure for hearing loss. Paul knew full well that some medical professionals were unwilling to acknowledge any problems with cochlear implants (CIs) and hearing aids because, for them, deafness was a problem that needed to be resolved with medical intervention. Robyn asked Paul to sign his name on a legal document that stated that as Ella's legal guardian he was waiving EIHD's advice about the surgery. He grudgingly added his signature, but only as a way of getting Robyn out of his house.

Paul shared his thoughts on the meeting with Eliza that night, describing how shocked Robyn had seemed and his irritation that she had needed to verify their choices using legal means. It was not that he and Eliza wanted Ella to go without cochlear implants for the entirety of her life even if she one day thought she wanted them. They had considered that implants might be something both girls would end up with when they were older and a little more aware of how to move between the different social spheres of hearing and deaf people. These early years of language development required one thing at a time. Paul just wanted them to be a family who communicated with each other the way deaf people were used to communicating naturally. Was that so terrible? He thought implants were awful things, mechanically artificial, like a robotic appendage. He never would have chosen to have them on his own and had no real desire to see his daughters get them.

Robyn called again a few days later, timing her visit to when Eliza was home, perhaps because she thought she could wheedle a little more compliance out of Ella's hearing parent. Robyn told Eliza she wanted to provide more educational information about the implants and show her the educational plan based on their use. Paul felt a little harassed by her inability to understand his perspective, but he and Eliza ultimately agreed to another meeting because they wanted the speech and language therapy sessions the EIHD program was required to provide.

Eliza and Paul requested that the agency arrange either an interpreter or a parent educator who was ASL fluent for all future interactions as a courtesy to Paul and the girls. Robyn had actually arranged to have someone new attend. Robyn had realized she was out of her league with the family and had asked her supervisor to hire someone who was well versed in Deaf community issues. The EIHD office hired someone to help with educational decisions with this family specifically, a woman who had a degree in Deaf education from Gallaudet.* The agency needed another early intervention parent advocate anyway, so this was perfect timing. Both Paul and Eliza liked the agency's hire, Leslee, even though she was not a trained SKI-HI consultant.**

Leslee told the family that she was working on finding a Certified Deaf Mentor who had an early intervention degree as well as SKI-HI training to work with the family. Until Leslee was able to do that, in the weeks that followed, Leslee accompanied Robyn on visits to their house and answered many of their questions as Robyn tested and worked with Ella. Robyn was often left out of the laughing and joking that took place because she did not sign and Leslee did not SimCom. Instead, Leslee used only ASL, which made Paul like her even more. Robyn persisted in asking why they were disinterested in cochlear implants, making arguments about their efficacy that both Paul and Eliza already understood. Leslee, knowing that Robyn could not communicate, went ahead and picked up the role of the interpreter at times, which was a conflict of her duties, and sometimes awkward. Paul felt as if they repeated a blunt *no* at least twenty times, and the ordeal irritated him

* Gallaudet often provides state-of-the-art information in the field. However, the person hired had no early intervention degree nor was the person deaf.

** SKI-HI is the oldest and largest institute of its kind in the U.S. Some benefits may be seen by having a Certified Deaf Mentor trained in the SKI-HI curriculum to help comprehend the deaf child's challenges and build language acquisition. SKI-HI programming helps families learn how to promote communication and language with the child in ways that best match the child's needs (SKI-HI, "What Is a Deaf Mentor?").

further. He was appalled that EIHD was attempting to do a hard sell of cochlear implants on its clientele. If they used this strong-arm tactic with him, what were they doing to parents who had no clue about communication options for their deaf children?

And then one day, Robyn showed up at their house without Leslee. It took a long time with their communication barrier for Paul to understand that EIHD was no longer agreeing to pay Leslee as a parent mentor. Eliza, breaking her usual habit of not giving Robyn the crutch of spoken language in front of Paul, asked what happened, and Robyn was evasive, only saying that her organization had made some changes and Leslee had been let go.

Later, Paul learned through mutual acquaintances that Leslee had been fired. EIHD wanted workers willing to advocate for cochlear implants and not for the Deaf community, which, in his opinion, was entirely backward. The real tragedy, Paul felt, was that Leslee had been far more help to Ella than Robyn had ever been. He believed Ella was being denied the full benefit of services because the agency wouldn't provide communication access through ASL. Why couldn't the people at the EIHD office help all families regardless of their choices? Why did they push an ideology about what type of communication they thought best? The poor treatment stood to delay Ella in her preparation for school. He felt like EIHD had put them on a track to wait, wait, wait, instead of doing what they could now to help their daughter grow and learn.

A week later, Paul received a job offer from a deaf charter school in Minnesota where there were solid services for their family. Minnesota had a large Deaf community, and St. Paul had a good deaf elementary school. Even though the salary was not much more than he was already making, Paul and Eliza discussed the situation and agreed—he didn't hesitate to accept the job.

13
Sign of the Times

Eliza found some respite in their new home. Their move to Minnesota freed her from her share of the battle with EIHD. But even after they relocated to where deaf services were generally culturally sensitive, she occasionally ran into well-meaning doctors and education professionals who asked her if she had considered fitting Kimmie or Ella for implants. These people sang the praises of the devices. Not only did the salesmanship regarding implants continue, but often these same people would emphasize listening and spoken language, sometimes over other academic learning, prioritizing spoken language with a forcefulness that bordered on unconscious bigotry. At least Eliza and Paul knew how to respond. They politely thanked whomever they were speaking with before changing the subject. It helped that Kimmie and Ella were both thriving. Kimmie's reading level scored among the highest in her first-grade class. Ella had begun adjusting to a routine at her new preschool and had made several new friends among children who could hear and a few who were also deaf.

From a political perspective, it was disconcerting to Eliza to continually confront the advice that the girls "needed to learn to listen and use their hearing and speech" from so many people she would otherwise consider intelligent and perceptive. She had become something of a stalwart on the issue of leaving the girls to their signing world long enough for them to feel a bond with a community that would always embrace them. Why couldn't her family feel free to expend its energy on living the way that naturally made sense for them? Why did other people want to impose their views when all she and Paul and the girls wanted was the liberty to exist in a familiar, comfortable unit among people who shared their means of interacting with one another? Why would Paul, or the father of any family, want to be surrounded by those who spoke in ways that he and his children could not master with the same fluency no matter how hard they tried? If professionals wanted the girls to talk so badly, what about encouraging the development of their minds so that they had something to *talk about*?

Hearing people didn't seem to understand what it was like to miss incidental information delivered in spoken language or sounds like the furnace coming on (or not) or the water running or overflowing in the kitchen sink. Eliza had not fully understood either until she had married into the Deaf-World. She discovered through her intimacy with Paul that she took her ability to hear for granted. Eliza believed that people naturally adopted a bias based on their own communication choices and abilities.*

Eliza was relieved to find out that a different service provider, the Deaf Center in Minneapolis, was a place that embraced Paul's Deaf perspective. She valued their intervention and educational services and respected their case managers, who, unlike the case manager from EIHD, were ASL fluent. The Deaf Center case managers signed with the girls

* Deaf people experience differences in taking in auditory input, even when using devices like implants or hearing aids. To use assistive listening devices sometimes means accepting a lesser status in a world that is not their own rather than competency in a world that is theirs. There are millions of people in the world who are born with hearing loss. There are billions of hearing people on the planet who do not need assistive listening devices. This could be one reason assistive listening devices are desired by some people with hearing loss. Media messages report the benefits of cochlear implants and other devices, which may perpetuate the hope of a cure for hearing loss (Padden and Humphries, *Inside Deaf Culture*).

when they visited and engaged in the kind of small talk that helped them know the Jean-Baptiste family in a deeper way. Through the Deaf Center, Eliza successfully negotiated extra speech/language services and accommodations for Kimmie outside of her deaf school. It wasn't always easy having children who were "handicapped" in the eyes of the government and the public. Eliza felt as if she spent too much of her free time trying to undo well-intentioned people's placement of her girls in a "less-than" box.

One day, when she took Ella and Kimmie to the local playground for a few minutes after picking Kimmie up from school, a mother of a hearing child approached Eliza and asked her what was wrong with Ella. Ella was standing at the base of the slide arguing with her sister about whose turn it was to climb the ladder. She signed emphatically as she demanded her right to go first. She moved her hands wildly and could not hear her own small high-pitched vocalizations. To someone who didn't know she had a loss of hearing, she possibly sounded as if she was in pain.

Eliza waved at the girls to get their attention and then left the park without bothering to answer the woman's question. She felt embarrassed despite knowing that it was neither her actions that had created the tension nor the other mother's actions since her question had been based on an innocent assumption. Once home, Eliza retreated to her garden to plant tulip bulbs and reflect on what had made her so angry. It had been the word "wrong" that had delivered the sour note. The word had caused Eliza to momentarily lapse in her tendency to educate, to take advantage of a teachable moment. If Eliza had explained that her daughter was deaf, she feared the woman might have categorized her as "one of those signers, those deaf-mutes, those poor unfortunates who make those odd sounds." The woman had probably felt pity toward Ella.* *Not today, please God, not today.*

Eliza sometimes felt as if her family had to battle for every scrap of validation and every educational choice that allowed her girls to flourish. Kimmie received some speech and language therapy, but Eliza spoke with the specialists at the school and asked that her education in this area not be at the expense of her learning to read, write, do math, and develop creative thinking skills, all things she could do as a visual language user. Expecting that the girls would somehow miraculously one day lip-read so well they could communicate effectively via spoken language represented a sort of pipe dream on the system's part.

The woman in the park reminded Eliza that not everyone saw the world the way she did. As Eliza dug holes for her bulbs, she remembered the day Roz had visited. An anxiety that Roz harbored certain prejudices about her daughters ate at Eliza all through the afternoon. Roz could easily one day demand changes in how she and Paul were raising Ella that would further undermine their decision to remain sovereign from the biases of the hearing community. Eliza and Paul had not seen Roz since that uncomfortable afternoon in Kentucky two years earlier; however, the image of the biological mother of the daughter she was changing her life to raise often appeared in Eliza's mind. She envisioned Roz's delicate features, her facial expressions, and the awkwardness of her attempt to hug Ella.

The expensive locket sat in a drawer in Eliza's bureau, waiting for a day that Ella could reasonably wear it without damaging or losing it or asking questions about why it had been given to her in the first place. The college fund sat in a

---

* Deaf people report encountering differing levels of understanding from the hearing world, including encountering questions such as "Can deaf people think if they can't speak?" "Should deaf people drive?" and "Is sign language a real language?" (Lane, "Do Deaf People Have a Disability?")

bank, growing interest. Neither of Roz's gifts addressed the most immediate financial questions related to her future, however. If Roz was going to throw money away, why not do it in a way that benefited Ella now? Or help some other deaf child with the cost of a private school, or if a family chose implants, help defray the cost of therapy or other expenses post-surgery.*

Eliza was not simpatico with Roz at the moment and had not gone to see her recent film. She also refused to watch more than part of an episode of either Netflix series Roz starred in, not because both weren't getting good reviews—they had received high critical acclaim, and people Eliza knew had enjoyed them. No, Eliza avoided reminders of Roz because it made her uncomfortable to think about a well-known person who had authority over her family. Why had she and Paul allowed the adoption agreement to be so one-sided in Roz's favor? Viv had assured them that they had the blessing of both Viv and Roz to raise Ella as they pleased. Sometimes, on days when she was feeling stressed, Eliza indulged in a little bit of

---

* Cochlear implantation costs between $30,000–$50,0000 per ear and is usually covered by insurance. Hearing aids may or may not be covered by insurance. Results with CIs may not make significant differences in sound discrimination, making the investment a gamble. Scholars in the article "Bilingualism: A Pearl to Overcome Certain Perils of Cochlear Implants" discuss salient issues in cochlear implantation of deaf children. Cochlear implants (CIs) have shown improvement in some young deaf children's speech articulation, but speech gains do not always correlate with language acquisition/fluency. Recent research has indicated risks of language deprivation during critical brain development periods with potential for gaps in cognitive and social skills. The authors of the article propose that before, during, and after implantation, deaf children simultaneously acquire a signed language along with a spoken language to safeguard full language access and optimal long-term outcomes.

Some who are implanted may experience success due to having heard prior to losing their hearing, but children who receive implants as young as twelve months of age sometimes face poor results due to a variety of factors. Success of implants depends on the age of surgery, type of implant, therapy after implantation, motivation level of the person with the implant, and how people around the person receiving the device interact with the individual newly learning to hear. For some deaf children who are getting CIs, it could be that implantation is seen as a possible "cure" for profound hearing loss. (Humphries et al., "Bilingualism").

rancor at the thought that Viv and Roz weren't the only ones with a say-so.

Eliza would give her blessing to implants when and if Kimmie and Ella were old enough to compare pros and cons and wanted to have the surgery. If either decided the surgery was for them, she and Paul would find a way. She feared that Roz might develop so strong a desire for Ella to speak like a "normal" child that she would interfere with Ella's chance to have autonomy about her communication choices. It could be a hard conversation to have with people who had not lived inside the Deaf community, but what parent would not wish their child to speak the language they spoke?*

Roz had done a PSA about the #MeToo movement and seemed to be sensitive to issues of race, gender, and class, but her open-minded public statements had not yet, as far as Eliza knew, extended to disability issues or issues of the Deaf community specifically. It was possible that Eliza, after her terrible morning, was exaggerating the threat Roz posed. Normally, Eliza hardly ever thought about Roz since Viv was the one who visited and made an effort to connect with the family. Viv had become one of Eliza's dearest friends.

With clouds beginning to form overhead, and rain looking like it might interrupt her gardening project, Eliza decided to leave the rest of the bulb planting for another day.

---

* Brenda Brueggemann, an English professor specializing in disability studies, describes the audist (discriminatory) mindset that historically led to bigotry about the Deaf community. People who harbored unconscious prejudice in previous ages reasoned, "Language is human, speech is language; therefore, deaf people are inhuman and deafness is a problem." (Bauman, "Audism"). Because some deaf people choose not to verbalize their communication, have experienced difficulty speaking, or speak with an obvious accent, they may seem "different" to hearing people, but should this difference disqualify them from the full rights of their society?

PART III

Division Signs

14
Radical Sign

One day, two years after she had visited the Jean-Baptiste family for the first and only time, and the same day that Eliza fled the park, Roz met Quinn for lunch. Roz learned that Quinn was dating a six-foot-four production assistant who worked for *Good Morning America.* Quinn had taken selfies with this new boyfriend on a date that had included a Lakers game. She passed her phone across the table to Roz so she could check him out and offer an opinion. Roz scrolled through the images. In the best photo, Quinn's face was pressed close to what seemed to be a very attractive person with strong masculine facial features.

"Well done, girl."

She returned the phone.

Opportunities to get together with Quinn in the last year had been rare: Quinn had become an outstanding publicist after taking over Roz's media issues (Roz's new personal assistant mostly annoyed her). But now that they were together, it seemed like no time had passed, and they picked up just where they had left off. Roz expressed excitement about the boyfriend, happy that her ride-or-die had found someone to be with, but also wistful because she had little change to share in her own life, beyond work and more work and, okay, an Emmy for the last season of her Netflix series and critical acclaim for her latest film. She had also had an opportunity to work with an extremely prominent director. But it had been a long time since Roz had dated, and even longer since she had felt any kind of attachment to another person. She'd acted in multiple steamy scenes, and the tabloids often paired her with her costars, but ever since the drama of Elle's birth, she had been hesitant to accept offers to dinner or romantic outings and was unwilling to have even a light fling. When it came down to it, she had become less trustful of intimacy and more willing to go it on her own. Her Hollywood clock was ticking, and she couldn't afford a second mistake.

She had little to offer the men she did casually get to know except the occasional conversation between media commitments. How could you get serious if you couldn't take a few weeks off to know someone new? When she had been out of the country a year earlier, Roz had arranged for Quinn to correspond with the Jean-Baptiste family in order to keep up with how Elle was managing. And yet Roz paid very little attention whenever Quinn reported the details of her daughter's life or shared snippets of news that Eliza or Viv had passed along.

In the last few minutes before falling asleep every night, Roz mused about her daughter and wondered whether she was happy and what it might have been like to raise her. She imagined what Elle liked to eat and what her favorite toys were and wondered whether her hearing loss had made her life hard or if she had learned to speak as Roz hoped she might. She dreamed about the four-and-a-half-year-old Elle, but when it came to absorbing the details of Eliza's interactions, Roz couldn't acknowledge anything but her fantasies. It was like there were two Elles: the nighttime Elle, who belonged just to Roz and who was the one she had named with her heart, and the Ella Eliza had adopted, someone she had said goodbye to long ago.

Roz enjoyed the photos Eliza sent to Quinn and Quinn passed along because these allowed her to look at her daughter and access her in a private way. Elle had inherited Roz's curly brown hair and had a smattering of her father's looks, especially in the shape of her mouth. Her face resembled Roz's. She had Belinda's features above the nose, and her eyes were a mixture of lighter brown with tinges of hazel, which Roz recognized as a combination of Roz's father's eye color and the eye color of her ex-boyfriend. Elle had somehow gathered the best of them all. Roz kept the book Elle and Kimmie had given her tucked away in a shoebox in her bedroom. She deleted the photos Quinn passed along from her phone after looking at them once, saving only one or two so that if anyone accidentally saw them, she could say they were photos of herself when she was younger, or, if that didn't seem plausible, that they were photos of a niece she visited occasionally.

Quinn waved her fork in front of Roz's face. She had been saying something, and Roz had not been listening. She reigned in her wandering thoughts and gave Quinn her attention. Quinn said that Andrew (that was her boyfriend's name), or Andy as she called him, was a producer for *GMA*. Roz had heard that much.

"So, would you consider promoting a segment?"

"I'm sorry?"

Quinn repeated that as a producer Andy scouted locations and researched some of *GMA*'s planned specials. Would Roz be willing to pursue a socially relevant topic as a co-host to Robin Roberts?

"Are you kidding, Biff?"

Roz latched on to the idea—she had pictured herself sitting next to Robin ever since she had been a teenager watching *Good Morning America* with Viv. She expressed her gratitude by moving around the booth and kissing Quinn lightly on the cheek.

"I'll do it for you."

Roz wasn't sure what she had to offer *GMA* in terms of content, but this was something Quinn could help with. Sales representatives frequently approached her to endorse fashion and beauty products or to act as an influencer. This sort of work could get serious, and Roz was the right person to push it up to *GMA*'s standards. She had also happily done publicity for artistic projects and had openly promoted important causes on social media that benefited the African American community or brought awareness to human trafficking. But she had never appeared as any kind of expert on a topic. She just had opinions, and she shared them.

"Hear me out."

Quinn took a sip of ice water and waited for Roz's full attention.

Roz enjoyed her friend's habit of saying, "Hear me out," one of her favorite introductions to the schemes they had enacted over the years. Quinn would say the words, and then Roz would have to wait sometimes up to five whole minutes before she pitched her idea because she loved keeping Roz in suspense. They had been scheming on behalf of each other for many years now.

"What about doing a segment on the Deaf community?"

"Are you kidding me?"

"In talking to Viv and Eliza Jean-Baptiste, I have learned a lot of interesting things in the last few months."

"It's hard to talk to Viv and not hear about the Deaf community."

Quinn told Roz that she had also been to a reading of deaf poets with Andy and that they had watched a movie that had won the Oscar for Best Picture for 2022, *CODA*, as well as two excellent documentaries concerning cochlear implants called *Sound and Fury* and *Sound and Fury: Six Years Later*.

"And?"

"Heather Artinian, the focus of the documentaries, also has a TEDx talk about what it is like with cochlear implants—those surgical hearing devices. She was a law student at some

Ivy League college, I think." Quinn pushed her empty salad plate to the side of the table.

Roz sucked in her breath and prepared herself to shut the conversation down.

"It's possible," Quinn plucked her napkin off her lap and laid it on her empty plate for the waiter to collect, "that Andy could get Heather to appear with you."

"Just how much have you told Andy about me? Am I about to open the *National Enquirer* and see my story spread across the page?"

"No, no. I didn't tell Andy anything." Quinn crossed her heart with her index finger. "After we saw the deaf poets, Andy did some research about CIs because the *GMA* team had mentioned wanting to feature hearing loss and ways to deal with it in the twenty-first century. It kind of occurred to me that you might do it, though I didn't tell Andy why. I just said that your mother knew ASL and that discussing the topic on the air might be something you would be interested in."

Roz pushed her tongue into her cheek. Dare she do it? The *GMA* team had no idea that she had a deaf child living in Minnesota. It seemed that no news outlet, even the tabloids, had picked up the story. She respected the Jean-Baptiste family for being so discreet, even if she had found them a bit standoffish the one time they had met.

Roz slid the bill for lunch over to her side of the table, and Quinn pounced in an effort to steal it back. Roz still made more money, but it didn't matter which one of them actually paid because a lunch like the one they had just experienced was no special luxury.

"I will think it over and get back to you." Roz didn't usually speak to her friend in such a professional tone.

She felt as if she had no other way to answer the proposal. She raised her hand to hurry the waiter over to their table so that he might take her credit card instead of Quinn's.

15
Signs of Cracking

Quinn was reluctant when Andy moved forward without waiting for Roz to make her decision about whether to accept the *GMA* segment. Instead, in his excitement about the possibility of a different angle for the show, Andy started digging right away, using Quinn as a link to Roz, as a sounding board for his ideas, and as his research assistant. Andy contacted and tentatively scheduled possible speakers: even if the episode did get approved, it wouldn't air for a year or more. Andy believed that if the project was good enough, it might propel him up the industry ladder and make him an executive rather than assistant producer. Andy told Quinn that with a spokesperson like Roz, the project would have "legs," one of his favorite things to say. Quinn believed that Roz would eventually accept, especially if they had the details of the show mapped out, making it easier for Roz to justify the time she spent on it to her agent.

In the meantime, Quinn called the producers and writers of the *Sound and Fury* documentaries she had watched with Andy. Doing this type of work was a way to get her foot in an industry door, not knowing what the future might hold. She may want to work her way into becoming a producer herself.

The first of the two films, *Sound and Fury,* featured members of the Artinian family. Some, not all, members of the family and the extended family were deaf. The film focused on decisions the Artinians made about communication options among deaf and hearing family members. One branch of the family—Chris and his wife, Mari—had a deaf infant son named Peter III (named after Chris's brother Peter) who they believed would benefit from cochlear implants. Peter III's cousin Heather, who was older and also deaf, learned about Peter's surgery through her older relatives and asked her parents for implants so she could talk with her hearing friends at school. Her hearing grandmother was in favor of implants, but Heather's deaf father and mother, Peter and Nita, opposed them. They supported the Deaf-World and were happy with their status quo. Heather's grandmother wanted Heather to avoid the difficulty that she perceived her son had had growing up deaf. She hated seeing Peter teased by hearing classmates for his inability to verbally communicate and discriminated against when he looked for work.

Peter and Nita agreed to at least discuss the procedure with Heather and to permit her to do research. Nita even entertained the idea of getting an implant herself, but as Nita and Peter learned what Heather's prognosis would be following implant surgery, they became more resistant to her proposal.* Part of Heather's parents' objection had to do with the possibility of her being rejected by hearing people. They felt they possessed stronger social bonds within the Deaf community than they could ever achieve within the hearing world. They wanted Heather to remain in the Deaf-World without a cochlear implant. Family members eventually encouraged Heather to interact with both the hearing and Deaf-Worlds and utilize her signing communication options first, before getting an implant. This first film ended with Peter III's surgery and family members reacting to its completion in the hospital waiting room.

* Spoken language acquisition differences are sometimes seen in children with cochlear implants, depending on a variety of factors (Newman, "Language Development in Deaf Children").

The second documentary, *Sound and Fury: Six Years Later*, followed up on Heather and the aftermath of her choice to be implanted after meeting her parents' conditions. Quinn also watched Heather's TEDx talk, the one she had told Roz about, in which Heather explained the outcome of her implant surgery.* Like Viv, Quinn thought it might be a good idea to take classes as she worked on the *GMA* episode, and so she, too, began a regular habit of studying ASL a few nights a week through an online university. She wanted to surprise the girls by being able to sign to them as best she could on the VP or when they went for a visit.

She and Andy eventually finished enough work on the project to take a vacation to Telluride together. Andy promised some fun times on the slopes away from the research that had been consuming them both. The physical jolting of learning a new sport—downhill skiing—and falling six hundred times exhausted Quinn and pushed her into thinking about the project more than she thought about Andy. He showed her how to snowplow so she wouldn't tumble face-first all the way back to the chalet, and she even enjoyed gliding down some of the gentler inclines, but the glittery luster of their earliest weeks together faded as she fought back frostbite. The Deaf community project had begun to feel very meaningful to her after all her years of playing fetch and carry for a superstar.

On the third day in Telluride, Quinn and Andy argued about what restaurant to pick since Andy was pressuring Quinn to go vegan. Tired of the constant battle over eating meat, they decided to give each other more space. He went to the top of the mountain to ski black diamond slopes, and she stayed

* Heather's experience exemplifies the experiences of a generation of deaf youth who have more communication options than those before them, with implant technology becoming more sophisticated with each passing year and children receiving implants at very early ages. Deaf life in twenty-first century America still includes dynamic controversies and communication obstacles, which may impact choices made by those in the Deaf community.

inside the lodge with her laptop and a hot chocolate, scrolling through stories about deaf families. Quinn respected Andy as an ambitious person, but understood that part of his interest in her derived from wanting Roz for his project, whether he would admit it to himself or not. It wasn't the first time Quinn had been caught in this trap. She refused to pressure Roz to sign on and assured Andy that Roz would make up her own mind in her own time. It wasn't for either one of them to try to force her into doing the project with them.

Quinn kept the backstory of Roz's relationship to the Deaf community from Andy. It seemed that she skimmed the surface of giving the secret away. It was Quinn's respect for Roz that made her see that combining her love life with a piece of Roz's past could cause serious trouble.

Assuring Andy that she would stay in touch, she left Telluride two days before the end of her vacation and used those extra days from work to get in touch with the Artinian family.

16

A Bad Sign

Roz turned down the appearance on the *GMA* segment, as the filming dates conflicted with another more lucrative project that took nearly a year to complete: a new romantic comedy with a very interesting and gorgeous costar. To make up for her refusal, she invited Quinn to celebrate and preview the television segment in a special way. She uncorked a bottle of Penfolds Grange and organized a kind of picnic in the screening room at her house in Beverly Hills for just the two of them. Quinn seemed to be nursing some sadness, or at least had seemed to be preoccupied since she had broken off her romance with Andy, news Roz learned not from Quinn, but from a gossipy stylist who knew them both.

Roz thought of Andy as a potentially nice guy, just not the best Quinn could do. He had called Roz on her private number one day, a naughty move, though typical for West Coast wannabes. (He had found Roz's number on Quinn's phone). She went to lunch with him, very much keeping Quinn's interests in mind. For example, as soon as he arrived at her house, Roz asked Andy not to mention the date to Quinn in case it upset her in some way. They spent a lovely afternoon driving down the coast to San Diego to a little place he knew where she could go unrecognized. She found his strong masculine features magnetic, even if she had to say no to the show. He pressured her throughout the meal, promising that she and Robin Roberts could do a private meeting together.

Roz urged him to give Quinn assistant producer credit for the segment. Quinn had helped Andy with so many aspects of the program's completion that a newer, better job title seemed the least Roz could try to do to make her friend happy. Roz learned a few weeks later that Quinn had turned down his offer.

"So, tell me where you are at with the man." Roz brought up the subject of Andy as soon as they had fully relaxed in her screening room's big, comfy recliners.

"Who?" Quinn fiddled with the remote to get the program to come up on the screen.

"You know . . . the big hunk you went to Lakers games with. Don't tell me he had wandering eyes?"

"No. He was fine." Quinn smacked the remote and the show cued up. "I kind of needed to turn the volume down and friendzone. We had to keep working together, and egos weren't going to help."

Roz thought there must be much more to this piece of news.

She wasn't skeptical exactly. Surprise summed up her first thoughts on the matter. Once upon a time, at one of their many sleepovers at Viv's, Roz could get Quinn to open up and divulge lots of juicy details of her likes, dislikes, or loves of the moment. She had just been so all work and no play lately. Roz had suggested they dress in pajamas to make the evening more like the old days. But even in this intimate setting, with the wine and pajamas, Quinn seemed different. Like Aunt Viv a few years earlier, Quinn had started studying ASL at night, which had reduced the number of evenings she was available for parties and that sort of thing. Roz didn't see how knowing how to sign could help Quinn's career or her social life. Who would she sign to once this project was finished? Out of nowhere, Quinn raised the subject of Eliza Jean-Baptiste.

"By the way, I sent a new packet of photos to you."

Roz had directed Quinn to correspond with the Jean-Baptiste family at her discretion. Every month, Quinn was to gather details of Ella's life, which she would then forward to Viv and Roz. The information soothed Roz's guilt about only seeing the two-and-a-half-year-old Ella in their home the one time and yet still having her name on Elle's birth certificate. The idea of having to use some magic way to talk to Elle frustrated her. Elle's shyness after she had bestowed her with so many gifts had also put her off, but maybe that was just how little kids were.

"Thank you," Roz said. "I'll look at everything later. Let's do your show and have more wine."

Quinn seemingly talked to Eliza and the nearly five-year-old Elle whenever she gathered a new file: some of Quinn's reports seemed to have come from a deeper intimacy. Roz didn't imagine the two adult women as a natural match, but anything was possible. Most of Roz's female friendships fell into a pattern of fast and furious, which was why, besides Quinn, she never gave new friends enough space to get comfy. Roz hoped that in viewing Quinn's *GMA* segment (she thought of it as belonging to Quinn rather than Andy) and putting her focus on her achievements for a night, she could win her friend back from this weird connection to Eliza Jean-Baptiste. She wanted Quinn back in her role as her one and only best friend.

After Roz had passed on Andy's offer, he had secured the deaf actress Marlee Matlin, who had won an Oscar for her role in *Children of a Lesser God* and was fresh off a Best Picture Oscar for another movie she starred in, *CODA*. Roz had to admit getting Marlee Matlin was a pretty big coup, even though Roz thought she could go toe to toe with Matlin in the acting department. Quinn and Andy had also booked Heather Artinian, the young woman Quinn had discussed when she had pitched the idea. Apparently, the first of the documentaries about Heather's family had also received an Oscar nomination. It seemed to Roz that almost everyone involved had an Oscar or an Oscar nomination, something she didn't yet have herself. Her new romantic comedy could mean she would set a statue or two more on her mantle one day if some critic didn't turn on her before awards season.

"Have all these people won something?" she asked as *GMA*'s opening music began to play. Robin Roberts appeared on the big screen in front of them. She had won three consecutive Emmy awards. Well, at least she didn't have an Oscar either.

"Some of these people have also written books and things like that."

"What do you know." Roz couldn't imagine a book as being the same thing as a Golden Globe, which she did have.

She pictured herself and Quinn walking a red carpet and accepting a set of Oscars together. What a perfect girl power moment for the two of them. Of course, the Oscars for feature films were usually awarded on the air, while the academy presented honors to lesser categories at a smaller ceremony. Still, Roz lifted her wine glass to toast their future success, and they clinked. Quinn looked good wearing the silk sleep set that Roz had purchased for her earlier: she hardly ever wore anything but business suits, which sharpened her softer aspects. The top half of the pajamas had Q embroidered on the front like the style Laverne from *Laverne and Shirley* wore. Roz's ensemble was pale pink with white piping on the lapels. They stretched back in the recliners, and Roz crossed her feet at the ankles, staring toward the screen over the top of her fuzzy pink mules.

As Roz understood it, the root of the communication debate for deaf people was over whether or not to teach deaf children to speak or to use sign language, an either-or in her mind.

Everyone Quinn and Andy booked on the show represented a particular stance on communication questions. Some of the panelists were using ASL, with real-time captioning appearing on the screen from a team of interpreters who were working into spoken English. Two other ASL interpreters facing the stage interpreted the material delivered in spoken English. Roz tuned in to the moving hands, sometimes distracted, but also fascinated by tracking how the words and the signs matched or not.

In addition to Heather Artinian, Andy and Quinn had brought in other members of the family, including Heather's mother, father, and grandmother. Quinn pointed each out on the stage and in the studio audience, pausing the video to tell Roz about them, but, of course, Roz didn't care. The expert panel members had a focus on either bilingualism with ASL/English acquisition for young deaf children or for the medical intervention of cochlear implants. Roz was surprised to see that the exchanges between the academics became heated at times, with the multilingual experts focusing on the acquisition of multiple languages (English *and* ASL). Quinn pointed out who each one was and what their credentials were, as if she were speaking of old friends.*

"Wow," Roz commented. "You would think they were discussing Coke versus Pepsi."

Quinn did not laugh, but wholly concentrated on the screen as if she were watching all of this for the first time instead of having orchestrated it herself. One of the experts, a woman in her late fifties, tossed out the statistic that over ninety percent of deaf children are born to hearing parents. She demanded to know why they should adapt their language patterns to meet the needs of their children.** The conversation erupted. Backing

---

* The details of this *GMA* segment are based on a hypothetical scenario. Some of the experts who could defend the ASL and English bilingual stance include Dr. MJ Bienvenu, Professor Emeritus of Gallaudet University, and Dr. Laurene Simms. Representing the pro-cochlear implant and spoken language stance could be auditory-verbal therapy participants or persons who work to promote oral Deaf education.

** A possible argument favored by advocates for oral education of deaf children.

her up, a woman in a pair of rimless glasses spoke about the miraculous twenty-first-century technology available to assist deaf children. She spoke of the cruel "deaf ghetto" some children who learn sign language find themselves in, and how their isolation in ASL dominant families leads to educational deficits, problems she felt could be resolved through implants and speech therapy. Roz shuddered at the word "ghetto." She did not want to see the Elle of her dreams subjected to a ghetto.

ASL/English bilingual experts stated that deaf children are human beings who can come to bilingualism naturally and are part of the fabric of society, which includes vast diversity.*

All this back and forth began to cause a throb in Roz's head.** Of the deaf individuals on the panel, Heather Artinian impressed Roz the most. She was a self-assured speaker who carried herself at a slight distance from the rest. Roberts turned to her often. Heather wore a cochlear implant. All this time, Roz had felt a slight fear of her daughter based on their inability to communicate with each other on their first meeting at the home of the Jean-Baptiste family. The segment that Quinn produced showed her that with a little financial investment, Elle could one day place her hand on her arm, as Robin had done to Heather, and they could be the mother and daughter they had been that moment in the hospital after Elle's birth.

---

* Some ASL/English bilingual experts argue that since over 90% of deaf children are born to typically hearing people, the parents should be the ones to learn to communicate through a common visual language, which the family learns together. Instead of conceptualizing ASL as a punishment for children who fail to speak, it is instead a distinct characteristic of family life and part of how a family forms its social bonds. The parallel to other bilingual families, such as those who speak Spanish or Italian, should be considered. Deaf children who learn authentic bilingual and bicultural methods of communicating often achieve educational targets on par with their hearing peers.

** The book *Never the Twain Shall Meet: Bell, Gallaudet, and the Communications Debate* (Winefield) outlines the extreme polarity of people's thinking on Deaf culture and education. Also see information about the Milan Conference of 1880, a touchstone historical event from which results still reverberate today.

Elle was her closest blood relative, and wouldn't it be wonderful if, on the stage of life, they became each other's greatest potential ally.

17
Risky Signs

The credits rolled, and Quinn consumed the rest of the wine in her glass. She asked Roz if she was ready to look at the photos from the Jean-Baptiste family. Roz stretched her arms overhead and let out a big, comfortable yawn.

"I suppose."

She picked up her phone and skimmed through her texts.

"Would you like me to send the file again?"

"I found it."

She flicked her finger across the screen. Gliding through the images inside the folder that Quinn had sent three days earlier, she perused images that included scanned artwork and homework. Roz looked up a few times and smiled absently at Quinn. The light of the screen shone on her face, creating ripples of light, almost as if she were underwater. She scrolled quickly, like she did when browsing Instagram posts. Sometimes she would pause over certain portraits of Elle that didn't include her family members. Once, she made an affectionate comment about her daughter's smile.

"Wait? Here *you* are?" Roz faced her phone toward Quinn. The photo was of the whole Jean-Baptiste family sitting at the table of a restaurant. Roz enlarged Quinn's face just to be sure.

In the last email she had sent, Eliza confessed that she was afraid of Roz and worried she would disrupt their life the way she had when Ella was a toddler. Quinn discouraged Eliza from confiding in her too much, but she understood Eliza's fears and where they were coming from. Roz could intimidate, especially when she strove for something she thought others were keeping her from. In changing the subject, Quinn brought up the research she had embarked on. Eliza had pointed Quinn in the direction of multiple useful sources and had truly helped her bring the project together. After Quinn had hit several serious roadblocks getting in touch with the Artinian family, Eliza had made a few calls and fixed everything.

Quinn was sure that Roz was missing out on an opportunity to build a really important connection that would help her get to know her daughter. Roz and Eliza both contributed to Ella's being, but the times Quinn brought up the Jean-Baptiste family, Roz usually changed the subject.

"I visited them last month," she admitted.

Minus the script reading she sometimes did for Roz, the best work Quinn had ever done was the *GMA* segment, and she had Eliza's generosity to thank for some of what she accomplished. Other opportunities were arising for Quinn to distinguish herself that didn't involve borrowing from an ex-boyfriend or her best friend's reputation, opportunities that felt more meaningful than preparing for galas or working on ways to lose weight. Once Quinn had begun talking to and learning from Eliza and then some of the segment's guests, she had yearned to share what she was learning with Roz too, but she had so often found herself rebuffed. The natural person to turn to had been Eliza, then one weekend, Eliza had invited her out to St. Paul.

Roz retrieved her phone from the table where Quinn had set it back down and continued her scrolling. From where she was sitting, in the parallel recliner in the screening room, Quinn couldn't see whether she was still browsing photos or looking at something entirely different. If she was still browsing, she was doing so too quickly to read the blowout grades on Ella's report card.

"After all this research on deaf families . . ." Quinn embarked on the risky discussion of her show's controversies. She lifted the remote and shut off the screen. The room became slightly darker with the television off.

Quinn continued, "I have to say that the Jean-Baptiste family really lives a compelling set of circumstances. You know, signing has afforded Ella and the family the chance to be bilingual and flourish. Since we have the Deaf community so close to both of us, you more than me, of course, I feel like I should do what I can to try to understand things from deaf people's points of view. You know, it is like being sensitive about human rights, that kind of thing. Like some of the other issues you have been asked to comment on . . ."

Quinn staged the perspective she hoped Roz would eventually adopt.

"Mmm." Roz placed her phone on the table between them and poured herself a final glass of wine, draining the bottle.

"I mean, how do you decide which projects to take on and prioritize? There are so many interesting topics out there."

If they had been in an open field, Quinn would have been able to hear crickets. It was possible she was being too indirect. She tried again.

"I know you must get kind of tired of hearing about people's problems all the time. I mean, what are you, the wizard of Oz? One Oscar, Best Original Musical Score, 1940, by the way."

"Hooray for *The Wizard of Oz*."

Roz set her empty glass on her lounge chair's armrest next to her phone. "I want an Oscar," she admitted.

"Okay."

"And yes. It does get draining sometimes. So glad I have an amazing staff. You all take a lot of the pressure off me. You go way above and beyond." She plucked at a loose thread on her lapel. She looked glamorous in her pink silk pajamas, and Quinn wondered when her transition from aspiring TV star to bona fide movie star had happened.

She was now, for certain, behaving like an icon and a diva.

She might be pleased to know that Kimmie, the older of Eliza's two girls, remembered her and had begged Quinn to come again with her movie star friend. Thankfully, she was fuzzy on the name and had confused Roz with Halle Berry.

Quinn had taken ASL 1–4 online through Troy University and had been able to earn an ASL certificate. She signed with both Ella and Kimmie and had befriended them enough that they started calling her Aunt Quinnie in texts and had bestowed a name sign on her in ASL. Quinn had no nieces and nephews, and with Andy out of the picture, she was overwhelmed by the thought that these girls might be the closest thing she would ever come to having daughters or nieces. Yes, her sudden interest in deaf people and Deaf-World culture was strange. Yes, psychologically, she might be compensating for Roz by playing perhaps the only role that her friend couldn't quite play herself, movie or otherwise. She was drawn to the girls and their lives because they made her feel needed and wanted in a way that came naturally to Quinn. She understood the Jean-Baptiste family and accepted what they were doing, and it scared her that Roz did not.

"I couldn't believe the passion on both sides." Roz provided a critical analysis of the show. "I mean, what was the argument about? It's not hard to understand that most people on the planet can hear or can get help to hear—"

Quinn rolled sideways in her lounge chair to absorb what her friend was about to say.

"And so it would make sense that a person would be motivated to communicate with most other people. I mean, who wouldn't want that?"

"I agree."

"I don't want Elle growing up in a deaf ghetto." Roz dropped the phrase with a hint of repugnance in her voice.

She shivered to hear Roz speak the word. The bilingual ASL/English representatives who had appeared, those who were deaf, had provided numerous examples of how they navigated a hearing world with two languages and weren't, in fact, forced into the margins of society or any form of ghetto by an inability to hear.*

Roz continued, "I think if someone used the phrase 'hearing ghetto,' or ghetto something, like, fill in the blank, it would be offensive to people."

Quinn felt a tinge of stress widen across her forehead.

Quinn could not understand how Roz had missed several of the excellent points the bilingual advocates had made about the pragmatic use of signing—simply another language. She had collaborated on Andy's project out of her interest in him romantically but also, quite blatantly, to get her friend to see that just because her daughter was deaf and she was hearing, it didn't mean they should remain strangers or that Roz shouldn't find ways to connect with her.

"The cochlear implants seem like they offer some hope," Roz said.

Quinn knew that some experts approved of implants, but she also knew that implants didn't offer the kind of miraculous cure her friend hoped for. They were not foolproof. Her research had unearthed evidence of their fallibility. And what she had learned in class about some of the communication

---

* There are and have been deaf and signing communities in the U.S., and the National Association of the Deaf (NAD, a Deaf civil rights organization) has been in existence since 1880 (NAD, "NAD History"). Many American Deaf community members live honorable, productive lives. Deaf community members generally live a more collectivist culture perspective (Mindess et al., *Reading Between the Signs*) and often strive to navigate American culture as multilingual and multicultural individuals.

controversies in the Deaf-World was coming true, up close, before her eyes.

"Do you think Ella should have one?" Quinn said as she rubbed the space where her head hurt with her thumb.

She hoped her friend might say no or state that the surgery was something for her daughter to decide on her own or for the Jean-Baptiste family to decide together. Roz looked stunned, as if Quinn had read her innermost thoughts.

"I don't know if she should—and anyway, I am not sure Eliza and Paul would want that for her. It might not be a bad idea to at least think about it before it is too late. For example, look how that Heather girl's speech improved with her cochlear implant. I would think anyone would want the same thing for their deaf child."

Roz had started by offering her opinion tentatively, but Quinn saw signs that her passion was increasing.

Why did the decision about implants have to be like life or death in the Roman Colosseum, choosing to give ASL a thumbs up or a thumbs down—an either-or choice between cochlear implants and sign language. Can you not choose both? Heather Artinian had found a way to toggle between two worlds successfully, and her experience as a deaf person could be instructive to those who were bilingual, using both a spoken (or written) and signed language. Quinn felt that she should not take anyone's language for granted and that ASL was a natural choice that worked the same way as spoken language, with a difference only in the way it was presented.

Quinn remembered the words of a deaf professor: if deaf people could detect sound easily, then speech and language would develop, and there would be no need for communication intervention. But with sound being inaccessible to deaf people, why pine away to hear? Why not choose a perfectly complete language, sign language, and move on with life? Learning to sign happens naturally—being born deaf is an act of God. If one is born deaf, then why not use the eyes and hands to produce the language that deaf people have themselves created and used since time immemorial?

Quinn found something beautiful in the idea, something honorable. There was an essential nature to it that she couldn't quite explain, an innate finesse that she had witnessed in signing poets and in her time with Ella and Kimmie.* Deaf children of hearing parents who do not sign often have difficulty developing spoken and maybe signed language naturally. Roz needed to move on from her fantasies about who her daughter should be and begin to embrace who she was. If she did, Quinn believed she might escape the restlessness that had surrounded her ever since she had given birth to a deaf baby.

"What do you think you are going to do? Say something to Eliza and Paul? Maybe run this by Aunt Viv?"

"Oh, that is a good idea. Yes, let's run it by BB. You know, I heard that there aren't going to be any more deaf people in a few years because of the cochlear implants!"**

---

* An example of the merger of need and ingenuity would be DeafBlind people having created access to signed language via the use of tactile ASL and Pro-Tactile (*Pro-Tactile: The DeafBlind Way*). Has human ingenuity and nature combined to create organic means of communication? Some deaf children are never exposed to natural, fully accessible visual language but instead are introduced to auditory/verbal language (the oral method). Deaf children with significant degrees of hearing loss vary in their ability to acquire spoken language (Seladi-Schulman, "How People Who Are Deaf Learn to Talk").

** Cochlear implants have been around since the mid-1980s to mitigate hearing loss in adults. Since the year 2000, implants have been FDA approved to be surgically placed in eligible children twelve months of age and older (ASHA, "Cochlear Implants"). The NAD's stance on CIs states that cochlear implantation is a technology capable of being used as a tool for some forms of communication. It may not be appropriate for all deaf and hard of hearing children and adults (NAD, "Assistive Listening Systems and Devices"). The book *The Mask of Benevolence* includes a discussion on a quote from George Veditz, president of the National Association of the Deaf in 1913: "As long as we have deaf people on earth, we will have signs" (Lane, *The Mask of Benevolence*). There are approximately 500,000 ASL users in the United States (Mitchell, "How Many People Use ASL").

Quinn discovered that as she sat next to Roz, she was talking to herself in signs, her hands moving in her lap, emphasizing points and reacting to what Roz said. Roz had repeated the line Quinn had heard her ASL teacher say about implants taking over and eliminating the Deaf community, according to some oral advocates. She blinked her eyes so as not to fall asleep in her comfy chair. Why did she feel as if she and Roz were in a dream? Quinn recalled a quote from one of her classes: the French author Victor Hugo wrote, "What matters deafness of the ear when the mind hears? The one true deafness, the incurable deafness, is that of the mind."

18

Where Do I Sign Up?

Ever since Quinn had visited and befriended her daughters, Eliza had stopped thinking about Roz other than the once or twice a month when she prepared a photo update for her. These updates often went unanswered—months turned into years. Then, one October day, a week or so after her last file delivery, Eliza got a text from a person whose number she didn't recognize. Her iPhone read "Maybe: Roz," and it was. She wanted to know if Eliza could talk on the phone. Roz asked if Eliza and her family could attend a catered dinner at the St. Paul Hotel. The girls were at school, Paul was at work, and Eliza was resting after spending the morning interpreting for a class at the University of Minnesota. Although Roz casually extended the invitation to meet, Eliza sensed a danger in refusing. But if they all were to attend, they would have to miss Kimmie's fifth-grade art show. Ever since her one surprise visit when Ella was a toddler, Roz had not spoken to her, and Eliza had received all her correspondence secondhand. She tried not to sound astonished or annoyed as she explained their conflicting family engagement.

"Tell Kimmie I will make it up to her."

Roz's voice sounded just as Eliza remembered it, deep and confident but also aloof and airy as if she were not quite in the same space as the people with whom she was conversing.

As proud as Kimmie was of her creative abilities, Eliza suspected she would drop everything to meet Rosalind Taylor again. Kimmie's one meeting with a movie star had stuck with her, and she had asked Quinn and then Viv on her last visit when her famous daughter was coming back to see them in their new house. Kimmie, being ten years old, was very interested in pop culture and Hollywood gossip. Since Ella generally became excited with whatever impassioned Kimmie, Eliza felt as if she couldn't refuse the invitation. Ella wasn't a follower exactly. She was just sure of her older sister's ability to know a good or bad thing when she saw it, and the two together represented an immovable force.

Eliza asked Roz what the occasion was, and Roz replied that she wanted to see Ella and observe how she was doing. Unsure how much Roz had kept track of or engaged with her updates, Eliza bragged that her Ella had recently started third grade and, according to her teacher, was the class brainiac.

"We can catch up more when we all see one another."

Eliza suddenly felt as if she had been babbling.

She ambushed Paul at the door when he returned home and immediately began with a description of the call before he had even taken off his jacket. His dark eyebrows tilted in a comical expression of astonishment when Eliza told him about their invitation to the best suite in the fanciest hotel in St. Paul. He hung up his coat and began to sign rapidly. Neither Eliza nor Paul believed that the well wishes and holiday gifts Quinn delivered for both girls at their last Christmas celebration had been chosen by Roz. What did she want now? Did she want to bring more presents? Perhaps she regularly paid for them, but Quinn's influence was obviously all over the gifts since they were things both girls liked. Though expensive, the gifts were not as exorbitant as the locket Roz had given Ella when she was only two. Eliza had still not let Ella wear it, not when she played sports and was still going through a tomboy phase.

Viv visited twice a year and never pretended her presents were from anyone but herself.

"This should be 2-5-8," Eliza signed to Paul.*

Eliza had not exaggerated when she had told Roz that Ella's progress at the Twin Cities Deaf School (TCDS) had been exceptional and that she was making terrific academic progress. Ella was happy, popular with other children, and thriving in difficult subjects like math and reading. Every teacher, aide, administrator, and student at the school were ASL fluent, and so Ella and Kimmie could attend TCDS without a lot of typical accommodations or intervention. If they attended a public school, they would be assigned interpreters and various services and might have been "othered" because of their differences. Most of the parents or guardians of the kids who attended the Twin Cities Deaf School could sign, were enrolled in an ASL class, or were working with a deaf mentor to gain communication skills. The student population also represented St. Paul's vast diversity of cultures. In the few years they had attended, the girls had acquired sophistication about the city around them and perceptiveness befitting their intelligence.

The school stimulated and challenged both girls and enhanced their bilingual development in written English and ASL. The school also offered trilingual opportunities in spoken and written Spanish and Mexican Sign Language—Lengua de Senas Mexicana—for children of middle school age. Eliza felt sure she would one day enroll her girls in this program.

She had a last-minute inspiration that Roz might want to stay at their house in Highland Park. She had been too flustered to ask Roz when they had been on the phone together, so after her conversation with Paul, she called Quinn.

* In ASL the combination of the numbers two, five, and eight represents a play on the production and sequencing of the signs and colloquially translates to mean "very interesting" (ASL University, "INTERESTING").

"Another time," Quinn said. "You know Roz, everything on her own terms." Eliza did not know Roz, but she didn't want to contradict Quinn. "I'm coming too."

Quinn had booked the Ordway Suite at the St. Paul Hotel for herself, Roz, and Viv. These were the best rooms in the Twin Cities area (Eliza had looked them up online). This was a chance for a girls' weekend for Roz, her mom, and her best friend. According to the schedule Quinn provided, Roz would arrive sometime in the early afternoon on Friday, spend a few hours on the school's campus where she would speak to the executive director of the TCDS and then convene with the Jean-Baptiste family for dinner.

Eliza asked what Roz hoped to learn at the school.

Quinn blew Eliza off with a flippant comment: "Oh, just this and that. I suggested she pretend to do research for a film, by the way, so the school won't know of her relationship to Ella."

"Why would she need a cover?" Couldn't Roz all on her own develop an interest in the Deaf community as a civic individual? Eliza felt some hopefulness about Roz's interest in the signing school and thought of all the other celebrities who had openly assisted with fundraising efforts for the benefit of school programs.

Quinn expressed excitement about getting to see them all, and Eliza politely signed off with her with no sense that she understood what was happening any better than she had before the call. On Friday afternoon, Kimmie and Ella tore through the house, assembling their best clothes. Kimmie was determined to find ones that befit an audience with a movie star. Eliza frantically pled with both her and her sister to look for items that weren't spangled with sequins and hadn't been worn as Halloween costumes. Kimmie fixated on a dress she had worn at a dance recital that would not be appropriate for the occasion. The Jean-Baptistes were regular churchgoers, and the girls had what amounted to dressy casual church clothes, a smattering of Christmas and Easter dresses, and more formal dresses for the one or two weddings they had attended or for school dances. They pieced together outfits, with additions provided by an after-school shopping trip. Ella set her heart on accessorizing with a boa, and Eliza decided she could wear it like a scarf if she also promised to cover her arms with a cardigan.

Somehow, with the addition of the sweaters, the girls managed to assemble individual looks that satisfied both parents, and they made it to St. Paul without snagging a pair of tights or mussing their neatly coiffed and braided hair. The Ordway Suite's formal meeting and dining room overlooked the city and was large enough to seat Paul, Eliza, and the girls on one side of a long table. Quinn, Viv, and Roz sat on the other side, a seating arrangement that felt professional and potentially adversarial. An employee of the hotel handed out cards that listed a choice of baked stuffed lobster, steak, braised scallops, walleye, or chicken cordon bleu. Eliza ordered the scallops. Paul steered the girls toward the chicken but told them they could have his lobster bib. The girls chattered with Viv across from them, their hands moving in big gestures interspersed with sounds Eliza recognized as giggles.

Roz ordered two bottles of wine, and Quinn tasted each after they were uncorked and approved them with the steward. A waitress poured out large glasses of either the red or the white to each adult while the girls sipped their first ever Shirley Temples. Viv interpreted from the girls' end of the table, and Eliza interpreted for the adults. During dinner, Roz shared a few stories about working on film sets.

After dessert, the girls skipped off to the interior of the suite to play with the American Girl dolls Viv had given them. They returned occasionally to take more bites of their chocolate mousse or to ask Paul or Eliza to settle a dispute about which doll was smartest and which was prettiest. Since the dolls looked like each of the girls, the answer Paul routinely supplied was "both." Viv slid down to the adult end of the table next to Eliza. She took over interpreting Roz's spoken conversation, while Eliza managed Paul's contributions. Viv's familiarity with Roz's discourse, cadence, and perspectives made interpreting from English to a signed form of English a doable task.* Eliza felt more comfortable working from ASL to English, especially with having to interpret for Paul on so many occasions. Because English was her first language, it made sense that she felt more confident working into English than working into ASL. She was not a native signer, and her attempts at ASL showed definite telltale signs of a hearing accent. Working as co- or team-interpreters opened the way for normal dinner conversation about politics, Hollywood, the weather, and the quality of their meal to occur, but there was no mention of what had inspired Roz to visit them. After two hours of nonstop interpreting, heavy food, and some very good wine, Eliza's shoulders ached, her forearms were numb, and her thoughts were foggy. Viv looked bushed too because she signed coded English, where Eliza was interpreting language to language. With the nearly nonstop nature of the interpreting, informal as it was, but sustained for almost three hours, both Viv and Eliza were making mistakes.

Quinn signed her part of the conversation during the evening, her proficiency developing quite nicely. Eliza was never so glad to see someone tell a nice long story as when Quinn would chime in with some details on her love life or her ASL studies. Viv talked often and was able to hold her own with

---

* Some people sign conceptually accurate signed English (CASE), which is a communication method incorporating ASL signs in English word order. Basic grammar of English is applied with some parts of speech generally omitted (e.g., articles "the" and "a," or linking verbs "is," "are," "was," etc.) (CDC, "Conceptually Accurate Signed English").

mostly English-like signing. Quinn was quickly following in Viv's signing footsteps with conversational fluency.

Then there was Roz who only used the signs GOOD and THANK YOU, which are similar in the way they are produced. Roz added her ASL proficiency to the conversation once or twice throughout the evening. Eliza hoped she hadn't knocked herself out learning those two words. Tired and perturbed that so much physical work went into making Roz understand their discussions when everyone else could have held their own with signing alone, Eliza distanced herself from some of what Roz had to say. But the meal was fantastic, and you don't bite the hand that feeds you.

A little hungover the next morning, Eliza woke and ate a small breakfast before leaving the girls with Paul. She had agreed to meet Roz on a second visit to TCDS. Roz wanted a meeting with the executive director of the school, Dr. Kathy Geething, along with Ella's speech therapist and a third-grade teacher, a youngish woman named Lori Smith. All of the school personnel had agreed to come in on their day off. As cover, Roz had told them that she was scouting information to use in a new film and that Eliza was a friend and contact of her friend Quinn. Roz said she wanted to speak to an elementary level speech/language professional and a teacher of younger students.

Despite Ella's resemblance to her biological mother, no one seemed to suspect her explanation was a ruse, or if they did, they didn't raise questions. They were excited to meet the star of *Hopeless in Love*, one of the blockbuster movies of the previous summer. She rewarded them with gossip about the leading man and the films she had appeared in. Roz seemed more comfortable with the Hollywood chitchat than the school-related material she had claimed she wanted to learn. She quizzed the TCDS group on deaf children's standardized test scores and the services they received. The teachers answered the strangely framed questions as best they could. Everyone in the room signed ASL, and so, for long gaps, the only voice belonged to the interpreter, a youngish woman who wore her hair in a braid like Eliza. Eliza and the administrators signed ASL every day as their natural language and were therefore familiar with the nuances of the language, for example, physically tapping one another to get attention instead of using verbal cues.

"What about speech?" Roz asked.

Her question seemed slightly out of place since most of the emphasis up until that point had been on signing.

Dr. Geething frowned.

Kathy was from a multigenerational deaf family and believed in emphasizing signing in her school. Instead of reiterating her school mission to Roz, who should have been able to understand without the benefit of more explanation, Kathy sat back in her chair and crossed her arms, a gesture Eliza had only ever seen her use on naughty children.

"Would there be a report I could get that presents statistics on reading levels, speaking abilities, and just general educational landmarks?"

"Do you mean benchmarks?" Ms. Smith asked. She was shy and only recently married. Ella adored her and had begun saying she wanted to be a teacher when she grew up.

Roz frowned, perhaps because she had been called out by a teacher and felt like a fish out of water. As much as Roz frustrated her, Eliza felt sorry on her behalf.

"Yes, benchmarks." Roz coolly corrected herself.

Ms. Smith explained the grade-level benchmarks to Roz and the ways a majority of children met them.

When they were leaving, everyone politely separated and crossed the parking lot to their vehicles without more fanfare. The excitement of speaking with a movie star had worn off, and it was Saturday. Eliza was preparing herself to head home, but Roz pulled her aside.

"Would you be willing to meet with me one more time tonight?" she asked. "I have an early flight tomorrow."

Roz's voice softened as she made the request, a change in her demeanor Eliza hadn't expected. Leaves blew across the parking lot, the day unusually warm.

"Certainly." Eliza sorted her keys until she'd found the one for their Jeep.

Roz slipped into the rented BMW parked next to her. Eliza got her attention to pitch a different idea.

"I am planning to make lasagna for dinner if you would like to come to the house?" She shouted over the roof of her Jeep toward the window that Roz had rolled down.

"I would prefer to meet at the hotel."

Eliza felt embarrassed and wondered if Roz thought she had misunderstood the request. How did you say no to *the Roz*, the one and only Rosalind Taylor, the queen of the silver screen, the rich and imposing Hollywood power player?

"I can make that work."

She wondered what it was that Roz wanted to talk privately to her about. Viv and Quinn had flown home. Eliza asked if Paul would mind feeding the girls and getting them off to bed if Eliza was delayed in the city past their bedtime. He negotiated for a night out with some friends he liked to go bowling with as trade.

When she arrived at the hotel at the planned time of seven, the concierge was able to key the elevator so that she could get to the top floor and meet Roz in her suite without her having to send anyone down. Eliza was once again struck by the size and splendor of the rooms and the opulence of the furnishings. A bottle of wine was being chilled in a bucket near one of the couches, and a charcuterie board covered with cheeses, vegetables, fruit, and crackers sat on a sideboard. At least it wasn't another full four-course meal. Eliza's skirt already fit too snugly after the meal they had consumed the night before.

"This place is so beautiful!"

Roz shrugged. "It's comfortable."

"What did you think of the school?"

Eliza laid her coat on the back of the couch, admiring the broad view of the city from the windows. "It's pretty modern and state-of-the-art, don't you think?"

"Yes, the meeting was what I wanted to talk to you about."

Roz invited her onto the couch and settled into one of the overstuffed chairs, crossing her legs and carefully balancing a plate with crackers and cheese in front of her. She nibbled on the appetizers as if they were without taste. Eliza recalled the Ritz Crackers she had served the day Roz had visited their house for the first time.

The lights of St. Paul twinkled below, the view ninety degrees different from the one they had had from the suite's dining room the night before. Eliza felt as if she were sitting in a birdcage, high up and exposed to the world below.

"The school meeting was somewhat frustrating," Roz admitted. "There was a lot I couldn't follow that I am hoping you can help me understand. Like landmarks and benchmarks. What was with those school people? They seemed full of themselves, didn't they?"

Roz was being candid, and Eliza found she liked that better than the Roz who had honeyed the women at the school and who had regaled them with Hollywood stories during dinner. Eliza sensed that admitting any kind of insecurity was hard on Roz.

"You have to understand the perspective of the Deaf community. Dr. Geething is an advocate for deaf civil rights."

"I know all that stuff they were trying to argue. I have heard it. But my concern is about Elle right now as an eight-year-old."

“Elle? Oh yes, Ella.” Eliza couldn’t get used to Roz using a nickname no one in the family used. Nobody had explained to her why Roz did this.

“Do you know about Heather Arti-Artisan something. Have you seen the films, and do you know the story?”

“Artinian, yes, but—”

“I have been doing research and talking to some people. Someone on Quinn’s show called the signing Deaf community a deaf ghetto. Ella’s school is for deaf children exclusively. That doesn’t sit well with me.”

“ ‘Deaf ghetto’ is a figure of speech some people who don’t know better use,” Eliza tried to explain. Roz’s greenness related to anything deaf required patience. “Just ignore—”

“Ella should go to a public school in the fall and get away from the purely deaf environment. If it is not too late, she should get cochlear implants and start learning to speak. I noticed she was not able to speak very clearly last night, even when I asked her to try. Some deaf children speak fairly well from what I understand. I want that for her. I mean, you would support this type of decision. Of course you would, correct?”

Eliza felt a horrible sense of déjà vu, having once had a similar conversation with her own mother. She had not understood why Kimmie wasn’t learning to speak at age two and why Eliza and Paul were focusing their energies on ASL. Eliza felt helpless in offering a satisfactory explanation. Both Roz and her mother had clearly made up their minds about what they valued: speech proficiency over deaf autonomy—same old story. Eliza knew how Paul would react and did not relish telling him about Roz’s—what was it?—request? demand?

Eliza resisted saying she agreed or disagreed with Roz. She avoided inciting her to be even more emphatic about what she wanted done. Eliza even agreed to keep their discussion from Viv and Quinn, even though she felt both would support her perspective over Roz’s.

As soon as she agreed to take Roz's suggestions into consideration, Roz's face crumpled into a mask of anxiety. Her hazel brown eyes glossed with tears. Eliza was bowled over by how emotional Roz had suddenly become. It should have been Eliza who was losing her cool.

"Your girls are the most important people in this discussion—especially Ella." Roz used a tissue to wipe her eyes.

"I understand that you want what you think is best, but I need to talk to Paul."

Roz nodded as if she were a little girl and Eliza an angry parent about to punish her for some infraction.

Eliza left the hotel sure that Roz had no idea of the enormity of the ask she had just made. Ella and Kimmie had classmates at TCDS from generationally deaf families, and many of their peers believed cochlear implants were not for them, so Eliza was not some rabid advocate forcing a way of life others didn't share. Ella was too young to make any sort of informed choice on her own, and so the difficulty of deciding what happened next would fall to Eliza and Paul. Changing course could potentially change everything about the life they had assembled for their family. It was too soon, way too soon for Eliza.

19

Signs of Independence

Paul had difficulty getting the girls to bed the night Eliza went to St. Paul. Kimmie and Ella were getting older, and they fought more with him than their mother about bedtimes and other things like brushing their teeth and getting chores done. Eliza had developed strategies for getting them to toe the line, whereas Paul was lacking in that department. He knew the real reason for the upheaval was the girls' tween-ager-hood and their growing need for independence. He had been irritated ever since Eliza had announced Roz's surprise visit, and all through the difficult dinner, which, to him, seemed to have no purpose, he had blamed Roz for disrupting their easygoing life a second time. It was hard watching the girls grow up and thinking about the day they might date boys or go off to college or want to wear fancy movie star clothes. They had always been his pair of spitfire princesses, and he had always been the best father he could be to them. He wished time would stand still forever and ease him of worries about the day they would leave the sanctuary of their signing home. He loved them snuggled on the couch, watching *Sesame Street*. Never mind that it had been years since Kimmie had taken an interest in a Muppet.

Paul and Eliza had talked to Kimmie about her adoption a few years back. They had assembled a slide show of their travel pictures from China and photos of the orphanage where she had spent the first six months of her life. Kimmie had asked lots of questions about her origin story. As for Ella, they were already a year past their promised timeline for speaking to her about her biological mother. Kimmie's bio parents were a world away. Ella's blood mother was stateside, a regular headline on the E Channel, and made occasional appearances in their lives. The more complicated circumstances—there was so much more to say—had forced them to spend too much time deliberating. Having another parent out there that Ella could run to made their role as her adoptive parents much more tenuous. It wasn't likely that one of Kimmie's bio parents would hop a plane to the U.S. and show up on the porch. You never knew when Roz might get it in her head to make an appearance.

Paul sensed that the girls, as perceptive as they were, had already suspected a relationship between Ella and Roz, but he couldn't be sure. When Eliza arrived home after her second evening at the hotel, her nose was raw, a condition that had afflicted her the two times Paul had seen her really upset during the years of their marriage: when her father died suddenly of a heart attack and when Kimmie ended up in the emergency room after falling from an apple tree in the backyard. Kimmie had been diagnosed with a concussion—so, was this situation worse than a head injury? He assumed Roz had expressed anger with Eliza for delaying speaking with Ella. He prepared himself to defend his wife and their choices as he hung her purse on a coat hook.

But no. Instead, the problem bothering Eliza was worse than Paul had guessed. He signed, "What's wrong?" and Eliza responded by signing, "I'll tell you later."[20]

Paul viewed postponements like "tell you later" and "never mind" as insults and the kind of wording hearing people used when they were too lazy to repeat themselves, when they convinced themselves there was no need to be clear with him, or that he would be too stupid to understand their talk (limited by an inability to lip-read or piece together speechreading with residual hearing to figure out a message). Eliza knew better than to sideline him with a "tell you later."*

He signed, "That is so unfair when you say that you will tell me later. We need to stop right now and talk. I want to know what Roz said."[21]

"I am so sorry, you are right." Eliza's tears began to flow as her hands formed her apology. "What is wrong with me? How horrible for me to tell you to wait. It is so unfair and hurtful to you. I am so, so sorry."[22]

She signed a description of Roz's request that Ella be implanted. Paul was horrified. Eliza confessed she knew he would be.

"That's why I tried to put off telling you."[23]

Paul viewed implants as completely ancillary to their family life. Even though he had agreed with Eliza that there might be a time when they let the girls make an autonomous choice about CIs, he had hoped it wouldn't arrive until they were in their teens or twenties. He knew some deaf people who had chosen implants. More than a few people he knew had quit using them because they did not work in the way they hoped. He also knew people who still wore theirs, but he knew no one who KISS-FIST (ASL for love with an intense passion) cochlear implants. Maybe it was the crowd he ran with; after all, he was a part of the Deaf community. There seemed to always be a problem that reared its ugly head with a CI. All these years, he had been agreeing with Eliza that the final choice of whether to get a CI or not belonged to the girls. He had privately been hoping that they would decide the surgery

* The film *Audism Unveiled* describes subtle and not so subtle ways hearing people discriminate against deaf people. The film features a segment where various deaf people echo, in ASL, the phrase "tell you later" when they express a desire to be part of a conversation or to know what people are talking about (Bahan, Bauman, and Montenegro).

wasn't for them. Kimmie and Ella were his daughters, and they lived in the safety of the space he had helped create. They went to a school he and Eliza had chosen because there was no other place as capable of making them feel like insiders instead of a school where they would be alienated in the world of sound. Deaf individuals are, after all, people of the eye.* Didn't Paul and his friends love their signing lives?

"Should we offer CIs as a possibility to the girls?"[24] Eliza began to sniffle again.

Paul suspected Roz could legally demand an implant for Ella if she became stubborn enough. The two-party open adoption agreement the couple had signed when Ella was a baby stated that Roz had a say in vital health decisions. Paul didn't count implant surgery as a vital health decision as much as he felt it was a medical intervention. However, he'd been around the block enough to know that any court rulings would likely skew in Roz's favor since the *medical* definition of being deaf was pervasive and preferred in the majority of mainstream hearing society. He remembered the ugly court scenes from the film *Sweet Nothing in My Ear,* where a deaf and hearing couple battled over the decision to implant their deaf son.

Viv had always been very positive about their family choice to sign ASL and had been an advocate for deaf rights, which was why he could not have foreseen a conflict coming and why he had consistently urged Eliza not to concern herself much with what Roz might or might not do. Viv was why he had never questioned the clause in the adoption agreement about health concerns or worried how it might be used against them.

Paul retreated to the basement for the next few days and spent more time on his woodworking projects.

As part of their traditional weekly movie night the following week, Eliza followed Quinn's lead and suggested the

---

* Lane, Pillard, and Hedberg, *The People of the Eye*.

idea of having a documentary event with three separate films regarding deaf issues and cochlear implants. What was there to be afraid of? The truth would set the discussion free, at least that was the hope. The family started mid-afternoon to watch the two Artinian documentaries, *Sound and Fury* and *Sound and Fury: Six Years Later*. After eating dinner, they watched the foreign-made documentary, *Voices from El- Sayed*. A beautifully filmed movie showing a Bedouin town in the Negev desert of Israel, the film tells a story about people who lived in the area with the largest percentage of deaf people in the world.

Paul grudgingly acknowledged that movie night was a good idea and was really jazzed about watching the Israeli movie. They also ordered a copy of the *Good Morning America* episode Quinn had assisted in creating. They set themselves up in the living room with M&M's, popcorn, and Pellegrino water with lemon and lime slices. These were family night favorites for movies they had watched on other occasions, films like *Back to the Future* and *Star Wars*, which did not bog them down with life-changing conflicts. The girls were excited about getting to see cinema about deaf people.

Kimmie signed that she had a friend at school, Mazie, who had a cochlear implant and had to go to speech therapy a lot. She lay on her stomach as close to the television as she could get, rapt with curiosity. When the movies were over, Paul signed his opinion on implants and emphasized what he thought they had gained from their signing experiences.

Kimmie signed, "I want to get a CI! CIs can work! Ella wants one too!"[25]

Ella looked less sure than her sister that this was true.

She had also moved from the couch to the floor to better see and watch the films but had looked to Paul every time Heather Artinian's father, Peter, spoke about his fears and hesitations. Paul knew full well that wherever Kimmie wandered, Ella often followed, but he also knew his opinions could deeply influence her as well, and he did truly want her to choose for herself—just not now. He and Eliza had decided not to let Ella know that their sudden family focus on the question of implants was because of her and ostensibly for her benefit.

Paul signed to both girls that it was very late and they needed to get to bed. While Eliza cleared the dishes, Paul followed the girls upstairs to supervise them as they washed their faces and brushed their teeth. Since they seemed to be moving along with their bedtime responsibilities, he offered to read a chapter of *Harry Potter and the Sorcerer's Stone* to them in ASL.

Kimmie signed, "I don't want to read a book now. I want to talk about CIs."[26]

Paul signed that he didn't think right then was a good time but that they could discuss it in the morning.

Kimmie stood up and stamped her foot.

Sensing a bigger blowup about to occur, Paul closed the book he had taken off the shelf and set it back where it belonged. He told Kimmie to say her prayers and go to sleep and that if she demanded anything more with the gestures she had just used, he would cancel her sleepover in a few days.

Still angry with him, she signed, "Dear God, thank you for a good day. Thank you for the movies about CIs. Please make sure I do get a CI. Also, that Ella will get a CI too. Amen."[27]

Paul's eyes began to sting.

He left the room before Kimmie caught on to how hurt her stubbornness and rebellion had made him. Downstairs, Eliza was carrying their water glasses in her fingers from the living room into the kitchen to place them in the dishwasher. He touched her arm and described what had taken place with Kimmie. Where would her new independence end? All because a woman they hardly knew had decided she now wanted to be his youngest daughter's "real" mother? Eliza set the glasses down. They stood facing each other until the sink filled with water and Eliza turned to shut it off.

20
Give Me a Sign

Just after Christmas, Roz texted Eliza a video that Eliza instantly recognized as inspiration porn (IP), what she and others in the Deaf community called some of the YouTube videos of deaf people hearing sound for the first time. This one was of a baby recently fitted with a CI turning her head left and right at the sound of her mother's voice. Some of them were adults who had become deaf and now were given the ability to hear again through the miraculous technology. These videos were meant, somehow, to be so persuasive that they propelled deaf people into scheduling implant surgery the next day, but, of course, Eliza had seen the clips and knew the score. Some of them obscured the fact that the person receiving the implant had heard sound all of their life and that the neuropathways that transferred and translated sound within the brain were already intact.* Sometimes your horse comes in, the implant works, which is a cause for celebration, but there are few videos available showing a deaf person experiencing an implant failure.

All Roz had to do to find IP on the internet was Google "hear for the first time," and a host of sentimental clips was bound to appear to make any kind of argument she wanted.** Eliza had

* For deaf people with significant hearing loss, ease of understanding and discriminating sound may not be readily detectable, even with a hearing aid or cochlear implant (Medline Plus, "Cochlear implant").

** Stella Young, a disability rights activist speaking at a TEDx talk in 2012 coined the term "inspiration porn" (IP) and argued that IP engendered feelings of seen and talked to enough disgruntled CI users in her career to stand back and take a breath before launching into an opinion either way. Whenever Eliza received one of Roz's links, she sent Roz a short update on their family and what they were accomplishing, treading lightly on giving her hope of any firm decisions. Eliza wasn't sure what was behind Roz's interest in CIs. Did she feel guilty and want to fix Ella's hearing loss? Did Roz feel like she wanted to try to mitigate Ella's deaf status for Ella or for herself? Viv accepted the Jean-Baptiste family, why couldn't Roz see what Viv saw? Everyone in Roz's orbit seemed to give in to her, not only because she was so beautiful, but because her bank account had 100 times what the average person's had. No doubt, Roz was a powerful presence, but at least she had given them space and a few months' reprieve to let the family work out their concerns.

The Jean-Baptiste parents were determined to be careful with their daughters' futures. Eliza asked Dr. Geething at TCDS for a recommendation of a good family therapist with expertise on deaf issues to help them iron out how to proceed. Dr. Geething referred them to a Deaf-centric therapeutic practice at the Volunteers of America in North St. Paul and a therapist used by other families at the school, a woman named Paula Keener. Eliza and Paul invited Aunt Viv and Roz to their first session with Paula, but both begged off, stating they had other commitments. Roz, however, did send Eliza videos along with the information that forty percent of deaf children received implants, another fact Eliza was already well aware of. Viv declined the offer to attend because she

---

sympathy for individuals with disabilities as a way of denying them access to rights inherent in their humanity (Disability Visibility Project, "Stella Young"). Depicting videos of children "hearing for the first time" further marginalizes a culturally Deaf perspective. Contrary to what these videos lead people to believe, culturally Deaf people take pride in their community. Inspiration porn often does not show the full story. A moment in time is shown that is not true to the real lives that Deaf people live, and it influences how the situation is viewed by the rest of society (DiMarco and Siebert, " 'Baby hears for the first time' videos").

was temporarily invested in a case in Columbus and wouldn't be able to get away for months. Viv urged Eliza to have faith in what they all might learn in having such an important discussion and in sharing their feelings.

Paula turned out to be a woman in her mid-fifties with medium brown hair. She was impeccably dressed in expensive designer clothing. She gained remarkable rapport with Paul and Eliza Jean-Baptiste, despite Paul beginning their initial conversation by stating he didn't want to be there. Children's art covered almost all of one of her walls, some of it framed, and some of it tacked onto a corkboard. Several stuffed chairs in different colors were set up in a semicircle on the other side of the room from Paula's desk. She invited the couple to take a seat wherever they were comfortable, then she settled into one across from them. Eliza was intrigued that none of the chairs seemed to belong strictly to Paula, that each was equal in its relation to the other and that Paula merely sat where she could see them the best.

At the end of the first session, Eliza and Paul aligned themselves over the idea that their individual needs could be met if they all proceeded carefully. On their fourth visit, they committed to revealing to Ella that Roz was her birth mother. They decided that in order to break the news in a way that gave the girls time to process the information, they should take them on an early spring camping trip to Lake Mille Lacs.

Paul taught both girls how to paddle a canoe and how to fish. He let them sleep together in their own tent. On the last day of the vacation, Eliza shared Ella's birth story and how she came to be adopted into the Jean-Baptiste family. She described Charles Stacker's phone call from out of the blue and how each event of Ella's adoption spiraled out to the day that Roz visited them in Kentucky, a day that Ella did not remember because she had been too young.

Eliza served the eighteen-inch walleye Paul and the girls had caught earlier that morning. She had grilled it on their camp stove and arranged it on paper plates at their campsite's picnic table. The girls both looked at Eliza with wide eyes, the excitement of catching their first fish absorbed into the whirlwind of this bigger news that Roz Taylor was Ella's mother. Kimmie slapped her hand over her open mouth, looking so much like Paul in her astonishment that Eliza wanted to pinch his arm and remind him that neither Roz nor any other person could ever claim that these girls weren't all his.

"I can't wait to tell my friends,"[28] Kimmie signed.

"You can't do that, Kimmie."[29]

Both girls flew into a kind of happy circling of the campsite despite the fact that they had yet to finish their fish. The dog in the site across from them began barking.

"Me too,"[30] Ella signed, waggling her hips as if she were now Beyoncé.

Eliza patted the picnic bench so that Kimmie would sit.

Eliza looked to Paul for help. They agreed that Eliza would say she needed to take a ride into town to get a few supplies at the general store and take Ella with her. They both thought Ella's reaction was not characteristic of who she was; they had expected more maturity from their youngest daughter, who always seemed much older than her years, even though she was not yet ten years old.

Ella and Eliza headed out to the store, leaving Paul to deal with Kimmie and to put away the bow and arrow he had been wanting to try out for a while now. He had gotten it at Cabela's but would have to wait until next time to try it out. *Fatherhood sure does cut into one's plans, but certain topics have to be dealt with and some can wait.*

"So, are you surprised that Roz is your bio mom?"[31] Eliza started out. Might as well put it out there.

"Yeah, I guess, but Kimmie and I have talked about how Aunt Viv fits into our family. I mean, we love her and are glad she is in our life, and we know she is Roz's mom. But we did wonder sometimes . . ."[32] Ella was such a bright girl—being a bookworm helped her thinking and understanding.

"Sometimes families come together in different ways. Your dad and I are just glad that we have the family we do. We are glad that Viv is part of our lives, and Quinn too. Roz has a hard life. You know it can't really be easy to be so famous."[33] Eliza tried to live by the idea that the glass was half full.

"But I wonder why she didn't want to keep me. Do you think it was because I am deaf? And why does Quinn sign and Roz doesn't sign much? What is next? Will Roz take me away? Is she going to become more of a mom to me now? I can't really talk to her very easily. I hope she doesn't want to take me to live somewhere else."[34] Now the questions were coming.

"Oh no, Roz doesn't want to take you from us. But you might want to talk to her more about her plans. Why don't we have a conversation about this with Dad and maybe a counselor? That way we can discuss more of your concerns."[35] Eliza was never so glad that they had found Paula Keener.

The girls needed to keep the news quiet. Roz had told them she was not yet ready to come out in the open with the story. Back at the campsite, Eliza explained to Kimmie and Ella that Roz's career depended on hiding her relationship to Ella. They could under no circumstances tell anyone their news until Roz said it was okay. This was a difficult constraint for both girls to readily accept. Such exciting news, in their opinion, should be broadcast on TikTok. They were even making up a song in ASL that had to do with them both being famous. In Eliza's opinion, it was definitely a case of too much fresh air. Paul promised them iPhones if they kept the news on the down low. Kimmie had been begging for a new iPhone, a CI, and her own bedroom all through the spring. Although Eliza normally did not approve of bribery as a means of getting children to behave, in this case, the risk of a tabloid bombshell outweighed the notch on her good-parenting belt.

Eliza and Paul did not share with Kimmie or Ella that Roz was pushing for Ella to have the implant surgery. They treated both girls as if the subject had been raised within the family because they were old enough to decide for themselves. They hoped that at some point Ella would voice thoughts one way or the other. Contrary to their earliest expectations, Kimmie did not let the topic go, and Ella did not immediately follow her lead. Ella seemed somewhat ambivalent about the whole thing. Paul and Eliza felt that if they ignored Kimmie's interest and followed Roz's requests for Ella, they would be forcing both girls into situations that may or may not correspond to their individual choices. If they were to maintain any control over their family life, they needed to have Kimmie work out her decision before approaching Ella and divulging Roz's wishes. The decision was to have Kimmie talk with Paula and to bring Ella along so she could witness her sister's arguments for and their reasons against CIs.

Roz held off on her plans to move full steam ahead to push for Ella's surgery to give the family time to make their own arrangements. Roz wasn't a completely unreasonable person, Eliza was discovering. She was just used to having things her way—and most people gave in. Under different circumstances, Eliza might have admired her strength and stubbornness.

For all of them, the process was probably hardest when they thought about what opportunities the girls might be denied if they chose one path over another. Paul prioritized all the joy and benefit he got from the Deaf-World: the opportunity to represent the United States on the 2010 Deaflympics track team, being a delegate from Kentucky at the NAD convention, playing basketball in the American Athletic Association of the Deaf tournament, and his deaf poker nights. He desperately wanted to keep a sense of community with his girls and admitted to Paula that he realized his loyalty to the Deaf community was alive and well. Eliza, who was hearing but had chosen a signing life because of her husband, had mixed feelings about her daughters becoming more like her and wondered if something closer to her own life between the Deaf and hearing communities would be possible. Paula, who had grown up with a deaf brother, helped them look objectively at their perspectives and how to best convey their feelings to each other. She convinced the couple that neither one of them was betraying the other no matter how they resolved the issue. She invited them to bring Kimmie and Ella into the office on a Tuesday not long after they returned from Lake Mille Lacs.

Kimmie led the way into Paula's office building, marching up the steps two at a time, Ella dawdling behind. Kimmie's hair was newly styled in a short haircut that made her look five years older than before their school spring break had started. Paula introduced herself to both girls, signed with them informally for a short time about school and their interests and hobbies, and then began using more formal ASL, as the proceedings were recorded. To speak what was being signed for the recording, there was a team of two interpreters present at the meeting who had signed a nondisclosure agreement.* There was no one in the room who required the services of interpreters, but Roz had requested a video recording of any conversation Ella was involved in, and Paul and Eliza had decided to allow it. Because Roz wanted to know what was going on in the meeting, she paid for the interpreters so that she could watch the video at a later date.

* Certified ASL interpreters are bound by the RID Code of Professional Conduct (CPC), and one tenet relates to confidentiality of information during the interpreting assignment (RID, "Supporting Quality in Interpretation"). It is not standard practice to sign an NDA every time one works as an interpreter.

Paula asked Kimmie directly about her interest in a cochlear implant, and Kimmie responded with a seriousness that caught Eliza off guard. Like the haircut, her words exhibited a maturity she was newly growing into. She told Paula that she believed she was ready to begin trying to speak and that she wanted more communication options. Ella sat quietly in a chair next to her, a tiny bit closer to Paula than Kimmie. Ella had always been the bigger empath of the two, and perhaps she read Paul's hopes differently than her sister. Eliza wondered what was on her mind. She and Paul couldn't hide every sadness they felt about their children growing up. They had known all along that each would one day become of age and enter the adult world. Kimmie's surprising eloquence proved that a girl her age could make up her mind independently.

Kimmie signed, "If I hear better and talk clearer, it will help improve my written English. A CI is a tool that can help me."[36]

Paula signed with Kimmie in a way that made the conversation seem as if it were just between the two of them. "What if the implant doesn't work like you hope?"[37]

"I know it might not work, like Dad says, but I want to try."[38]

Kimmie's decision on this day was the one that both parents agreed to accept. They were both beaten, and Kimmie's future would be the future she chose.

Ella shifted in her chair, looking uncomfortable. Eliza wondered what kind of pressure she was feeling because all the recent events were huge and life changing.

"We Googled Roz. Wow, is she well known!!"[39] Ella signed when Paula asked how she felt about learning who her mother was.

"True, but telling other people about your biological mother includes written and spoken English and signing with other people. Maybe you think signing to someone is no big deal—not the same as telling someone in English."[40] Paula reminded her not to divulge the information to anyone in the Deaf community, even though they might seem not to know who Roz was or care much either. "It will be hard not to talk or sign about it, but I know you can keep a secret."[41]

Eliza appreciated Paula's encouragement of her younger daughter. The girls were still bursting with Roz excitement, and stories could spread like wildfire in the Deaf community, especially on some social media platforms. Once the cat was out of the bag about Ella's birth and biological mother, Eliza feared the roar could be that of a raging lion.

21
Signs and Symptoms

One day, when Kimmie had her friend Mazie over for a sleepover, Kimmie converted her and Ella's bedroom closet into a clubhouse and did not let Ella join. Mazie had an implant and was teaching Kimmie how to speak various English words and phrases. Kimmie didn't want Ella tagging along, because she said Ella was too young. During Mazie's visit, Kimmie wasn't friendly to Ella, but then the next day she was, and then she wasn't again. She kept the closet as her clubhouse and filled the space with some of their best books and pillows, a place away from Ella. Kimmie got mad when Ella wanted to visit the closet: Ella used her iPhone as a flashlight to signal Kimmie through the crack in the closet door.

Ella went to their parents and told them that Kimmie wasn't sharing. Ella's mother told her that Kimmie was going through a phase. Ella knew what phase this was because Kimmie was almost a teenager. All of Ella's favorite characters in books had trouble with their teenage brothers and sisters. Like in *Diary of a Wimpy Kid*. And Harry Potter had trouble with Dudley Dursley after his thirteenth birthday. Kimmie was getting bossy, and Ella wished she could just not care about what her sister did, but then her sister would be friendly again.

"Big, big secret,"[42] Kimmie signed on one of her friendly afternoons.

"What?"[43]

Kimmie slid open the door of the closet.

"Come in here."[44]

Ella had already been inside the closet to peek at what Kimmie had in there on a day Kimmie was at karate class. Ella thought Kimmie didn't know, but at dinner afterward, Kimmie said her stuff had been touched. They fought over how Ella had invaded Kimmie's privacy. Paul told Ella to leave her big sister's things alone. Ella refused to go in now that it was the next day and Kimmie was feeling friendly again. Kimmie assured Ella that she had an invitation from the club's vice president, so it was fine to go into the clubhouse. The space was about four feet wide and eight feet long. Kimmie crawled over the shoes and boots on the floor to the far corner, and Ella followed. Ella sat on some shoes with her back against a dry cleaning bag that held her mother's winter coat. Kimmie nestled into some pillows with her back against the wall.

Kimmie laughed when the bag clung to the side of Ella's face and rubbed her hair on the plastic to make the strands stand on end. She looked like a lion.

"Wait,"[45] Kimmie signed.

She slid the door closed while pulling the string above them to turn on the light so they could see each other.

Ella wondered if the secret Kimmie wanted to tell her was about Kimmie's birth mother. Since Ella's birth mother was Rosalind Taylor, maybe Kimmie's birth mother was a famous person from China. But come to find out, Kimmie's birth mother had not given her real name to the orphanage where Kimmie had been adopted, so they might never know it. Ella guessed Kimmie had found out about her birth mother somehow and was going to tell her. Ella thought not knowing who her birth mother was would be better than having a birth mother who wanted her to speak instead of sign. Kimmie could be a queen's daughter. Ella considered her secret about Roz a good one because it meant Viv was her grandmother, but it also meant Roz texted her sometimes, and Ella didn't know how to say anything back. She and Kimmie KISS-FIST the way Aunt Viv was more like their real grandmother than Eliza's mother. Kimmie also KISS-FIST Roz being famous. Maybe the clubhouse could be her and Kimmie's new secret. They could keep other people out.

"Roz is hoping that you get a CI,"[46] Kimmie signed. The girls always used her sign name: the letter R following the movement made by producing the letter Z.

Ever since they had gotten their new phones, Kimmie had been trying to find out things about Ella's birth mother. They weren't allowed to watch Roz Taylor's movies because most were rated R. So they watched her on YouTube movie trailers. One was about a man who fell in love with her on a street in Paris, in another she was a police officer, and she was once an action hero.

"I am wondering why you are telling me this."[47] Ella said.

"I saw Mom and Dad talking about it last week."[48]

Ella was surprised by a few things Kimmie said. She sometimes didn't believe Kimmie and thought she made up stuff to cause trouble. Ella was surprised to think that her mom and dad would have secrets about Roz and CIs. Why did Roz care about CIs? Her dad didn't care about them, and she didn't care about them. Kimmie sure did. What was the big deal about CIs anyway? Ella loved her life, when Kimmie wasn't annoying her, and she didn't cause trouble and drama like Kimmie did.

Ella was also surprised that her sister would spy. Ella spied on Kimmie and her friends and what they said, but Kimmie had no reason to spy, because she wasn't left out. There was a gap where the doors of the closet folded, and Ella had looked through it when Kimmie and Mazie were inside. They talked about girls in school and a boy who made them mad. Ella spied on her parents sometimes too. She knew her father was unhappy sometimes about Roz Taylor because his face said so.

"Why do you care?"[49] Ella asked.

Sometimes she wondered if her mother had made a mistake about who her birth mother was. Roz was both African American and white—mixed race, like Ella, but Ella was even more mixed because Roz had mixed her again. Kimmie was from China. Ella's mother had ancestors from Ireland, and her father's were from Canada, which made Kimmie and Ella everything, all jumbled together. Roz did not want to raise Ella, and her mom said that Roz's career and movies were important to her. But maybe the real reason was because she was deaf, and maybe that was why she wanted her to have a CI.

Another thing Eliza had told Ella about Rosalind Taylor was that Viv had adopted *her*, so Ella was adopted-adopted. Eliza told Ella that Aunt Viv could not have a baby because her husband had died, and then God had asked her to take care of Roz. Aunt Viv learned ASL without having a deaf person in her family as a way of showing how much she loved Ella. Quinn could also sign. She asked Ella questions about school and didn't call her a different name, Elle. Ella saw her birth mother boss Quinn at the hotel dinner the way Mazie bossed Kimmie. Kimmie sometimes bossed Ella now that she was an almost teenager.

Ella hated bosses.

Roz also did not use ASL, so she was part of all the people who didn't use ASL outside of Ella's family. She visited one time and did not send letters or birthday cards, like Quinn and Viv, and only sent texts now that Ella knew her secret. Ella decided she was angry at Roz and that next time her bio mom texted, she would say "drop it." She shared her plan with Kimmie.

"Don't act stupid,"[50] Kimmie bossed.

Ella started to climb under the coats to leave the closet.

Kimmie signed that she wasn't friends with Mazie anymore. Ella knew this was a lie and that Kimmie and Mazie were only having a fight and would be friends again the next day. Kimmie said she had seen Mazie being mean to a girl.

"You still want a CI?"[51] Ella asked.

Kimmie had only started wanting a CI after Mazie had gotten one.

Ella felt sweaty in the closet and wanted to go.

"Of course I do!"[52] Kimmie answered.

Ella was sure that Kimmie was just in a fight with Mazie. Kimmie said she wanted to meet famous hearing people and become a movie star, and Mazie told her she only could if she got an implant. Kimmie went on and on about all the famous people she would meet one day. After Kimmie was done showing Ella pictures on her phone and talking about plans for her future, she told Ella that she could be in her club instead of Mazie, and Ella decided to join.

22
Signs of Change

Paul had an idea that they should sell the house in Highland Park and move to the Tangletown area where one or two of the public schools provided services to mainstreamed deaf children. Eliza did not object, although neither one of them was happy to leave the neighborhood where their girls had mastered their first two-wheeler bikes and learned to climb trees, where they could walk to a grocery store or play in the beautiful nearby parks.

Before they decided to move, Paul would sometimes catch Eliza watching him. She seemed to be trying to think of something to say to distract him or make him feel better about Kimmie's CI. When she asked him what he was thinking, he had trouble answering. He spent a lot of time being "too quiet," but it was hard to say what was on his mind, and he didn't want to talk about anything that might hurt Eliza's feelings. After all, Eliza was hearing, and he was saying that he did not want his girls to become like what she was. How could hearing people understand the idea that a deaf father would not want his deaf daughters to be able to hear because he really did not value something he could not achieve, they may never achieve, and he simply did not want to be bothered with? It might look like he was being selfish.

It had always been his and Eliza's joke that he was the tall, dark, silent type even though his quietness mostly arose from being deaf. His tendency to shut down had brought occasional trouble to their marriage, but he was working hard to assemble his thoughts so he could state them correctly.

Everything had snowballed since Kimmie had confirmed her decision to have implant surgery. Ella had also tentatively said that she wanted to be at the same high school as Kimmie in two years, which meant she would need to go to a mainstream program in a public school instead of staying at TCDS. The family discussed the future on several occasions, once after a long weekend trip to Wisconsin Dells. Paul and Eliza knew Kimmie wanted an implant, but after discussions and seeing Kimmie's strong-arm tactics to get Ella on board too, they thought it was time for a serious conversation about it. They talked to both girls about the surgery, what it would entail, and the possible aftermath. Ella, not wanting to be left behind in terms of her big sister's life choices, finally admitted to wanting an implant. Paul and Eliza checked in on her decision on several more occasions and got some confusing messages, but in the end, it always came down to an affirmative response from Ella.

Paul in particular was suspect of Ella's acquiescence to a CI. He really didn't want her to get the surgery, but he had also taken the lessons they had learned from the *Sound and Fury* movies to heart. Perhaps Ella was tired of discussing it, but she insisted she wanted to go through with the procedure. They took Ella's choice as the opening Roz had hoped for and scheduled implant surgery for both girls the following summer. They wanted to leave enough time for them to recover before school started in the fall. It took six weeks after the implants were inserted to have them programmed and mapped by an audiologist. Paul, having seen other deaf students he worked with go through these same procedures, wanted to give the girls plenty of time to adjust. There would be new language plans and curriculum considerations since, at public school, they would be educated differently than they had been at TCDS. They would also have speech therapy at school as well as privately. If the girls were getting implanted, he wanted to do it the right way with plenty of auditory supports. The girls would be adding to the spoken language they had already developed through speech therapy sessions at the various programs and schools they had attended.

Paul thought the planning phase had finally been brought to a close, but Ella started a conversation at bedtime one night when Kimmie was still downstairs.

"Dad, you had a CI in the past, right?"[53] Ella signed.

"Yes, but I was much older than you are now. CI technology was not sophisticated like it is now. Why do you ask?"[54] Paul dreaded this conversation.

"Your experience with a CI was not good, right? I saw you and Mom talking before. Can you explain what happened?"[55]

Paul broke out in a sweat, and he really didn't want to talk about it. "Why do you want to know? Do you have a specific reason for asking?"[56]

"Some kids at school do not like CIs. They have said that deaf people who have CIs are trying to become hearing. They say those people are choosing to live as a hearing person and are rejecting the Deaf-World."[57]

"Well, um, I am not sure . . . Oh look, Kimmie is coming upstairs. Hurry up, girls, it's late and time to go to bed!"[58]

Kimmie was bubbling over with excitement. "I can't wait to go to school tomorrow! There will be an assembly for people who got good grades. I will get two awards!"[59] Paul told both girls that he was proud of them, read them a story, and tried to calm their excitement.

Paul signed, "I am going to try to make it to your school tomorrow for the awards ceremony. I am so proud of you two!" Ella looked disappointed, like she had more to say. "Remember to enjoy the last assembly at TCDS. Soon you will transfer to a new school. We'll have to take plenty of pictures!"[60]

The girls had a bittersweet perspective on moving from TCDS. They would miss their friends but were looking forward to new challenges. One of the schools in St. Paul that provided quality services to deaf children was called All Seasons Elementary. The other was East High School for grades six through twelve. Neither was all that far from TCDS, but it would be easier all around if they found a house within the district, which meant living directly in the city. Kimmie and Ella would still attend different schools until Ella graduated into sixth grade and could go to East High too. Both would need communication access services to participate in inclusion programs since most of the academic content would be delivered in spoken English. The change would also mean an interpreter, or interpreting team, for both of them.

The search for a new house came at the right time since they had outgrown their current place. Making moving arrangements gave Paul something to keep his mind off his negative thoughts. Despite rehashing his traumatic experience with Paula, then his conversation with Ella, he agreed to be open-minded; however, his bad experience of having to have an implant removed when he was younger nagged at him. His CI had failed to work, and after years of speech therapy, Paul still wasn't able to speak like a typical hearing person. He suffered extreme self-consciousness when he tried. As a teenager, the pain of being teased for his "weird" muddy speech and language had led to him once attempting suicide. He had moments since they had decided on Kimmie's and Ella's cochlear implant plan when he wanted to call the surgery off.

Moving to a solid public school district would at least ensure that the girls would get the best possible support for their transition. Roz had offered to help them with a new mortgage and the cost not covered by their insurance for the implants. Paul refused until Eliza convinced him that accepting would be best for the girls and would be the only way they could afford a house in Tangletown. Paul planned to keep a careful eye on how the implants functioned, especially since he had two girls with seemingly different views on CIs. He was apprehensive because he had never been able to benefit from his implant. Part of what had gone wrong when he was young was that no one had correctly diagnosed the cause of the implant malfunction.

Paul's parents had taken him to numerous doctors to attempt to get answers. Finally, they found out about an otologist who specialized in implant failures. The doctor told them that the implant electrode array had been damaged, probably due to being put in incorrectly. He would have to have the implant removed and reinserted. By then, Paul was sixteen, and he and his parents decided that enough was enough, it was too late. What a relief it had been to finally give up.

At least his girls were starting in a better place than he had, already proficient in ASL, before they embarked on learning spoken language. Also, the CI technology had come a long way and was much improved compared to the almost primitive technology he had been offered. He would keep an eye on Ella because he knew what a potentially emotionally explosive situation was in front of her. Kimmie seemed fine.

On a day when the girls were at a TCDS friend's birthday party, he rolled the lawn mower from the garage and began taking the engine apart to sharpen the blades and mow the lawn in preparation for their open house. Eliza had done a nice job designing the flower beds and nurturing the perennial garden. The outside of the house had what their realtor called curb appeal, and they would likely make money on selling it, given how prices had gone up since they first moved in. With a little planning, they could pay off any loan they took from Roz within a few years. Paul noticed a car slowing down to look the place over. The better the deal they got on the house, the less he would feel like he owed Roz afterward.

The house shimmered in the sunlight. Its big oak in front where Paul had hung a tire swing gave the place a storybook feel. One of the greatest frustrations of being deaf arose from people seeing only the outside and not acknowledging the life within. "Normal" people noticed people who had lost limbs, were blind, or who used a wheelchair. However, being a deaf person carried an invisibility that caused that reality to be undetectable by most people. Paul was grateful for his community, to belong. The Deaf community was often an enigma to hearing people, so it was easy for assumptions to be made about "the deaf." What isolated a deaf person wasn't necessarily the hearing loss itself. A famous quote from Helen Keller, who experienced both hearing and vision loss, described it clearly: "Blindness separates us from things, but deafness separates us from people." Of course, this meant those people who could hear and did not sign.

While he was working, Eliza stepped out onto the porch steps with a mug of coffee. It was a gorgeous May morning, and her feet were bare and her hair loose. They so rarely got time when they were home together without the girls, and he felt a pleasure at just looking at her. Paul felt lucky to have Eliza as his life partner, someone for whom deaf struggles were in plain sight, despite the fact that she had not been born or raised anywhere close to the Deaf-World.

When he finished with the first blade, he set it aside and wiped his hands on the tail of his shirt. Eliza had been watching the birds at the feeder, but she turned toward him as he rose from the grass. She swept her hair off her shoulder.

He signed, "What is your role as a hearing person who happens to be the mother of deaf kids?"[61]

His question caused her to bobble her coffee mug. She carefully set it down on the step beside her. They had been so unified in all they had done as parents that it was easy to forget one was deaf and the other hearing. However, Paula had urged them to talk about their cultural differences as a way of acknowledging and working through any variations that might cause resentment. After what seemed like a long minute, Eliza answered.

"First and foremost, I am able to provide clear access to a full language, ASL. How many hearing people, not from deaf families, can sign ASL? Of course, I am not fluent like you, people can see my hearing accent. Also, I help the girls in terms of their English."[62]

Paul nodded. "Right, and you are a former deaf ed teacher too. You know the educational needs of deaf children related to language."[63]

"You bring up a good point! Also, I understand various types of educational settings for deaf and hard of hearing students."[64]

Paul could see Eliza's face light up at the reminder of her brilliant knowledge. She was showing off, and he was proud to see it. Not many people were bolstered by education and specialized classes to be parents to their children. As Paul's wife, they shared cultural knowledge, some of hers learned from classes, but for both, what they learned from the experiences of deaf friends and actually being members of the community. He had greater intuitive access to the girls coming from a common deaf experience, while she traveled a great distance for her knowledge.

Thinking this idea over, he signed, "Also, as a woman, you are a role model. It is important for the girls to have a female role model. Did you forget that?"[65] Kimmie, in particular, had baffled him with her new girlish interest in makeup and crushes.

"Oh, you are right! I know what you mean. As a woman, the girls look to me as a role model, and I am able to explain hearing culture. Oh, I forgot something really important. Doing the cooking, cleaning, and driving to activities."[66]

"That's true," Paul signed. "But, hey, I also cook, clean, and do a lot of driving to activities too."[67] They both laughed because they did share quite a few duties, and the overlaps bound them together.

Eliza had once confessed to Paul that her hearing friends who were not involved in the Deaf-World rarely broached the subject of her mixed marriage. They just took it more or less for granted that it was the same as their hearing/hearing relationships but with a slight twist. Eliza's friends who were also involved in the Deaf-World seemed to assume she was rolling with the punches, figuring it all out. More often than not, her deaf friends expressed awareness of what it took for her to sideline the hearing world to primarily live in the Deaf-World.

Paul tried to be attentive to who Eliza was. She might never know the inside pain of audism or the frustration he felt at being left out and having to fight for equal access to services and accommodations. And yet, Eliza's life had been altered more than his when they had married and adopted children. She was often called upon to be the family interpreter whenever they interacted with the hearing world so that hearing people were not communicatively inconvenienced. They asked her all the questions they couldn't ask Paul or the girls directly: Do they read lips? Can they talk? Do they read braille? (This one exasperated Paul.) Can he drive? Hearing people would sometimes treat him as if he weren't standing right in front of them with his car keys in his hand.

Some hearing neighbors unintentionally put Eliza in the position of a communication buffer between the Jean-Baptiste family and themselves. She had seen deaf friends interact in the hearing world in a successful way, born out of need and common sense. Their ability to move through their day-to-day was part of how Deaf-World members lived the "Deaf way." Eliza wanted her girls to be able to interact in the hearing world, so she intentionally encouraged opportunities for them to learn bicultural deaf ways from their community. She picked appropriate times to sign more ASL or at times coded English syntax to help the girls track written English that Paul generally didn't bother with. Paul translated the books he read to the girls each night into ASL, whereas Eliza generally used a version closer to spoken English syntax,* with more English-like features built in. Seeing differences between ASL, spoken language, and written English helped the girls become more naturally bilingual. The habit of teaching multiple languages was not unusual because most deaf parents want their children to read and understand a second language outside the home. However, Eliza's knowledge, language proficiency, and teaching skills were better than average. She had lived and studied in both communities. Paul's contributions were key, though, because his ASL fluency naturally encouraged the girls to use a visual language in the home and had led them down a path to bilingualism. There were times, at the doctor's office or at school meetings, when Paul acted as an interpreter for the girls. Many times, deaf people act as interpreters for other deaf people. This is part of the path toward some Deaf community members, who are interested, developing their skills and becoming deaf interpreters (DIs).

Eliza asked Paul, "What about your role as a deaf dad?"[68]

"The girls know you are the only hearing person and that we are all deaf. I am able to model for them what life is like as a deaf person in America. They are able to see what it means to live the life of a deaf person who signs."[69]

Paul had experienced less angst of late, and the niceness of the spring day opened his mind to what the future might bring.

---

* Referred to as academic ASL, this discourse is what is seen in places such as educational, legal, medical, and some media settings. Language choices are made to fit in with expectations of these settings (Bahan, "The Whole Picture").

However, his temporary euphoria was shaken by the image of the conversation Ella had initiated. What was that about? He tried to shake the negative feelings, looking around at the charm of his surroundings and thinking about how much he would miss it. The neighbors they had gotten to know in Highland Park were from a variety of backgrounds, some Somali, some Hmong, some African American, others elderly, some people from Sweden and Italy, some Latina/o, and two houses over, a gay couple had moved in who were looking to adopt in China just as they had. They even had other deaf neighbors a few blocks away. A war amputee had returned home to live with his mother on the corner. Paul's family represented a community within the community surrounding them, and within their enclave were individuals who had learned to live with and understand each other. Paul thought about the changes coming their way, and it gave him pause. The new communication methods the girls would use after their implants, along with the extra hours of speech and language therapy, would tax them all. In two or three years, they would be different people than they were now. But if they blended into the tapestry around them, what a gift it would be.

23
Signs and Wonders

Kimmie's best friend, Mazie, invited her to Comic Con to see Sean Berdy,* a deaf actor from the television show *Switched at Birth.* Her parents had special tickets to meet Sean at his hotel because her father worked for the corporate headquarters of a telecommunications company, and he was part of the sales team who scored invitations to big events like baseball games and various community events. Paul wanted Kimmie to bring Ella with her, but Ella was too young in Kimmie's opinion and would be excess baggage. Ella was nine and a half, and Kimmie eleven and a half, which, in Kimmie's mind, was a huge difference in age. Kimmie also argued that it was unfair that Ella was getting so many presents from her birth mother, and she wasn't getting any. Eliza had shown Ella and Kimmie a special locket that Roz had given Ella when she was a baby. Eliza told Ella that she was old enough to wear it even though it had diamonds on the outside. Kimmie didn't think Ella could be trusted to keep it safe and was happy when Ella usually left it in its box. Roz had also sent Ella a full-sized Barbie house on Ella's birthday, which Kimmie liked but had told her sister it was a baby toy. Roz had never paid attention to Ella before, but now that Ella was going to get a CI, she sent her presents. Paul and Eliza finally agreed to let Kimmie go with Mazie without

---

* Sean Berdy is an actor who had a recurring role on the ABC show *Switched at Birth*, which aired between 2011 and 2017. Berdy is Deaf from a Deaf family.

her little sister tagging along. The other good news was that they were moving to a house where Kimmie was going to get her own room. First the phone, then the implant surgery, then her own room, and now a visit to see her very favorite actor. Kimmie predicted the best summer of her life.

Ella, when they predicted together, saw a hard summer on her horizon. She didn't want to go stay with her famous mother, even though she might get her picture in magazines and meet famous people. Kimmie wanted to visit in her place and thought it was unfair that Ella was saying no to the invitation to spend time with Roz. Kimmie *wanted* to be an actress and imagined what it would be like having a big mansion and a swimming pool. She could marry Sean Berdy or be his best friend.

Mazie's father picked her up in his car, a BMW, a status symbol lost on Kimmie. They went to the Minneapolis Convention Center Hotel. A man and a woman who worked for Sean Berdy met them and took them up to Sean's room on the elevator. The view from Sean's suite was nice, but not as nice as the one at Roz's dinner, where Kimmie had been able to see all the way to the airport. Mazie and Kimmie watched the cars on the street below until Sean came through the door from his bedroom. They could hardly breathe. They both stood frozen to the spot, holding their hands over their mouths. He had red hair and freckles like a cute boy at their school. Sean looked just like he did in the poster Mazie had in her room.

Mazie and Kimmie couldn't eat their lunch. After the meal, the woman who had taken them up in the elevator told them to ask any questions they wanted. Everyone at the table had things they wanted to ask. Sean knew a lot of famous people. He had once recorded a song in ASL and had been in commercials. Kimmie raised her hand. She was at the end of the table with Mazie and her parents. There were three other girls, three people who worked for Comic Con, and an ASL interpreter. Kimmie asked Sean if he had ever met Roz Taylor.

"No," he signed. "I really wish."[70]

"I have!"[71] Kimmie told him.

Mazie knocked Kimmie in the ribs with her elbow.

She probably thought Kimmie was lying just to get Sean's attention. But she wasn't. Kimmie held her phone so everyone could see a picture of her with Roz when she had invited them to her hotel. Eliza had taken it, and Kimmie had sneakily AirDropped it from Eliza's phone one day so she could keep it.

Kimmie suddenly realized she couldn't say any more to Sean about Roz or she would get in deep trouble. But if she told Sean Ella's story, maybe he would call and text Kimmie, wanting to know her better. She could get Roz Taylor to meet him, and Roz could get him a job in a movie. Sean said he was looking for a good movie to be in, and she wanted to watch him on the screen again and maybe act in the movie with him. Kimmie said that her aunt Viv was a relative of Roz Taylor. She didn't lie, and she kept Ella's part secret. Sean Berdy added her to his Instagram. Kimmie could DM him anytime she wanted, he said.

Kimmie and Mazie took lots of pictures with Sean, one with his arm around just Kimmie, which she posted on her social media right away. Maybe she could get one of Roz at her pool in California and then send it to him and invite him over. Roz might want to visit with Ella, and Kimmie could go and then invite Sean Berdy.

When she got home, she told Ella all about her day, but Ella wanted to finish drawing a picture of a horse. Ella didn't care about Sean because she didn't know about his show, or about movies, Hollywood, or any of that, or how hard it was to be famous. Ella showed Kimmie another present from Roz that had arrived in the mail, a little red handbag from Prada. Kimmie couldn't believe it. From Prada. That's when she knew that her sister was lucky, too lucky. If she wanted to be lucky too, she needed to get an implant and audition for Sean's television show.

24
Vital Signs

Paul and Eliza planned the girls' surgeries for the same morning so they could endure one hospital stay, one week of bandages and dizzy spells, and six weeks of waiting until the devices could be programmed together. The drive to Children's Minnesota, the children's hospital in Minneapolis, in the early, early morning fog felt surreal, hazy, chilling. The girls nervously fidgeted in the back seat, and Paul kept his gaze away from Ella in particular, not wanting to give her a chance to flash her doe-eyed look. Paul kept his sights squarely on the barely visible highway in front of them so Eliza couldn't talk to him to release her tension. With Paul driving and Eliza in the passenger seat, Paul usually did most of the talking so Eliza would watch him and he still could watch the road. Paul was an expert at driving and watching people sign, behavior that usually made uninitiated hearing people very nervous. Because he was not talking at all, it was obvious he did not want to.

One after the other, Kimmie and then Ella rolled into surgery. Eliza and Paul sat side by side in the waiting room with a big Thermos of coffee, trading out available reading material and crossword puzzles until that moment they were no longer waiting. A nurse told them to expect the doctor in a few minutes. Dr. Perry told them that the procedure had gone well (twice). She assured them that both girls had done well being under general anesthesia. Dr. Jean T. Perry was a world-renowned cochlear implant surgeon in the Twin Cities area, and she explained the surgery: much like they had already known both from prior appointments and a lot of Google searches. The incision was made behind the ear after the hair was shaved away from the incision site. The implant was then placed under the skin, and the electrode array was inserted into the cochlea in the inner ear. The surgical team performed some tests to ensure the implants were working properly, then the incision was closed using dissolvable stitches. The doctor said that the girls would be in recovery for a few hours, then would probably be ready to go home, if there were no complications.

Paul felt sick to his stomach but dared not tell Eliza. Eliza had mom work to do. She began reassuring, stroking hands, signing for the huge bouquet of flowers Roz had sent, and showing the girls text messages and cards from their friends from school, signing to them even when neither girl felt comfortable enough yet to sign back. Paul hung back, staring at the white walls, words escaping him.

The girls were groggy at first, and they looked exhausted and pale. The hospital had secured an interpreter so they could report any discomfort directly to the nurses and get more pain medicine if they needed it. Kimmie needed help getting to the bathroom. Ella threw up once. Paul brought the car around a few hours later and drove them home to Highland Park. Eliza had already prepared places for them to sleep downstairs. She wanted to keep a close eye on both girls for at least forty-eight hours. After all, the surgeon had cut through the mastoid bone behind their right ear and implanted the array into the cochlea, which would send signals to the auditory nerve. After six weeks, when the receiver was attached, the device would replicate sound if their brains could "translate" the signals. Kimmie complained of pain, and Ella cried off and on, her recovery slower. Eliza doled out medicine and felt like a full-time nurse for a while.

The girls opened the presents they received. Ella turned the Skullcandy radio Roz had sent to her over and over in her hands. Kimmie crashed to the floor the first time Eliza loosened her bandage. When she changed out Ella's, she unraveled the bandage slowly so the pressure in her ear didn't change all at once.

The girls snipped at each other, impatient to be moving around again. They fought over whose gifts were whose. That's when Eliza knew they were feeling a little better. Using a hand mirror, she showed them the space above their ears that had been shaved, and then when Kimmie shrieked and cried, she promised them new haircuts at a salon in St. Paul. She let them watch unlimited television and blew up an air mattress so either she or Paul could sleep near them at night. She promised them a cat when they moved to their new house.

They hired a mover to pack their things, though they could barely afford the cost. For three days, after the girls had returned to their bedroom, the place emptied box by box. Paul and Eliza reconstructed their belongings at their new destination. The boxes were getting thinned out as their furniture was arranged to fit into a new domicile. Their new home, a prairie-style craftsman in the Tangletown area, had a modern addition off the back that made it larger than it looked from the front. Compared to the other house, there were pros and cons: the yard was smaller, Eliza gained a small office, and Kimmie and Ella had their own bedrooms, but there was no tree for a tire swing. On the outside, the lot ran in a narrow strip to a small garage and a driveway used by all the neighbors. There was a large enough patch in the back that Eliza could plant a late tomato garden and the girls could play with their new kitten, a calico they named Gabby.

The family spent most of June and July watching the neighborhood through their big front window. People walked their dogs or rode their bikes by their house all day long. The traffic was heavier than they were used to, and they often had to keep the curtains shut. A few people who lived closest stopped by to introduce themselves, and the girls introduced them to Gabby (with Eliza's interpreting intervention). Eliza could smell the exhaust from the big roads that snaked over to the north. During the six weeks after the girls' surgeries, she missed her old home. In late July, they visited the audiologist to have the cochlear implants programmed digitally.

Eliza received a text from Roz asking her to film Ella's CI mapping since it would be the first time impulses would be sent through her implant to her auditory nerve and the first time Ella could "hear" or, at least, detect sound. Kimmie, who was wearing the red Prada bag Roz had given to Ella over one shoulder, watched Eliza text a response as they sat side by side in the audiologist's office. The waiting room's outdated dingy yellow chairs clashed horribly with the purse. Eliza answered Roz with a short note explaining that they wanted to keep the event private if that was okay. She had no idea how Roz had even learned the time and place of their visit since Eliza had been vague, even with Quinn, about when it would happen. She also wrote that she would update her and Viv at the earliest possible convenience to tell them what they learned.

"So, I am just wondering why you didn't share the video with Roz,"[72] Kimmie signed.

"There was no new information to share."[73] Eliza didn't want to pressure either of the girls into thinking the testing was an all-or-nothing event. It would take time for them to know how well the implants were working.

Paul had lapsed into another period of silence. He had busied himself with all the working parts of the new house. He had installed a fan in the living room and had put in a new garbage disposal since the one that was there wasn't working. He and Eliza tried to keep their promise to Paula to maintain their lines of communication, but there hadn't been much time to talk.

An audiologist appeared in front of Eliza and asked which one of the two girls wanted to go first. Kimmie sprang from her chair, raising her hand as if she were in a classroom and the teacher had just asked who could help the new student, Sean Berdy. Paul took Ella by the hand, and they followed Eliza, Kimmie, and the audiologist into a small examining room that also had a sound booth. Paul stood with his back to the door, and Ella and Kimmie shared a chair until the audiologist directed Kimmie to sit in the one close to her desk. She checked Kimmie's healed wound and attached her receiver. Using a laptop, she played differently pitched tones through Kimmie's new device.

Kimmie watched the audiologist's hands as they slid the mouse across a pad, changing the pitch of the beeps piping through the implant. As the audiologist clicked the mouse, Kimmie's face focused. She nodded to indicate when she was aware of the beeps that were presented. Tones were carefully chosen by the audiologist, moving from fainter tones to more intense and lower to higher pitches. The audiologist was mapping, or programming, the implant, trying to make sure each girl was comfortable with the auditory input she could handle right now. After a while, Kimmie acted like a mind-blowing auditory event had taken place, but Eliza could see that an equal amount of her senses was focused on the mouse and that she was watching what the audiologist was doing.

Kimmie spoke and signed, "I can hear! Will I hear better and better all the time?"[74]

The audiologist nodded and explained, "You should continue to hear more efficiently. Once you get used to the implant, and have auditory therapy, sound will become more understandable."

Kimmie looked from the audiologist to Eliza.

"What? I missed what she said,"[75] she signed.

Eliza interpreted. Kimmie had not understood the audiologist's spoken words.

The girls switched places, Kimmie holding her red purse in her lap as Ella slid into the seat next to the audiologist's desk. Ella claimed to be able to hear fewer of the beeps than Kimmie, though she seemed to track more of what the audiologist said in between the tests, her head turning to follow her voice. The two girls were having seemingly different physiological and psychological reactions to the sounds they were hearing or not hearing. What could this mean?

Paul watched the proceedings intently, his light jacket and both of the girls' coats gathered in his arms, his back against the door. The air conditioning in the building pumped out way too much cold air, and Eliza rubbed her arms. Paul frowned, his head bowed as if at a funeral.

After they left the office to celebrate at an ice cream shop, instead of texting Roz as she said she would, Eliza gazed across the table in the ice cream parlor at Kimmie and then Ella, each with cups of ice cream instead of the cones they had loved so much when they were little. What was this mood she had—why did she feel so morbid? Her thoughts once again turned to the huge life event they had all just experienced in the audiologist's suite. Bye-bye indigenous deaf ears, may you rest in peace.

25

Some Excellent Signs

The last chore of the summer was to secure ASL interpreters for the girls in their new school district. Paul wrote to the pupil services director who was in charge of special education programming and asked how the district handled interpreting services for deaf or hard of hearing students. The director's administrative assistant, Kim Bass, sent along notification that Kimmie's school interpreter would be a young man named Lucas Hamilton and Ella's a young woman in her late twenties named Ginger Noble. A lot depended on how each interpreter matched with the girls, so Paul formed a plan. From what he could tell, both were well credentialed, yet he wasn't sure he was ready to just accept the district's choices. Paul realized that parents usually did not select interpreters, but he asked the pupil services director if he could bring the girls to the school to meet their potential interpreters. The director said that this was an unusual request, but the school district had a staff of interpreters, so he felt that parents had the right to check the credentials of the interpreters. After the meeting was approved, Kim Bass arranged a mutually agreeable time for all to meet.

On their way to the meeting, Paul and Eliza stopped at the local Panera to pick up sandwiches, chips, and chocolate chip cookies.

They gathered, ate, and engaged in a lot of chitchat with Lucas and Ginger. Paul noticed that Lucas, tall and barrel-chested, wore a shirt with the name of a band Paul had never heard of under a cardigan sweater and had earrings that bobbled as he signed. He readily told them his life story. The adopted son of an ASL-proficient hearing mother and a deaf father, Lucas's childhood did not sound all that different from Kimmie's. His parents adopted him from Korea when he was a toddler, bringing him to America to round out a family that already included three biological daughters. Everyone in his family signed ASL. In addition to ASL and English, Lucas spoke Korean, which he had learned to know more about his birth culture. This made him an ASL/English/Korean trilingual, a very impressive thing to be.

Paul asked where Lucas had gone to school.

"I graduated from a school in Ohio, Kent State University's interpreting program, then went on to receive a master's degree from Gallaudet University."[76]

Kimmie watched him closely.

"I am going to college in California where Sean Berdy lives."[77] She spoke and signed at the same time.

"I just got back from a trip to Los Angeles and had a great time!"[78]

Lucas described his travels, which was all the encouragement Kimmie needed. They lapsed into praise of the flashier places, like Beverly Hills and Rodeo Drive, and Paul's family chat became a full-blown conversation between just the two of them. Paul was amused at how easily Lucas had learned to speak Kimmie's "language." At one point, she asked Paul for the car keys, ran out of the room, and returned with the Prada bag Ella had more or less given to her. Lucas held it in his hands and looked it over inside and out.

"Wow, it's real!"[79] he signed.

Eliza and Ella were talking to Ginger, with Eliza doing most of the talking. Ginger was much less chatty than Lucas, much more formal, and shyer. She wore a skirt and heels and had on a plain sweater that showed the contrast of the cross necklace she was wearing. She addressed Paul and Eliza as Mr. and Mrs. Jean-Baptiste rather than by their first names despite the fact that Paul had introduced the family casually.

Ginger told the group that she had recently been the interpreter for an older student, but the school board representatives thought she would be a good match to work with Ella. She explained that she would work with Ella in all school contexts, from higher level math to social situations. Since the cochlear implant had not been the remedy for Ella's hearing loss that Roz had hoped for, Ella preferred using ASL, or maybe Ella just preferred a visual language over a spoken one. Ginger was willing to provide effective visual language on all register levels and work with Ella in the way Ella wanted.

Paul was pleased with this academic approach to considering Ella as a whole person with her own preferences. Like with Lucas, Paul reserved his judgment in the hopes of discovering a bit more about her on a personal level. Eliza was better than he was at drawing out details. Ginger remained so entirely professional, she didn't use her side of their conversation to venture much beyond information about her interests or family background.

Eliza finally directly asked her where she had grown up and to explain her path to becoming an interpreter. Ginger explained that she and her husband, Alex, lived in a signing home, and they were both children of deaf adults (CODAs). Two of Alex's siblings were also deaf. His parents had attended Gallaudet, and Ginger had earned her master's degree there where she happened to meet Alex at a Gallaudet homecoming game. At the mention of Gallaudet, the reserve between the four adults at the table melted.

The girls had finished their sandwiches and had taken off for an impromptu tour of the school while no students walked the hallways. Ginger knew Viv and Paul's friend Dr. Charles Stacker and had taken classes with him.

"He was the reason we were able to adopt Ella,"[80] Paul signed.

They discovered they had other friends in common, neighbors from their old neighborhood in Highland Park who were members of Alex's father's congregation, Shiloh Baptist Deaf Church. Alex's father was a nationally recognized spiritual leader, not just in the Deaf community, but in hearing circles as well.

Paul was not surprised to learn the CODA connections of the two interpreters, which were sometimes called deaf-parented interpreters (DPIs). Both interpreters possessed multilingual and multicultural qualities of individuals connected with both hearing and Deaf communities.*

"Do you have hobbies?"[81] Eliza asked Ginger.

"Alex and I lead our church youth group."[82]

Ginger also had a five-year-old hearing daughter and an eight-year-old deaf son.

Just then, the girls came back from their foray around the school. Ella tuned into the conversation, and Kimmie was looking through her Prada bag, as if somehow something

* Another term for hearing people who use ASL due to significant relationships with deaf parents/individuals is "heritage speaker." Individuals who grow up in an ASL environment may speak the minority language inside the home and the majority language when interacting in the mainstream community. An important number of interpreters have deaf parents, siblings, or a relationship with deaf grandparents or other individuals (Kelleher, "Heritage Briefs"). However, the majority of working interpreters are without deaf familial connections, instead learning ASL within academic programs. Some people in the field refer to this group of interpreters as second language learner interpreters, non-CODAs, and a more colloquial term, NERDAs (not even related to a deaf adult) (sparkbot, "NERDA"). Second language learner interpreters often bring native spoken English abilities to the table and may lack significant time spent in local Deaf communities and a deep understanding of Deaf culture (Subak, "Becoming HEARING").

had appeared in it spontaneously and she had to check it out. Ginger came alive, her face animated as she told stories about her children. Ella, who had read every single one of Eliza's old collection of the *Baby-Sitters Club* novels, had a sudden burst of animation and asked Ginger if she needed help with her children. Ginger shifted her attention to Paul's younger, more serious, daughter. She said that she would be absolutely delighted to hire a babysitter, provided she was smart and responsible.

"Oh, I want that job!"[83] Ella signed.

As the informal interview was wrapping up, Paul was glad he had thought of the idea. He enjoyed meeting new people and was very supportive of the interpreting community. The girls walked out with Ginger and Lucas, then said they wanted to take some selfies in front of the school and would be right back, leaving Eliza and Paul to clean up.

"You think Lucas is gay?"[84] Paul asked Eliza.

"I don't know, maybe. The interpreting world has a well-established LGBT+ community."[85]

Paul joked with Eliza that if Lucas were gay, it would be a good thing under the circumstances. Given the depth and breadth of the crushes Kimmie had formed recently, a good-looking young man only eight or so years older than her would have to be gay to keep problems from occurring. Sometimes Eliza was glad that Paul's unsharpened comments were not made publicly in the hearing world. Deaf discourse is often more forthcoming, in-group, and in your face. There is something refreshing about it, but hearing people often find it jolting.

The girls came running down the hall and back into the room, something they couldn't do if school was in session. The girls looked for the last few cookies to grab off the tray. Paul asked Kimmie what her impression of Lucas was. She dramatically placed her hand under her chin as if lost in thought. She told Paul she was grateful that he did not look down on her for having a cochlear implant since a lot of deaf people and people in the signing community could be unfair about that kind of thing. And she liked that they talked in spoken English and ASL. She also said she really liked the way Lucas signed. She thought he was funny too.

Paul then asked Ella what she thought of Ginger.

"I hope I can babysit for her children! I love babysitting! And Ginger is sweet too!"[86]

Paul could see how a few years of maturity on Kimmie's part gave her deeper reflective abilities. It was fortunate that Ginger and Ella had more in common both in personality and seriousness, making a great match. It seemed Providence had had a hand in pairing the girls with the right interpreters. Paul and Eliza looked at each other, sharing an expression of agreement and familiarity. The trajectory of the unknown journey into the hearing world was working out better than they could have predicted.

Roz had managed to stay away and give the family space despite wanting to be in on what seemed to be even small decisions. Perhaps work on a new film had distracted her, or maybe she had a new boyfriend. Her texts trickled down to zero. Quinn and Viv were not due for a visit until Ella's birthday in October. It was unusual for them, too, to be out of touch. Paul enjoyed the break.

26
A Sign of Something Wrong

One of the prelaw student interns in the office knocked on Viv's door just as she was unsealing a Tupperware container with a chicken-salad sandwich she planned to eat for lunch. The intern was pleasant, about nineteen or twenty, and often shy when she subbed at the front desk. She filled in every day when the usual receptionist took her break, but because there were not many appointments scheduled for that hour, she almost always read or caught up on her homework instead of doing much else, her nose buried in the middle of a book. If the phone rang, she jumped in a nervous way and straightened her posture and her hair before she answered. She often had to summon Viv's secretary to answer complicated questions, or Viv herself, and she often sent calls to the wrong recipient and then went directly back to the partner's office to apologize.

"Come on in, dear." Viv invited the girl closer to her desk.

She had been meaning to tell her what a wonderful job she had done photocopying and filing some legal paperwork for a recent motion the partners were assembling for the state supreme court. New clerical help needed to ease into their office routines, and Viv provided all the patience in the world. Viv's partners had instituted a formal dress code, which the undergraduates from The Ohio State University had difficulty managing, not always owning a business wardrobe yet. This was how it should be. The intern's pretty cabana shift dress brightened the place up, the designed bottom trim and three-quarter-length sleeves appropriate for a summer wedding or a breezy afternoon garden party. Viv preferred happy clothes to suits and was always saddened when the interns grew up and dressed "appropriately."

"Ms. Brown, there is somebody here to see you." The intern glanced nervously back over her shoulder to where the person was.

"Oh, let me see." Viv hoisted herself from her chair. From her office, she could view the waiting room just around the corner.

"I don't think she has an appointment." The intern offered to just go back and dismiss the visitor.

"No matter, no matter." Viv's friends sometimes dropped in around lunch whenever they were in the area.

She crossed the office slowly.

She had recently had a hip operated on, and it still ached when she placed weight on her leg. These days she got herself almost everywhere with a cane, or sometimes a walker at home, but for such a short distance, she didn't feel she needed the support. If she just braced her hands on her desk and went slowly, she would make it just fine. The intern waited next to the door and helped her with the last step or two. An older gentleman with a beard occupied a stuffed chair near the lobby window. Viv recognized him as a client of one of her partners. A woman paced in front of the reception desk. She assumed this was her visitor.

She was a white woman of about sixty. Her hair looked as if she had once dyed it red. A stripe ran along her part with a mixture of brown and gray. Viv quietly shut the door. Something about the way the woman was standing made her suspect that she had been abrupt with the intern. She did not seem to have prepared for a legal consultation. Her jeans and threadbare sneakers suggested some other intention. She moved to cross her arms in front of her chest. On the back of the woman's left wrist, Viv saw a flash of some kind of tattoo. She had seen a tattoo like that before somewhere. Where had she seen one like that? Was it from a picture? Was this person from some of her pro bono work?

Sometimes she did free legal work for nonprofit organizations around the city, and, of course, because her grandbabies, Ella and Kimmie, were deaf, she also tuned into cases that involved the Deaf community. Not all deaf individuals lived the kind of lives the Jean-Baptiste family did. Some were very down on their luck since it wasn't always easy to find work when you couldn't hear. But the woman didn't appear to be deaf. Perhaps someone from one of Viv's pro bono cases had sent the woman to her as an intermediary. That was all right. Viv enjoyed work wherever it presented itself.

"What did she say?" Viv was beginning to feel very curious about who she was.

"Just that she wanted to see you, and when I told her she needed an appointment, she said something really—uh . . ."

"Strange?"

The intern shrugged her shoulders anxiously. "I tried telling her she could speak with your secretary, but she's at lunch right now."

"You did the right thing." Viv patted the girl gently on the arm. "What was it she said?"

"She told me you were a relative?" The pitch of the intern's voice scaled upward. "I might have misheard."

"A relative?" Viv jiggled with amusement.

The woman was as white in skin tone as Viv was black. She was tall, and Viv would barely come to her shoulder.

The intern responded with a small smile and then tried to adjust her face to a more serious, professional expression.

With sudden inspiration, Viv realized exactly who was standing in the lobby. The woman, though white, resembled

Roz. Viv had seen her body language many times during Roz's stubborn teen years and more recently when they had locked horns over Ella's implants. Viv had chastised her daughter for butting into private Jean-Baptiste family business. Viv recalled the tattoo because Roz's father had told her that Belinda had "Michael" inked onto her pale wrist, the letters too large and a big red heart dotting the *i* in Michael. He had showed her a picture of the tattoo, being very proud of the strange image. Viv was still very friendly with Roz's bio dad, Michael Taylor, and his family. Some of them attended her church. Michael himself had long since retired from the military and now managed a plant that made aircraft parts. He, his wife, and two teen sons lived in Oklahoma.

"Her name is Ms. Thomas, I believe." Viv told the girl how the visitor should be addressed. She hustled her toward the door. What news would Belinda bring?

"Are you sure?" the intern asked.

Viv nodded.

She leaned on the back of one of the office chairs and straightened her suit jacket while waiting for the intern to return with her guest. The door opened and she extended her arms. She clasped Belinda's hands in hers. This was the woman who had shared with her the most precious gift of her life. Without Belinda, Viv might never have known what it was to see a child flourish up close. The hard expression on Belinda's face softened as soon as they touched. Clearly, Belinda had not expected to be greeted warmly. She carried an air of guilt and defensiveness, but as far as Viv was concerned, she had nothing to apologize for. Viv showed her to a chair at her small conference table and took the one closest to her.

"So, you are my baby girl's birth mother?"

Belinda's eyes wandered around Viv's office, at the bookcases and heavy oak furniture and the photos on all the walls.

"I wish Rosalind was in Columbus. We could have a real reunion! She hardly ever comes home anymore."

Viv wondered how much Belinda knew about Roz's life. She could check out any number of media sources to find a Roz story. Had Belinda been sober long enough to pay attention to the daughter she had given birth to? Belinda must know that Roz was famous, but did she also know she had a granddaughter? Michael's people knew because Viv didn't feel right keeping it from them. They had gone to her church: there were no secrets there.

"I don't want anything from Rosie, but I hear she is rich and famous. You must have done a good job with her." Belinda brushed her hair off her shoulder.

"Well, she is yours too, even though she is all grown up."

"I just wanted to tell her that I have been sober for twenty-two months now."

"Oh! That would please her so much." Viv clapped her hands together. She had hoped this day might come. "Yes, Roz has done well for herself."

Viv had tried several times to get in touch with Belinda as Roz was growing up, even after Roz moved out to California. Later, when she discovered a hint of where Belinda had gone, she learned about her near overdose. After that, Viv followed Belinda's struggles through the courts, keeping tabs so as to know when it might be the right time to step in.

Belinda's addiction issues had been so intense throughout her life. It was probably all Belinda could do to try to stay alive. Viv was impressed that Belinda was working to reclaim her life. How difficult it must be to pull yourself back from addiction, and how important it was to have people who believed in you. However, she did not want to force Roz into a reunion. Instead, she promised Belinda that if she shared her contact information, she would pass her address and phone number on to Roz. In all these years of loving the same little girl, this was the first time Viv and Belinda had been in the same room.

As Belinda wrote down the information on one of Viv's legal pads, she noticed the framed pictures on Viv's desk.

"Is this her?"

"No, no," Viv said. "That's my Ella."

She could see Belinda speculating, possibly recognizing the remarkable similarity between Roz at four (the last time Belinda had seen her) and Ella at the same age in the photo that had caught her attention.

Viv accepted the piece of paper Belinda handed her and was not surprised when Belinda turned and abruptly left. She cancelled her afternoon appointment. Instead of meeting with her client, she called the community outreach pastor at her church and asked if he knew of a safe place Belinda might stay since the address Belinda had given her was the YWCA. No good could come of letting her live on the margin.

PART IV

Multiplication Signs

27
A Sign of Things to Come

Could Viv, Quinn, and Roz all have been limiting their visits and correspondence with the Jean-Baptiste family in Minnesota for a reason they had agreed upon amongst themselves? Eliza would not put it past Viv to have firmly enforced a moratorium on Minnesota to give Paul and Eliza space to help the girls handle the pressures of mainstreaming in their new schools.

The week after classes started ushered in the biggest changes they had faced yet related to the girls' new cochlear implants. With Ella in fifth grade and Kimmie in seventh, there were many orientation issues to consider, including curriculum differences in the classroom and not having full access to communication. Even with the support of excellent interpreting services, both girls at times drifted unhappily through their respective busy hallways. They missed their bilingual school. They were new to using so many verbal resources and were not familiar with some of the routines and norms used by the swarms of constantly chattering hearing children around them. A visual environment was all they had ever known. Eliza thought they were lucky to be armed with ways of negotiating hearing environments acquired in the Deaf community. Certain people gave them the space they needed to negotiate the transformation. The one person who unconditionally provided them with the right balance of kindness and emotional distance was Aunt Viv. Viv cancelled her usual late summer visit, saying only that she had a situation taking place in Columbus, but she sent the girls a pair of diaries to write in on a daily basis.

The girls' relationships with Eliza's family members hardly ever produced as great a level of understanding and affection. How could Viv have guessed that the diaries would be the perfect gift for two girls who were transitioning into an environment that brought such significant communication changes? As much as Eliza would have liked her mother to have also bolstered her suddenly stranded granddaughters, she could not imagine it happening because of her mother's lack of interest in learning ASL. Eliza's mother had limited interaction with either of her deaf granddaughters, though she had a close relationship with some of Eliza's nieces and nephews. She bought all of her grandchildren presents, but communication with Kimmie and Ella consisted of mostly texts and Eliza interpreting during live interactions.

On Labor Day the Jean-Baptiste family attended a reunion for Eliza's people, the Halischak* family picnic, and Eliza spent the entire day interpreting and SimComming to help Paul and the girls enjoy the day. The work of interpreting took away her chance to swim or play volleyball. At previous family gatherings, the girls had slipped away from the adults to run off with their cousins, but at this picnic, their usual ease faltered. The group of cousins had once shared a universal language of childhood, but since all the children had inched into their awkward adolescent years, they had lost some of their ability to be comfortable with each other.

Paul's parents had also never learned ASL, though his mother could fingerspell, which left conversations very limited. The communication and physical distance between the

* The real Halischak family is actually a multigenerational deaf family originally from central Ohio.

families were less of a problem only because the Jean-Baptiste family visited them rarely, the long drive or multiple flights to Canada generally out of the question with their busy schedules and Paul not as close with them or his brothers as Eliza was with her sisters.

Paul's parents stopped in for a day in late September on a long-awaited drive across America. Paul refused to use his voice around them, and he also discouraged Eliza from interpreting as a way of retaliating against his parents' resistance to learning or using ASL. Eliza was privately relieved he was so stubborn because he discussed awkward topics with his parents, including details of his father's prostate cancer and information about their will. They wrote notes to each other or texted on their phones sitting in the same room.

All in all, it had been a bleak month. Cheering up the girls required giving them space to unravel from time to time and letting them take personal pride in their ability to pull themselves together and get up and face a new school day. Eliza allowed Kimmie to invite her friend Mazie to the house for yet another overnighter. During the sleepover, Mazie shared gossip with Kimmie about old acquaintances and news of what Sean Berdy had done or said. Twice, Eliza went in and told them it was time to go to sleep. Mazie excluded Ella for the entirety of the visit, so Eliza was not that sorry to see Mazie return home the next day, though she had a positive effect on Kimmie's mood. The real turning point in the girls' ordeal occurred on a Friday afternoon in mid-October when Viv flew in from Ohio.

Viv gave Eliza three days' advanced warning, a courtesy Eliza appreciated. Eliza kept the news from the girls so it could be a surprise. They went off to school in the morning, and Eliza made up Kimmie's room and moved what Kimmie needed into Ella's. When they returned on the bus, Viv was sitting on the couch by the front window drinking a cup of herbal tea, her bags already unpacked, and her dresses hanging in Kimmie's closet. Both girls dropped their backpacks in the foyer and rushed over to hug her simultaneously, just as they had done when they were little. Instead of reaching only to her waist, they were as tall as she was. Eliza thought Ella might even be taller. She had gone through a late summer growth spurt and had overtaken Kimmie in height and probably Viv too.

"I think I shrunk since the last time I saw you."[87] Viv smiled.

Ella had grown very serious since her implants, as if she was trying to figure out "hearing-speak" when someone talked to her. She signed, "No. I grew two inches."[88]

"I know, baby. I know." Aunt Viv both signed and spoke. "How are my sweet, sweet, and perfect grandbabies?"[89]

Kimmie unburdened herself, some of her news exciting and some verging on very emotional: she had been sharing Instagram posts with Sean Berdy! She told Viv a story of three girls barring her from a lunch table, an incident she'd had too much pride to confide in Eliza, so Eliza's heart was breaking in hearing it for the first time. Viv listened to all the ups and downs the girls shared.

Ella described some of the same frustrations, although she described more about her schoolwork than Kimmie. She was just as studious as she had been at Twin Cities Deaf School, and her academics had not faltered after the move despite difficult classes and the uncertainty of having to follow along all day with hearing norms and auditory cues. She told Viv she was afraid of falling behind, something that had never occurred to her as a danger before. She said a boy in her class had laughed at her for getting a problem on a math test wrong. The teacher later said that Ella's answer was actually right.

"Of course it was."[90] Viv patted her on the shoulder.

Ella used spoken language with Viv, something Ginger had told Eliza she rarely did at school. Her spoken language, to Eliza's ears, sounded nearly as clear as Kimmie's. Kimmie worked on her speech relentlessly, always looking forward to her hour with the speech therapist and practicing with Mazie during their overnighters. Ella, on the other hand, had been much shyer, much more like Paul in how easily a mistake embarrassed her, and was hypersensitive to noticing someone's reaction to her speech.

Kimmie had an advantage in having more residual hearing than Ella before the implants, so the fact that the two were on par suggested that Ella must have also been practicing sometimes. Aunt Viv did not address the clarity of speech with either girl. She remembered the conversations she'd had with Charles Stacker about this. A highly taboo subject, he said. Don't go there. The implants seemed to have no bearing on how she related to the girls.

Eliza wondered if Viv had ever initiated a discussion with Roz about Roz's zeal to see Ella implanted. If they had broached the subject, what had the two of them said to one another? Viv spent the afternoon responding to the girls in ways that allowed each to express herself in whatever way was easiest, enjoying the mash-up of ASL and spoken language. It seemed to Eliza that Kimmie was using much more SimCom and taking a stab at using just spoken English. Ella did the opposite—less SimCom and more ASL. Perhaps she did this to keep Viv on her toes with her ASL skills. Eliza suspected that Viv would likely report to Roz after the visit, and that "checking in" was not the reason she had come to see them.

As it happened, there would have been quite a bit of news to share with Roz if Eliza and Paul had chosen to come clean. They decided not to share news about school and communication changes with Roz, thinking some things were better left unsaid. Also, it was a complicated series of events Roz had initiated and was heavily responsible for but probably would not understand completely.

Then, there was an incident with Ella. Just after school had started, Ella became upset when talking with Roz on a FaceTime call. Ella's biological mother insisted that she speak with her instead of signing or typing responses and to not have Eliza interpret. Ella was silent and evasive during the call, falling back on signing and attempting to bring Eliza or Kimmie in to help, something Eliza could see annoyed Roz.

Right from the first moment of receiving her implant, Ella had resisted opening her mouth, but Eliza had never seen her struggle as hard as she did when she was speaking to her biological mother. Roz's sign language repertoire had increased to include some words beyond her time-honored GOOD and THANK YOU: she had recently added PRETTY and WOW and signed them rarely at that. She seemed to demonstrate them, perhaps implying that she was meeting her daughter partway. Roz did not disguise that she was disappointed with Ella. After she gave up getting Ella to speak to her, she started interrogating Eliza about how often Ella practiced her speech. Another rejection from Roz.

A dark cloud came over Ella—what was becoming of the very easy communication she had had with her family? What was Roz doing? Yes, Roz was her biological mother, but they could barely carry on a conversation. Maybe the kids at school were right, and getting a cochlear implant was a way to leave the Deaf-World and try to become more hearing. Ella remembered the *Sound and Fury* movie where Heather decided in favor of a CI, but her father resisted her wishes because he did not want her to leave the Deaf-World.

Roz and Eliza continued their conversation. Ella's head was spinning, and she recalled something she had heard at school. Much like the fate of some of her mini unicorn dolls, Ella had heard of a few students flushing their CIs down the toilet.

"Why is her sister further along? Weren't they implanted at the same time?"

"They were, but growth happens at a different pace for everybody."

"Can we get her more speech lessons?"

Ella signed to her mother, "What is Roz saying?"[91]

"Oh, she is talking about your school. Maybe there is a need for more speech therapy for you. I will explain later. Let me finish my conversation with Roz. Hold on a minute . . ."[92]

Eliza turned back to talk to Roz on FaceTime. "She has school and schoolwork." Eliza had never heard of "speech lessons" and was sure that Roz meant speech therapy.

Ella fumed at the feeling of being ignored; a pit formed in her stomach. She went into the bathroom to cool down. She barely had room to pace back and forth, but she tried. She was light-headed and wobbly; what was she going to do with this situation? Her shoe caught on something and she almost tripped. What was that on the floor? A hair clip lay on the floor near the commode. As if she were seeing it for the first time—there it was, her escape route. Her thoughts flashed to one deaf boy in her class who had recently decided he did not want to wear his CI anymore—so he flushed it, never to be seen again. She could say that the CI came off and fell into the toilet. Could she do it? Feeling frustrated, she unhooked the headgear, which consisted of a microphone, an external magnet, a coil, and a sound processer. Taking a deep breath to try to cool down, she glanced out the window.

Her dad was mowing the grass. There he was, her deaf dad—she loved him to the moon and back. She felt herself calming down just seeing him. He was deaf too, and he understood what Ella went through. She wondered what he thought about when he was out there mowing. He always looked so relieved after he mowed, so proud of the neatness of the diagonal rows. And the smell of freshly cut grass—he said he loved that part. He said that the lawnmower was a good one—really powerful. He was always careful to clear the lawn because he said the blades could destroy things like twigs and branches. She remembered finding one of Kimmie's Lego hair salon parts that had evidently been mangled by the lawnmower. Ella wondered if the mower would be able to destroy something like her CI. The CI might not make it down the toilet, but it probably could not survive the lawnmower blades. She remembered seeing a YouTube video of a dad running over his son's video games with a riding lawnmower. Before she knew what was happening, she was outside, waving to her father.

"Hey, the lawn looks great! I see a flower and am going to pick it. Carry on, I won't bother you,"[93] she signed her lie to him and then waited until he turned his back. She made sure to look for a place where he hadn't mowed yet. The brown plastic piece would hardly be visible in the tall grass. She dropped it in what she thought to be a perfect spot and then walked toward the porch to watch the show. Her dad seemed to do his usual mowing, moving from row to row without really looking at what was in the grass. As the mower moved over the spot, in her mind, the mower seemed to sputter. To her relief, her dad continued mowing, making sure the grass was even. Ella slowly turned and walked into the house, hoping the mower wasn't broken. She saw her mother still talking to Roz.

"What is Roz saying now?"[94] Ella asked smugly, feeling powerful in the moment.

"Roz promised to call and help practice your speech when she has time."[95] By the next time she called, the news would be out that Ella had "lost" her CI.

After her dad put the lawnmower away and the coast was clear, Ella went outside to check the place where she had put the CI processor. Looking for the pieces of the processor near where she had dropped it, she pretended like she was smoothing over the grass with her foot so that no one would see her looking for something. She saw mangled brown pieces of plastic and metal. Sure enough, it had been chewed up by the mower—the cord was practically cut in two, hanging by a thread. Ella made a mental note to fish the processor pieces out of the grass tomorrow when no one was around.

That night, Eliza asked the girls for their headgear so she could check it. Ella went into the bathroom to figure out what to say. Should she lie? Should she tell the truth? She thought she would have had a few more days to fake wearing her processor. Why did her mom ask to see that stupid thing on the very day she decided to throw it in the path of the mower?

Eliza was on a mission. "Well, give me your CI."[96]

"My CI is gone." Ella decided to tell the truth. "I was upset so I threw it in the grass. Daddy mowed over it. It's gone."[97]

"Wh-aaaatt? Why?" Eliza was stunned. She decided she needed to talk to Paul before she said anything she would regret. "Wait here, I'll be right back."[98]

Eliza waved Paul down frantically as he walked to the refrigerator for a cold bottle of water. She signed wildly, "Hey, hey—something teeerrrible just happened! JUST AWFUL! Ella threw her CI in the grass on purpose, and you mowed over it! Can you believe it?"[99]

Paul stopped in his tracks, looked down, stared at the floor for what seemed like an eternity and then looked at Eliza. He started to laugh.* Eliza looked at him like he had lost it and

* The cochlear implant (CI) controversy includes medical-related and Deaf-centric perspectives. There are organizations that advocate medical intervention in correcting deaf persons' hearing abilities by retrofitting them with a CI to enhance hearing acuity. The action stems from the belief that speech and hearing development are essential to a deaf person's success in school and life (AG Bell Association, "Cochlear Implants"). However, being implanted can also be highly risky for some children, including partial facial paralysis, dizziness, and involuntary tics. Studies have shown the effectiveness of CIs in enhancing language acquisition in some Deaf children (FDA, "Benefits and Risks").

A Deaf community perspective of Deaf children encourages them to learn more about Deaf culture, traditions, language, and norms. For many Deaf children, total said, “Seriously? I am in shock and you are laughing? I will check with the insurance company tomorrow. I am so glad we bought that extra insurance.”[100] Eliza told Paul to go take care of Ella.

Eliza got in the car to drive around, not knowing where she was going. She tried to think of someone to talk to, but who? Should she call Viv? No, not a good idea. What about Ginger, she might have some words of wisdom. No, it was too late: she didn’t want to interrupt family time, especially with bedtime routines. There was no one she could think of to call. After all, who could really understand the whole picture—the full scope of CI complexities and issues? As mad as she was at Paul right now, she had to admit she understood why he had laughed. He had never really wanted the girls to get CIs in the first place.

The next day, Paul, Eliza, and Ella had a conversation about the missing CI. Ella made a case for being upset by Roz’s insistence that she speak and not sign. Paul backed up Ella, and Eliza was neutral. She knew how much time and effort had gone into the CI surgery but also knew how Paul felt about the CI situation. Paul still wanted to punish Ella, and he told her that the mower could be damaged (he knew, however, that this was probably not the case). Ella apologized for any damage to the mower and said she would not take allowance for a year to pay for it. They decided to go out in the yard so that Ella could show them where she had thrown the processor in case they needed the pieces for the insurance claim. Eliza

---

immersion in the Deaf community is necessary for their identity development and allows them to develop a Deaf identity. The National Association of the Deaf (NAD) shared their vision in part with the acknowledgement of and respect for language, culture, and heritage of deaf and hard of hearing Americans in the pursuit of life, liberty, and equality (NAD, “About Us”). NAD also approved a position statement on CIs stating that implanted children should be encouraged to learn ASL to support language development. It is strongly recommended that Deaf children and their parents consult qualified Deaf and/or parent mentors to obtain multiple resources before making linguistic decisions impacting the deaf child (SKI-HI, “Stories”).

called the insurance company and submitted the claim for a new processor.

Eliza was much more upset than Paul as she explained to Ella about the new processor, "The insurance company will pay for a new processor one time. Don't do something like this again—promise?"[101]

"I promise. I shouldn't have done that. Sorry," [102] Ella managed to say. Ella knew that they could make her wear the processor, but she didn't have to turn it on.

Eliza and Paul decided not to tell Roz, Quinn, or Viv about the CI incident. What they didn't know wouldn't hurt them.

Roz had not kept her commitment to work on Ella's speech by the time Viv arrived for her visit. Ella didn't care that Roz broke her promise. Speaking seemed much more important to Roz than to Ella anyway. The thought of Roz was a faraway memory when Aunt Viv was visiting. Auntie was closer to Ella, Kimmie, Eliza, and Paul than some of their blood relatives—it all had to do with Viv's attitude toward the family.

Eliza suggested they eat at Viv's favorite restaurant in St. Paul, Mamma Ann's on Rice Street, where the smothered chicken was excellent. The buttery gravy warmed Eliza inside and out.

"If you want to know what homemade smothered chicken tastes like, I'll bring you some of mine next time." Viv slapped Paul's wrist as he tried to pay the check at the end of the meal. "Then you'll know what good soul food tastes like."[103]

Kimmie had brought along the red Prada bag, which had become her favorite accessory. She laid it on the table as they were getting ready to leave, and Viv complimented it, not recognizing it as the one Roz had given Ella or that it was a Prada design. Or perhaps she thought the gifts that Roz sent from Armani Fifth Avenue, Prada, Bergdorf Goodman, and Louis Vuitton were meant for both girls. Viv had a real bias regarding her adopted daughter, and Eliza floundered trying to consider how best to bring up the idea that Roz might have been overwhelming Ella with some of her recent purchases. Instead of bringing up the subject, she asked what Quinn was doing lately.

"Oh, you know Quinn."[104]

Viv said nothing more until they reached the car. She pulled the seat belt over her shoulder as she caught Eliza up on the news that Quinn had cut back the work she had been doing on production projects in order to handle a public relations problem for Roz. Viv explained that a tabloid had claimed that Roz had a secret baby living somewhere in the Midwest. She called it the sort of nonsense tabloid writers always came up with.

"Elvis is another one having babies in the Midwest." Viv filled the car with laugher. "And he's dead."[105] She roared.

The big difference between Aunt Viv and Roz was that Viv always seemed to have something to talk to all of them about. She and Kimmie and Ella did a lot of speculating on Hollywood gossip and what could or couldn't be true. Viv lent an ear to Kimmie's gossipy chatter about Sean Berdy, a topic that never exhausted Kimmie but did tire the rest of the Jean-Baptiste family. When they were just about home, Kimmie tapped Eliza on the shoulder and asked if they could go to the Mall of America while Viv was visiting. Eliza could not think of a reason to say no. She waited until Paul had parked the car to catch him up on the conversation and tell him about the plans for tomorrow. Viv was over the moon with excitement, claiming she had heard tales about Camp Snoopy and wanted to see it with her own eyes.

"The world's biggest shopping mall,"[106] she gushed.

What a joy it always was to be in Viv's presence. She blamed no one for anything, and she lit up the world around her. Eliza intuited that the tabloid story weighed on Viv more than she admitted. Eliza also couldn't imagine her shy daughter, who was just beginning to adjust to her new school, having to deal with scandal seekers tracking her down and asking her if she was Roz's baby given up many years ago. Was the story the reason why Viv had not visited that summer? Did they have to worry about being seen together in a public place? Did Viv suspect that someone in the Jean-Baptiste family had somehow spread the news because they were angry about the implants? Eliza tossed and turned that night, but the next day as she and Paul followed Viv, walking hand in hand with the girls through the mall, her worries slipped away.

28
Just Follow the Signs

After Viv returned to Columbus, Eliza and Paul sat Kimmie down and asked her if she had been sharing anything on her social media that might have exposed Ella or Roz.

"No." Kimmie's eyebrows raised in the family expression of confusion they had all inherited from Paul. Eliza always teased him and called it his "mock innocence."

Kimmie spoke and signed to her father, "I wouldn't."[107]

"Sure?"[108] Paul asked.

"Sure." Her eyes began to widen.

Paul glanced at Eliza. His wife seemed to also doubt Kimmie's denial.

"Maybe," Kimmie confessed.

"I shared just the one photo with Roz and me. I showed it to Sean Berdy at Comic Con a long time ago. Mazie is the one who told me to show it. I didn't mean anything by it, and I only showed him the one picture with me; Ella was not in the picture at all."[109] Kimmie's hands, after moving rapidly through all she had to say, dropped to her sides. She collapsed onto Eliza's shoulder and sobbed. Her regret, in Paul's estimation, was real, and she had carried her guilt since she had first broken the rule not to share any Roz-related media. And she blamed Mazie for goading her to do it, a lie.

"NP [no problem]-okay,"[110] Paul signed over Kimmie's head as Eliza patted her on the back.

They took Kimmie's phone away from her for a week, a punishment she reacted to without pushback. She went off to apologize to Ella, something Paul said she needed to do to show her sister that she respected her privacy. Eliza thought they should report the incident to Quinn, and Paul agreed, but somehow neither one of them sent an email about the incident, even after a week had passed and Kimmie was back on Instagram.

The girls were showing signs of independence with their recent antics, spreading their wings, driving their parents crazy in addition to the many other things Eliza and Paul had to worry about.

Talking before bed one night, Eliza admitted to Paul that she was afraid to anger Quinn over something that might not have been the source of the leak at all. Quinn would begin to doubt everything they did, and Eliza didn't want to set that ball in motion. Whatever damage Kimmie's mistake had done was now far behind them. Kimmie had recognized her own wrongdoing, and what did it matter if Roz got one obscure instance of the same press and scrutiny that nearly every big Hollywood star faced?

Paul was pleased to see that, a week later, Kimmie took down the Sean Berdy posters from her wall and replaced them with posters of Sean Forbes. She also stopped talking about all things Berdy from Instagram. Instead, she started singing and signing Sean Forbes songs, sometimes she hit the notes, other times not so much. Eliza never wanted to discourage Kimmie's exploration of sound and language, so she did not tell her to stop or dare make fun of her attempts to sing. Kimmie still occasionally showed off Roz's expensive presents, pretending that they were hers. Doing so seemed to help her make her first new friends at East High, and since Ella didn't seem to mind, they let the situation go.

Social media permitted Kimmie and Ella to find friends in ways that initially didn't seem possible. No longer were the girls cut off from kids who only used spoken language. Students in their school spent a lot of their time texting, TikToking, and sending each other photos and memes. The girls, having atypical hearing, only encountered complications when face-to-face or in a classroom learning situation, but otherwise, they quickly discovered they could use technology to run with the pack. Paul sometimes chastised the girls' (especially Kimmie's) neglect of homework in favor of checking social media sites, but like lots of twenty-first-century dads, he was slowly drawn into complacency because he began to understand that this was how the girls' generation hung out. When cyberbullying wasn't taking place, the cybersphere offered a real chance for kids of all backgrounds, even deaf kids or kids with speech issues, to interact. What a bonus! No new rumors about Roz circulated that spring, or at least any that Paul caught wind of. Paul thought that he might be the last person on earth who picked up on juicy Hollywood gossip, but the girls would have heard something if stories were floating around, and he would have eventually tuned in.

Despite his great fears that the girls' cochlear implants would upend their family life, changes happened subtly and slowly. They spent more time in speech therapy than they once had, they also still played soccer, took karate classes, participated in the deaf quilting circle, and went on adventures with friends. Ella stayed after school for a number of academic clubs including Math 24 and Camp Invention. They still gathered on the couch on school nights for family time and took turns reading and signing, with a smattering of spoken language, as a way to improve reading fluency and language literacy. Kimmie continued to be highly motivated to develop her speech abilities and had switched to SimComming during almost all her conversations. Paul occasionally noticed that

Ella disconnected the receiver on her implant and returned to a deaf space, something he used to do when he was at war with his device as a teenager and wanted some privacy. Around Paul, Ella rarely used her voice, and Paul was surprised when Eliza told him that her speech had improved nearly as much as Kimmie's.

A year passed, then both girls were in the same school, Kimmie in eighth grade and Ella in sixth. Kimmie noodled for a second implant for her left ear, and Paul and Eliza began making new appointments with the ENT. Paul was surprised that Kimmie had stepped so confidently into the hearing world, something he had not done even as an adult. Though he had also attended a lot of speech therapy sessions when he was young, he had not believed the therapists when they said that he was progressing. He found some of their encouragement deceitful. He would try to use his voice around his peers, and he could read in their faces that he was making mistakes. The feeling of humiliation reached its worst in middle school, which, by all accounts, is a horrible time of life for everybody.

Eliza tried to convince Paul that Ella, like Kimmie, could one day possibly attend an Ivy League college, but Paul didn't believe that Ella would go to a hearing university. With her grades she could certainly get into one of them, but she avoided a lot of contact with the hearing world. However, at a recent student-teacher conference, a teacher reported that Ella was developing a close friendship with a hearing boy. Paul was not, and never would be, ready for his daughters to have boyfriends. Paul decided to relax and take pride in the fact that Ella did not let differences in one's hearing status prevent her from making friends. One day he asked his little girl about her friendship with the boy. She said his name was Nick. She was teaching her hearing friend ASL at the same time as he was helping her pronounce words in spoken English. The teacher might have thought it nice that Nick was guiding a shy deaf girl, but that shy deaf girl also had a language to teach him. Fair was fair.

Paul remained friendly when Roz met with the Jean-Baptiste family one afternoon during their vacation in Chicago. She spent a weekend shopping with Ella and Viv, then planned another weekend in New York—a weekend that Ella did not seem to enjoy and did not tell him much about when he picked her up at the airport afterward, though he lobbied hard for details.

Quinn and Viv had been much more regular about staying in touch with Ella and observing both girls' triumphs and special occasions. Viv and Quinn learned new ASL from the girls and even picked up some of their teenage slang. Paul had begun to feel about their encounters with Roz the way he did about the times members of his family stopped in, believing that, in the Paul Jean-Baptiste home, no one had a right to make demands on how members of the family interacted with each other. Roz wanted Ella to use her voice and relied on Eliza to interpret her calls. On a visit, which lasted only an afternoon, just after Ella turned fifteen, Paul convinced Eliza to take Kimmie ice skating so that only he and Ella would be home.

Roz breezed in as per usual, bestowing presents and waiting awkwardly for other people to break the ice. Paul signed hello, spoke with her for a few minutes through their phones, and watched as Ella used her voice with Roz, then left them alone. When Ella and Roz talked, Roz wrote her part of the conversation on her iPhone and showed it to Ella. Ella did her best to use her voice. Paul sensed that to do otherwise would upset her biological mother. After Roz left, sooner than she had said when she had arranged the visit, Paul asked Ella what they had discussed. Ella seemed embarrassed to tell him.

"You don't have to divulge it. The conversation can be kept private,"[111] he assured her.

"She wanted to know what we said about the adoption."[112]

"What do you mean, what we said?"[113]

"To the media."[114]

Ella collapsed in the chair Paul had been sitting in. She glanced out over the gift bags she had yet to open, looking at them as if she thought they might contain snakes. Paul, who had decided he would go out and mow the lawn in a few minutes, tousled his daughter's hair.

"We didn't say anything," he signed. "Hey, I am going to mow. Do you have your CI on? There is no CI processor in the grass today, right?"[115]

"Maybe I am wearing a 3D fake processor now, and the real one is in the yard?"[116] Ella teased. But Paul knew that she could very well do something like that. Sometimes teenagers could be fun but oh so challenging. He was trying to take her mind off what Roz had implicated.

Paul didn't feel that Ella should concern herself with her biological mother's worries. Roz was famous enough, and he did not think that the story of Ella's birth would do great harm to her career anymore. In any case, all of the Jean-Baptiste family members had been very careful about not bragging about their relationship to Roz Taylor. Kimmie's minor slip a few years earlier with Sean Berdy hadn't caused more than a minor ripple.

Paul sent Ella to put her new gifts in her bedroom before Kimmie and Eliza came home. He took the opportunity to do a little investigative work on the internet. Why not surf around since it looked like it might rain, which ruled out mowing anyway. He was able to find a story that had appeared on The Scoop. It speculated on the possibility that Roz had a secret child. The article read, "The Scoop has learned that *Love on 42nd Street* star, Roz Taylor, is said to have a secret hearing-impaired daughter she gave up for adoption fifteen years ago. The child is said to have been placed with a family with other hard of hearing members and goes to a school in the Midwest. There is no information about who the father of the child might be. How could Roz keep this a secret for all these years? The story is unverified at this time." The story was just a simple blurb that named no member of their family.

When Ella came downstairs after taking all the presents up and storing as many as she could before Kimmie came home, Paul closed the laptop.

"I do not want any other family other than this one,"[117] she signed and sat next to him on the arm of the chair.

Paul KISS-FIST his youngest daughter's attitude.

He felt a little sorry that Roz had missed out on Ella's life, but when he thought about the years together—their trip to Mille Lacs, their mornings in front of *Sesame Street*, family dinners and movie nights, their drive to see the Grand Canyon—he came to the conclusion that he wasn't that sorry after all.

29
Exit Sign

A slew of minor and inaccurate tabloid stories had circulated regarding Roz's pregnancy fifteen years earlier, and then suddenly, after all those years, a very accurate one appeared in *TMZ*. Roz begged Quinn to look into how they had broken it, explaining that Ella had told her that Kimmie had once shared her photo with a young deaf actor. Seventeen-year-old Kimmie was the biggest social media user of the Jean-Baptiste family by far, so Quinn began her search for possible media leaks with her pages. Kimmie posted several selfies a day, usually one that revealed her morning fashion choice, then a midday post with her friends all squeezed together at a school lunch table. Later in the afternoon, Quinn would see the same girls in their soccer uniforms or dressed for football games. East High School seemed to be more richly diverse than Quinn and Roz's high school had been, and Kimmie seemed to move freely between different groups in a way that made Quinn smile. She hadn't known any deaf girls in her high school, or even any who had worn hearing aids. The girls themselves were more self-confident than Quinn remembered ever being.

Toward the end of the day, Kimmie often used her social media posts to express her dejection about homework. She would photograph herself among the books she had to read and the essays she had to write. She shared pictures of boys intermixed with those of her female friends in the late, late evening. Quinn could roughly map Kimmie's moods, her social aspirations, her crushes, and her disappointments. She also recognized the bling that Roz had sent Ella in quite a few of the photos, a set of gold bangles here, expensive makeup there. Once Kimmie even took an unfiltered shot of herself wearing Ella's Tiffany locket, and the biggest reveal was the time she wore the several-thousand-dollar gown that Roz had given Ella earlier that year. Kimmie had borrowed it for her junior prom, and there were scads of photos of her on the arm of a boy while she was wearing it as well as lots of other pictures of Kimmie's friends and their dates. Surely, other people had recognized that the dress was far beyond what Paul and Eliza could afford. And yet, like the more mundane posts, the junior prom photos tickled Quinn in a fond way.

To make it look as if she weren't stalking (which she was), Quinn commented on some of Kimmie's selfies the way a friendly aunt might, choosing a funny emoji or a GIF as a response. But since her thumbs up or smiley faces also left trails, Quinn rationed how often she interacted with Kimmie to keep anyone from tracing her as Roz's publicist. The oldest Jean-Baptiste girl could sometimes be so overt, Quinn feared Kimmie was leaving breadcrumbs with every selfie and expression of her moods. And yet, how to stop her? Or should she be stopped?

Quinn dug deep to research who else was looking at Kimmie's posts and how often and in what way they responded. The vague story of Roz's lovechild had grown in detail since the first couple of media mentions. To trace them, Quinn asked herself who had closest ties to the information. The gossip followed a pattern. A news outlet or entertainment columnist would say an anonymous individual had tipped them off to a child in the Midwest that belonged to Roz. The anonymous source seemed to know that it had been an open adoption with private arrangements, and most recently, they had added the new wrinkle that the girl was deaf, which not only gave the story momentum, but also began to narrow the possible threads other outlets could follow to discover more. Quinn thought that if someone was getting information from Kimmie, a minor, they might try to frame her as an anonymous informant.

Quinn learned from her forensic investigations that two years earlier Kimmie had befriended a deaf actor named Sean Berdy who had appeared on the television show *Switched at Birth* and had faithfully followed him on Instagram for more than a year. The premise of the show Sean was in involved two infants mixed up in the hospital. One baby was born with a hearing loss and was raised by a single woman, the other in an affluent home, a kind of *The Prince and the Pauper* or *Parent Trap* dynamic that Quinn had to admit had weird similarities to Ella's situation (although reversed since the riches Ella lived among were simple). Quinn surmised that Kimmie had a puppy-love crush on Berdy, and maybe the show's premise had triggered her imagination, but she was unable to uncover anything that had been shared between the two about Roz except a single post in which Berdy had asked Kimmie to remember him to her famous friend. It was cryptic evidence at best, and Quinn was not at all sure that Kimmie had anything to do with the Roz baby story that was unraveling in the present. Quinn was careful about monitoring visits to the Jean-Baptiste house, preventing Roz or Viv from too much contact in case the story exploded.

Quinn warred with herself over the loyalty she still showed her oldest friend and how it contrasted the affection she felt for a family that inspired her with their ability to live on their own terms. They would never intentionally spill Roz's secret, she felt sure, but she sensed they did not share Quinn's devotion to keeping Roz's career on an even track or fully understood the reasons for protecting her privacy. Better that Roz and the

Jean-Baptiste family keep their lives entirely separate, at least until Ella was eighteen, the age that Roz and Quinn had agreed that Roz might "own" her daughter publicly. Eighteen was an age that would not embroil Paul and Eliza in a storm of speculation and press inquiry and an age that would not trigger more difficult legal questions.

Quinn called Roz and discussed using a better platform than the FaceTime app she usually used with Ella. She also suggested cancelling her next visit until they understood where the new outbreak of stories was occurring. Roz willingly agreed. Viv was not so compliant. She told Quinn she was attending Kimmie's graduation in May and refused to budge. Quinn, too, had been looking forward to watching Kimmie cross the stage.

And then the baby story exploded, not on its own, but because someone, somewhere had given everything but the Jean-Baptiste's name to a *TMZ* reporter. Roz had become something of a scandal queen lately, having had back-to-back relationships with married male costars and consequently having broken up a marriage. The news of a deaf child wasn't about to touch Roz's popularity, in Quinn's opinion, and the reasons for keeping it secret squarely rested on what all that media attention might do to Ella. Roz no longer represented the bright new face on the scene but, instead, had earned the reputation of a woman who knew how to work her public image. Female actors seemed to acquire less naïveté as they grew into their career, got savvy, and handled the pressure of judgmental eyes dissecting their every move. It was the reality of Hollywood that people only stayed young on the outside.

30
Signs of Trouble

Roz Taylor - Secret Baby!

Roz T's Baby Deaf!

Rozzy Dumps Deaf Baby!

Ella's sense of normal cascaded into confusion. Even Quinn couldn't stop the media blitz or keep reporters from following her to after-school activities and trying to take her picture or get a statement. When Roz's secret baby story broke, it must have been a slow news day because it went viral, bowling the Jean-Baptiste family over and making it hard for them to go anywhere in St. Paul. Ella skipped school (on a day she had a test—something she would otherwise never do) so that Quinn could brief her on how to handle reporters. She lingered in bed, her shades shut and her laptop propped on her knees. Everyone else in the house had gone off to school or work.

"Who do you think told?"[118] Ella steered the conversation away from what she should say to a plan of what should be done. Quinn's training boxed Ella into an artificial feeling—having to be fake. Who made detailed plans about how to talk to other people?

"We think someone at your school, maybe."[119]

"It can't be!"[120]

Lucas, Kimmie's interpreter, wouldn't have known enough about the family to provide them with information. Kimmie could also speak and hear well enough her last few years of school that he mostly assisted her in her classes by signing Manually coded English (MCE) and at times sign-supported speech.* That meant that Quinn believed Ella's interpreter, Ginger, was to blame. Quinn suspected Ginger because Ginger had become one of Ella's best friends and knew about Roz, having interpreted sometimes when Ella talked to her bio mother. Roz wouldn't let Eliza act as an interpreter anymore and often called Ella at school on the district's VP. Ginger would stand behind the computer and interpret. Ella had tricked Ginger into interpreting by telling her that Roz preferred it that way. Roz finally figured out what was happening because Ella's eyes followed Ginger instead of watching Roz's face.

Ella told Quinn that she was wrong about Ginger being the informant, which turned their FaceTime conversation into a big stressful fight.

"Look, you may be right. But please stay quiet until we find out for sure. Ginger maybe violated your rights; she may have done something illegal."[121]

"But this all is so unfair to Ginger!"[122]

"We will see. But there is another reason for this call. Reporters from *People* magazine will come to St. Paul and interview you. Roz will be on the call too—from California."[123]

Afraid she was going to have to speak instead of sign, and afraid of what the reporter would write about her, Ella refused. She didn't want to be famous. She was already very tired of the attention.

"Please cooperate!"[124] Quinn signed.

Ella felt a catch in her throat. Quinn was practically her aunt. Now she *really* was getting an illness instead of faking one to stay home from school. She wished she had gone to school after all.

---

* Sign-supported speech (SSS) combines speaking English with producing signs from American Sign Language, also called SimCom. Structurally, SSS follows spoken English language grammar (Johnson, Erting, and Liddell, "Unlocking the Curriculum").

"If you tell the true story, that means it will be easier later for you and your family."[125]

"Let Kimmie do the interview. She enjoys attention and loves pictures of herself."[126]

"Good idea. Kimmie should be in the article, if it makes you feel more comfortable. I promise not to let anyone accuse Ginger yet. If she is guilty, the truth will come out later."[127]

"Ginger promised that she wouldn't say a word. I trust her."[128]

"Okay," Quinn signed. "I will keep our promise too."[129]

Ella felt somewhat ashamed of how angry she felt. Quinn was only doing the job Roz made her do.

That Thursday a woman from *People* magazine converted the Jean-Baptiste's living room into a mini photography studio. She brought along fancy video equipment, lights, and an ASL interpreter. Interpreters sure had caused a lot of stress between Roz and the Jean-Baptiste family, even though Ella's mother, Eliza, was one. The woman from *People* asked questions about her childhood and education, which the interpreter put into ASL, and Ella answered using SimCom so that Roz could follow along. Roz joined them over the reporter's iPad. She smiled more than Ella had ever seen her smile. They almost seemed like mother and daughter as they worked to make everything about Ella's life sound okay.

For the photo spread after the call, Ella and Kimmie hugged each other, smiling like they did in the pictures Eliza took for their family Christmas cards. When the story hit the newsstands a week later, the questions the reporter asked appeared in bold type, and Ella's and Roz's answers were printed underneath their names. Ella liked how her first interview in a big publication had turned out and felt more grateful to Quinn for taking the time to teach her how to respond. The magazine had let her speak for herself. The editors used what she had said in her own words, which summed up that she didn't want people to treat her differently and that she loved her adoptive parents as well as her aunt Viv. She even said that she loved Roz, which was true when Roz wasn't bossing her.

The photo of Ella and Kimmie together didn't appear on the magazine's cover (Roz had that spot alone), but theirs took up nearly a whole page. Eliza gave Kimmie permission to tweet it to all her friends. Meanwhile, Aunt Viv spoke about Roz and Ella to various other outlets so that the story eventually received a dignified telling and ruined any tabloid's hope that scandal lurked under the basic facts. Roz, in an article that appeared in *Vanity Fair* later in the month, mentioned the possibility of suing one of Ella's interpreters because Roz had wished to keep her protected until Ella had turned eighteen. Her protective mothering played well with the press, and the news was picked up by more media outlets as a little bit of juicy drama. Behind the scenes, she was so upset with Ginger that the whole family could see she wasn't going to drop the issue, and they were at a loss as to what to do.

Ginger had been Ella's interpreter for four years, helping her with hard subjects like math and science and making herself available anytime Ella had questions about her advanced coursework. For the last few months, Ginger had needed to miss time at school to visit an obstetrician (she was a few months pregnant with her third child). When Ginger took days off, Ella was assigned another interpreter, Jolene Heath.

Jolene had been working for the district in a floating capacity for several years. She was less qualified than Ginger and preferred gossiping over helping Ella decipher basic chemistry. After the district suspended Ginger for possibly breaching Ella's privacy per the Roz comment in *Vanity Fair*, Jolene lobbied hard to become Ella's full-time interpreter. She thought she would seal the deal by telling yet another instance of Ginger's unethical behavior so she could take over as the full-time interpreter for Ella. Jolene couldn't wait to spill the tea and was always coming up with dirt on people.

Jolene was jealous of another interpreter, Carrie Morgan, who was a much requested interpreter in the area. Jolene tried to block Carrie from getting work whenever she could, hoping instead to put herself in the position to take more jobs. In one instance, an interpreting agency wanted Carrie to interpret a wedding. The twist was that this was a Buddhist wedding. Jolene wanted the job, so Jolene dropped the rumor to the interpreting agency that Carrie was a staunch Christian and would not step foot in a Buddhist temple. The interpreter coordinator asked her how she knew that information. Jolene claimed that Ginger had told her in confidence, then asked the interpreter coordinator not to say anything. Because, you know, Ginger and Carrie were "those kind of narrow-minded Christians." Jolene had concocted the whole wild tale and tried to paint Ginger as the unethical person in the scenario.* Carrie was a community interpreter and needed to keep her reputation clean to continue to be contacted for interpreting assignments in the area.

Eliza, who knew many of the interpreters and ran into them regularly, was doing dishes alone in the kitchen one evening. She was listening to music. Ella could tell because she was swaying and her lips moved. It hurt Ella that people were not always who they seemed, but Eliza alone radiated a physical truth that Ella could see. This was her mother, and nothing would ever change that. The thought of her family made Ella happy.

Ella asked Eliza if Ginger was as guilty as Jolene painted her and if Carrie had not gotten a job because Ginger had spread gossip.

---

* Commenting about an interpreter's religious affiliation amounts to religious discrimination (U.S. Equal Employment Opportunity Commission, "Religious Discrimination").

"The story that Jolene told was not true, and she was trying to implicate Ginger as being unethical."[130] Eliza explained that even though Ginger's faith was Christian, she would still accept an assignment for a Buddhist wedding.* It must have taken a lot of thought for Jolene to concoct this tale to make it look like Ginger was a drama queen.

The real story was very different. In reality, the interpreter coordinator had contacted Ginger to ask if she might team interpret (work together) with Carrie for the assignment. Ginger had said that the coordinator should contact Carrie directly to make sure she was available and wanted to accept the assignment. The school district never got the full story of what really happened. Jolene had twisted the truth and had spun her own fake tale, trying to get Ginger in hot water so she would get fired.

"Ginger did nothing wrong."[131] Ella could see this was a very complicated tale.

Eliza continued to explain that details had been cherry-picked and twisted around to make Ginger look bad. Once the district realized what had happened, they made sure to apologize immediately to Ginger, and they lifted her probation.

"Poor Ginger."[132]

"Interpreters are sometimes involved with drama. Things happen and life is not fair."[133] Eliza placed her arm around Ella. Her hands were soapy from being in the sink, and warm water trickled down the back of Ella's neck. Faintly through her implant, she heard the tinny sound of Eliza's music.

A few days later, Ginger permanently resigned her position as Ella's interpreter, citing a desire to take time off to be with her new baby. Paul and Eliza were painfully aware that the real reason was that Roz had publicly filed a lawsuit against

* According to the RID CPC, an interpreter must be careful with assignments they accept, making sure they feel qualified, comfortable with the content, and have no conflict of interest (RID, "Supporting Quality in Interpretation").

Ginger. Ella tried for three days to reach Roz through texts. She tried Quinn and placed a FaceTime call to her personal assistant. She would have a hard time explaining all the twists and turns and who was really to blame for all the confusion with Carrie, Jolene, and Ginger. When she finally reached her bio mom, Roz refused to budge.

"Please," Ella begged. "Please leave Ginger alone. I will do *whatever* you want . . ."[134]

Roz frowned and said nothing. A week later she dropped her lawsuit.

31
No Signs of Stopping

Roz starred in another two films after the world discovered she had a daughter. The first one did fairly well at the box office, though no big critical buzz. The second one bombed. She and Quinn met at their old haunt, the vegan café attached to their workout club. Roz had shed two pounds over the last week and needed to drop twelve before she auditioned for a role in a thing Michael Bay was putting together at the end of the month. She was out of her comfort zone in the action genre, but the movies made money, the leading men were easy on the eyes, and she wasn't getting any younger. In addition to working with her personal trainer at home, which had become dull, Roz had signed up for yoga classes and had asked Quinn if she wanted to tag along. She hadn't seen her bestie in a long time, ever since the messy business with Ella's interpreter.

Quinn's stern advice at the time had been not to press any charges. Apparently, the interpreter had *not* been the source of the leak, but Roz had hoped to send her scurrying so Ella wouldn't rely on her more than necessary. Quinn thought that Roz had made Ginger a scapegoat, and that was unfair. But Roz was in the public eye and protecting her image. Plus, now that her daughter was a public figure, Roz wanted her to demonstrate that she was *more* than just deaf.

The cochlear implant *had* provided Ella with auditory input that helped her acquire more speech fluency. She spoke better than her sister, who had spoken much earlier than she had, and earned great grades in school. She had handled her first public interviews, even though her parents had often interfered and barred even the good entertainment outlets from getting close. In Roz's opinion, Ella's parents wanted to trap her in an exclusively Deaf-World. Roz thought Ella needed a push from the nest. Ella's resilient spirit and determination were lost on Roz. Roz failed to see what a capable young woman Ella was becoming.

Just before their workout, Quinn informed Roz that the Jean-Baptiste family had put their house in Tangletown on the market because they felt too exposed after the media had swarmed them. Quinn said they hoped to relocate to Maryland, closer to the University of Virginia–Main Campus where their other daughter would be attending college. Ella would finish high school in a more rural setting where she might be less hounded. After that she would apply to colleges on the East Coast. Paul Jean-Baptiste was trying to get a job as a psychologist at a deaf residential school in Frederick, Maryland, and Ella could attend too. Roz was happy to hear about the family's intention to move from Minnesota. She abhorred the Midwest. All of the news made her happy except the information that Ella would not be mainstreamed at a public school.

"Their other daughter—what's her name?"

Quinn coughed into her napkin.

"Don't laugh at me. I can't remember everything."

"Kimmie."

"Yes, that's right," Roz recalled. "My assistant said she emailed and asked for a college recommendation a few months ago."

"She was thinking of majoring in media relations at the University of California."

Roz poked at her spinach salad.

"So I assume she is now going with a plan B?"

"Yes, I think so."

Roz disliked keeping her figure. She poked at her salad again, looking for that one last hidden crouton. Why did she oblige all the constant pressure to be thin? Why not let Roz be Roz? What a waste of a personal chef and a city full of exciting restaurants. A waiter passed their table, a salted caramel dessert perched on his tray. The waitstaff at the club turned over quickly, everyone in town an aspiring something on their way from here to their next thing. All of it made Roz feel every bit her forty-two years. Could fifty really be on the horizon? With diet and exercise technology, fifty *was* the new thirty. Was she experiencing some sort of midlife crisis? Dreaming of letting herself get fat?

New light fixtures hung from the ceiling of the café, and new paint covered the walls, a color that Roz had not even known was in style. And maybe it wasn't. The club no longer seemed like the "it" workout destination in Los Angeles. The women surrounding them fit into their yoga clothes less well than they might. Roz recognized fewer famous faces and far more brassy hair color choices. She put her fork down, feeling all at once like she had to confess to Quinn everything that was on her mind.

"I had to say no." She started with the question of the recommendation. "I really don't know Kimmie beyond two or three quick visits with Elle. But on the subject of colleges, I wish Viv would talk to Elle. We need to get *her* application process started now."

Viv had looked so *old* the last time Roz had seen her. She was using a walker all the time now, like she had after her hip surgery, something Roz couldn't have imagined a few short years before when Viv was chasing down legal cases all across the state of Ohio.

Roz called the waiter over and ordered a caramel dessert.

"It's good that Ella is getting out of the Midwest and all that."

Quinn reached up and prevented the waiter from leaving. "Two forks." She flashed him two fingers.

Probably unnecessary, Roz thought. *Everyone here can hear.*

"Kimmie's really quite a nice kid these days—just a little too caught up with her Instagram, but what girl her age isn't?"

"I wouldn't know." Roz thought the comment made Quinn sound like an old hen. "How do you feel about also ordering a cheesecake and splitting both desserts?" They had earned some indulgence after their workout, stretches that Roz had hardly managed and which had left her feeling wobbly and like it might take some effort to get out of her chair after their meal was over.

The waiter pulled an ink pen from above his ear and wrote down the second order. While they waited for his return, Quinn talked a bit more about the Jean-Baptiste family. Roz complained that they had left her out of the loop with regard to this new move, and, in response, Quinn provided a few more dull details of their lives. The waiter brought two desserts and two forks. He had a series of interesting tattoos on the inside of his arm that reminded Roz of her birth mother, Belinda. She asked him about them, coming very close to flirting. He smiled in a dazzling way and explained they spelled out the name of his band. The nice thing was, as he spoke, he came very close to flirting back. Roz decided to leave him a good tip.

Quinn picked at her cheesecake and begged off their usual tradition of capping off their afternoon with a little shopping in the neighborhood. She worked for a new name in the business, someone who had her doing more research on social causes—dolphins or the ocean or that sort of thing, perhaps a cause Quinn had picked herself. The professional clothes Quinn had changed into in the locker room seemed as if they might have been made from an easily wrinkled eco-friendly fabric. Quinn didn't seem to need to fight the extra weight the way Roz did, but there were small signs that she was aging too. Her frame had always been tall and slender, but she had lost some of the flesh around her face. Maybe it was time for them to go in for a fix-it session. Neither one of them would look like Ella again, who Roz had to admit had become stunning, but with some alterations, they could get close.

The last time Roz had FaceTimed Ella, something they were doing every other week now, Ella had lip-read part of the conversation. She had also spoken instead of using sign, and though she had pronounced a few words in a weird way once or twice, she had not stumbled so often. When she was talking about her dad going to his bowling league every Friday, she had pronounced it "lee-gue" instead of "leeg." Anyone who did not know that she had a hearing loss might miss the telltale signs of one who did not hear well. Roz thought Ella's slight speech differences could be mistaken for a kind of accent. It seemed the CI had really advantaged Ella in her speech development. Remarkably, Ella's progress with speech had begun on the day Roz had agreed to drop litigation against her interpreter. She conveniently did not inform Ella that the real source of the leak had been her birth grandparent, Belinda. Why let on when her daughter for once seemed so grateful and appreciative?

When Viv initially asked Roz if she would reconnect with Belinda, Roz bluntly refused—the thought repelled her. After Viv's reasoning softened her to the idea, Roz agreed to meet Belinda, but she was not impressed by their first meeting. Her mother's hair was scraggly, and she was missing several teeth. Roz permitted the reunion because Belinda had managed over two years sober, a milestone Roz never imagined she could reach and had used as a condition. When they met in a small diner in Cincinnati, Belinda did something unexpected. Instead of asking for money, she begged Roz's forgiveness as part of her twelve-step program, so she gave Belinda the resources to visit a dentist and paid rent for a condo close to the beach in San Diego.

The fact that Belinda told the press everything that Roz had shared with her over their chat maybe happened for a reason. After the news about Ella was out, Roz's ex-boyfriend Kent, now a successful film producer, had called and asked if he could see her again. The reunion rekindled the intense feelings they'd had for each other in the past. She was over the moon. Quinn seemed not to read her bliss even though she was wearing a ring that Kent had recently given her. She made sure to wave the ring in Quinn's sightline, waiting for her to ask where it had come from. Kent was single now after being married at the time he had met Roz and they'd had their fling.

"I assume that Ella will go to Gallaudet. Her boyfriend started there this year." Quinn seemed more interested in the Jean-Baptiste family than the things Roz really wanted to discuss.

"Elle has a boyfriend?"

"Didn't you know? They have been dating for a while now. He is someone she met when she was a counselor at a deaf camp last summer."

"So, this boy is deaf too?" Roz was showing her bias.

"Yes. His name is J.P. and he's from St. Paul. She invited him to dinner once while I was visiting. He seems very polite and is very good looking."

"No." Roz slapped the table with the flat of her hand, surprising herself with how quickly emotions had risen in her.

Quinn reacted with surprise, bringing her napkin up from her lap and dabbing her mouth.

"She has done enough hiding. I want her to apply to a good school, Harvard or Yale, where she can make good connections.* I want her to have a choice of men instead of just the ones that are safe and deaf like she is. After all, her father is a Princeton grad."

"Her father?" Quinn raised her eyebrows.

"Kent and I are dating again."

"Kent?"

"Elle's father."

Quinn gaped at her, her mouth literally opening. Roz was tempted to reach across the table and lift her chin back into place.

"You remember."

Quinn had always pointedly taken Roz's side in the arguments she and Kent had once had. Quinn puffed her cheeks and let out a breath of air in reaction to the one-eighty. A large number of years had passed since Roz had given birth, enough for a daughter to grow up, enough for her and Kent to become different people. Surely, Quinn understood.

"Does he know—"

"Everyone knows."

"That's right. They do." Quinn removed her napkin from her lap. "Which reminds me. How did all this information about Ella really leak anyway?" Roz had kept her meeting with Belinda from her.

Roz shrugged. "Does it matter? A momma does what a momma does."

"I am so confused."

"It couldn't be you who told the world because you wouldn't have wanted to upset the Jean-Baptiste family. It couldn't be me, why would I do that? It turned out not to be that little

---

* Numbers of deaf students attending mainstream colleges are low. Of the 20,000–30,000 deaf individuals who attend college (or post-secondary training), only 25% graduate with degrees (Leigh, Andrews, and Harris, *Deaf Culture*). Gallaudet University, the National Technical Institute for the Deaf, and California State University at Northridge are the three largest post-secondary institutions established to serve Deaf and hard of hearing students.

interpreter. So, it was none other than Belinda Thomas, *my* real mother. It makes a certain kind of sense, if you think about it."

Their conversation slipped into the tone of an argument, though Roz couldn't understand why. The news she had delivered was entirely happy. Had anyone been harmed by Ella's birth story leaking to the world? How long had it been since Roz had seriously dated anyone? Yes, there had been many newsworthy flings, and some of them had lasted longer than her relationship with Kent, but she had not realized during all the years since she had last seen him how frequently he had entered her thoughts. The early months after she gave up Ella, she had cried herself to sleep night after night. Those feelings had intertwined with her feelings for Kent. Being with him made her feel young and in control of her life again. Her daughter scared her, growing up so fast. Maybe Kent could help her wrangle Ella into a solid family relationship one day.

"I have news too." Quinn pushed her half-eaten cheesecake to the middle of the table.

Roz extended her fork toward the dessert in a stealthy way since she had finished the entire caramel dessert herself.

"Well, what is it?" she garbled with her mouth full.

"I am moving to Paris."

"Paris?"

"The media organization where I am working has an opening in their European division. And I have always wanted to learn French . . ."

Roz took another bite of the cheesecake.

Quinn glanced at her watch. "I need to get back. I'll pay the bill on the way out."

After Quinn left, Roz stayed where she was for a few minutes, long enough to be sure that she had one more chance to smile at the waiter who was taking the orders of a table full of women on the other side of the dining room. Their laughter mocked an invisible presence. Roz had the feeling they were celebrating a divorce. After she handed the waiter her tip, she slid on her sunglasses and idled out onto the street. She browsed a few of the nearby stores all on her own. Why did it feel so nice to be alone? *I can't think about this now: I'll go crazy if I do. I'll think about it tomorrow.* She swapped her favorite movie line with the reflection of herself in one of the big glass windows.

32
The Signs Are Everywhere

Eliza sifted through the pile of college advertising materials Ella had received in the mail. Two of them were from Harvard. She thought there was a good possibility that Harvard or another Ivy League school would accept Ella because the Maryland School for the Deaf–Frederick Campus, where she had started her senior year, was a who's who of the Deaf community. Some other students who had done well with the school's curriculum had gone on to top-tier colleges.* Harvard had found the Jean-Baptiste's address ahead of other schools. Eliza sorted and threw out half of what she had just taken in from the mail. Who knew institutions of higher learning could be so aggressive? Ella had placed herself into a competitive category with her high academic achievement, but even so, there was simply too much advertising for any one high school senior to look at.

Paul had taken over the job of school psychologist at Ella's high school, a position he never thought he would get. Eliza had had to encourage him to send in his materials and calm his nerves when he had flown to Maryland for each of his two interviews. The board of trustees, faculty, and staff at the

* There are deaf individuals who attend institutions of higher education throughout the country. Colleges/universities have accessibility services to accommodate access to individuals who utilize various learning strategies (generally referred to as disability or accessibility services) per various U.S. legislative mandates (The University of Texas at Austin, "Deaf & Hard of Hearing").

school wielded enormous clout, including some well-known members who worked on civil rights cases and others who published important educational research. Their sudden fame (which Eliza would have happily done without) had led to their eventual move from Minnesota to Maryland, a move that had greatly improved the Jean-Baptistes' bank account. With the money they had made from the sale of the house in Minnesota, they had been able to find a quiet place in Frederick that reminded Eliza of their home in Highland Park. They hadn't needed Roz to help them afford the mortgage this time around.

Unlike Kimmie, Ella was curious about the cultural and political perspectives of the Deaf-World. She did not mind trading her mainstream high school for something steeped in Deaf culture. She made new friends her first day. Kimmie, a college sophomore at the University of Virginia, clung to vestiges of the hearing world she had adapted to at her St. Paul high school.

Eliza and Paul had moved Kimmie into her dorm the previous year. During the move, Eliza and Paul were on either end of a mini fridge, trying to figure out where it would fit into Kimmie's room, when her roommate shyly asked Kimmie if she was wearing hearing aids.

"They are implants," Kimmie said in spoken English in a way that Eliza registered as potentially unfriendly. "They make it so I can hear all the time."

"So you can't take them out?"

"Why would anyone want to take them out?" Kimmie asked. "Of course I want to hear."

Fortunately, Paul missed the comment. Eliza mused that Kimmie sometimes acted like a hearing person in a deaf person's body. Kimmie valued what Eliza thought of as "the status" of perceiving sound. The roommate had asked a question that, if a bit intrusive, at least got the ball rolling. Why couldn't her daughter get the chip off her shoulder and be more forgiving of what she perceived as a stupid question?

Paul and Eliza said their last goodbyes to Kimmie and left her to her college life, hoping she would enjoy the coming months. They wanted to see her bloom in her new independent environment. Academic work at the college level was not likely to come easily to Kimmie, and in her first phone calls, it became clear that she did not get along well with her roommate. Instead, it seemed to Eliza, she chased after the sorts of friends she had coveted in high school. Ella, who had more opportunity to observe Kimmie's day-to-day life because she followed her on social media, told Eliza that Kimmie pledged a sorority. Eliza didn't want too much information about what Kimmie was doing from then on. Kimmie might have to learn the hard way in tangling with Greek life or not. She earnestly prayed that her oldest daughter would survive her transition to adulthood.

Ella, going into her senior year, received her scores for the advanced placement classes she had taken at East High and the Frederick School and the SATs she had sat for over the summer. She earned a very respectable 750 on the math section of the SAT and was solid in the verbal. One of her favorite teachers at her new high school, an athletic, cheery woman named Sherry Bradley-Koo, dubbed her the Maryland School for the Deaf's top math whiz and encouraged her to research careers in engineering and science and to look at the STEM program at Gallaudet. It was maddening, in Eliza's opinion, that Ella's public school counselors, favorite teacher, and parents encouraged her to go to Gallaudet to solidify her Deaf identity, while Roz was pushing her to widen her perspectives and avoid Gallaudet. How dare Roz be so egotistical and unimaginative!

Ella FaceTimed her boyfriend, J.P. every night at Gallaudet so that the two of them could work on their homework together.

J.P. helped Ella with her English essays, and Ella walked him through calculus problems. J.P., following in his father's footsteps, was finding a major that fit him at Gallaudet. His father, Jimmy Beldon Jr., had been active in the school's Deaf President Now (DPN) movement in 1988. For 124 years, a hearing leader had run the most prestigious institution of higher learning for deaf individuals in the country, and then one day, thanks to pressure from the student body and a group of alumni, the school had stepped into its own.

Ella signed a quick movement of her middle finger to her forehead, meaning "duh," and said, "Of course." The first essay she submitted to her new English teacher analyzed the historic importance of DPN for the national Deaf community. J.P. knew his Deaf history. Ella only hoped to be able to catch up to him with Deaf-World knowledge someday.

Eliza kept sorting through the carpet of advertising materials they were receiving. Harvard continued to lead the pack in bombing them hard, even into late September, when most seniors had already made up their minds about where they wanted to go. Eliza intuited that Harvard was Roz's choice, but she couldn't decipher why it was Ella's. When they had their weekly FaceTime chats, Ella seemed to fear her biological mother less and defy her more, pushing back on Roz's suggestions about certain aspects in her life. At one point, Roz verged into the territory of Ella's love life and tried to discourage her from committing herself to J.P. Eliza heard the squeal of annoyance from downstairs and the slap of Ella's laptop slamming shut. Since Quinn had left the country, it was obvious to everyone in the Jean-Baptiste household that Roz had more time on her hands. Viv blessed them all with her company one weekend, but she had become more frail, and Eliza wondered if she was able to get out to California easily to see her daughter.

On the surface, Roz's career seemed to be traveling its same high speed. She gossiped with Ella about award ceremonies and galas and her public notoriety in general. In the photos Eliza sometimes glimpsed on the magazine covers at the supermarket, she seemed not to age. Where her timelessness had come from, Eliza couldn't say. There were men, or a man, in her life, according to the tabloids.

In October, Roz sent an Ivy League admissions expert to their house, a person who had a reputation for getting students into good colleges. Roz must have paid him well because he burst in promising them the moon and regaling them with a number of success stories among the children of Hollywood elite. Eliza interpreted everything he said to Paul because she knew Paul would be amused. The admissions counselor was so invested in his sales pitch he didn't even notice that Ella was deaf until Ella explained why her parents were signing. When he realized what was going on, he suggested she list ASL as one of her languages on her application. Ella had already prepared most of the materials she needed, including her essays and documentation of her bilingualism.

"What a huge waste of money," Paul signed after he was gone. "Who knows, it could be a scam. Do they think our family is stupid? Does Ella have to go to Harvard anyway? NO!"[135]

Eliza tried to encourage Ella to give Gallaudet one more thought. She and Paul could help her with vocational rehabilitation information or pay for some of the expenses to free her from feeling she needed to honor Roz's wishes or rely on the college fund she had set up. They explained that, with her grades, Ella could earn scholarships and that Gallaudet had a National Institute for Health program for STEM talented students.* Attending Gallaudet would mean leaving behind

* Gallaudet University is the only stand-alone post-secondary institution in the world for deaf students (Gallaudet University website).

the pretense that she had to adapt and assimilate. Attending Harvard would mean Ella would matriculate as a kind of token student, her deafness an exception and likely their primary reason for considering her. The admissions counselor had talked a lot about her niche qualities. Paul did not want to see her wrestle with issues of being marginalized while some people would act like the discrimination was not real. He had lived with the denial charade way too long.*

Ella remained constant in her desire to see her Harvard application through. She sent off her early decision materials just after Kimmie made a whirlwind visit home for her midterm break. Perhaps, Eliza thought, for Roz, Harvard was a chance to prove her daughter extraordinary, not just a hardworking young adult, but a miracle. Perhaps Roz needed the thought of constant miracles to keep herself happy since she had missed all of the smaller ones that Eliza and Paul had witnessed. Eliza reminisced back to the days before Ella had her implant and Roz was sending inspiration porn. Is that what Roz wanted to give her daughter? A gift that transformed her life? No matter the communication complexities and all that went with it, Ella seemed to ignore the negative aspects of her relationship with Roz and was growing to love her biological mother in a deep and thoughtful way.

When Kimmie's weekend home wound down, Eliza drove her back to the University of Virginia while Kimmie chattered about the exciting new people she had met. When they reached the school, a full-blown argument erupted over where to park. And then they were hugging again, and Eliza was weeping when they said goodbye. Where had the time gone?

* Plausible deniability is a concept in which knowledge of a particular truth is ignored and the existence of a fact is refuted to benefit or shield one from responsibility associated through the knowledge of that truth (Wikipedia.com, "Plausible deniability"). For example, Paul's parents in knowing Paul preferred to communicate via ASL ignored that fact and did not sign, hoping communication issues would just "go away."

Since it was on the way, she visited Gallaudet as she drove home and spent time with her old roommate Carolyn who worked in the provost's office. Even after the span of years since she had graduated, Eliza experienced a sense of coming home on the campus grounds. She and Carolyn fell into their old rhythm of signing and joking with each other. They ate in the cafeteria where Eliza had once confessed to Carolyn that she had a crush on a boy in her psychology class. They discussed the future of the Deaf-World.* Some things, she hoped, would never change.**

And suddenly, Eliza began seeing signs everywhere, not just in the language she and Carolyn spoke, but in the significance of Ella's possible early acceptance to Harvard. A gaggle of geese flew parallel with Eliza on the highway heading north, keeping even with her in their V-formation for what seemed like a hundred miles.

When Ella's early acceptance to Harvard letter arrived a few weeks later, Ella, Paul, and Eliza celebrated at the best restaurant in Baltimore, just the three of them. Paul, who rarely spoke in public, made a show of telling their waiter why they were so happy: "My daughter, she will go to Harvard!" The waiter brought them a free bottle of champagne. Paul signed to Eliza and Ella, "If I had a chance to go to Harvard, I think it would be great, but it would be too much for me. My English is not developed enough. But Ella has perfect English, just like a hearing person. I am very proud and hope that Ella is happy. She can succeed even if she is the only deaf student."[136]

The great honor of being accepted into Harvard transformed Ella. Whatever luminous genetic matter she had

---

* Dr. Carol Padden in a 1999 keynote address at Gallaudet stated that changes in Deaf culture would happen in ways that could not be predicted (Armstrong and Karchmer, "William C. Stokoe"). Cultures are living entities, in constant change, and this includes Deaf-World culture.

** "As long as we have deaf people on earth, we will have signs," a quote from George Veditz (Gallaudet University, "Visionary Leader").

inherited from Roz multiplied tenfold as she prepared herself to leave home. Eliza hardly recognized the young woman she had become and could not help but be in awe at the signs of maturity and wisdom beginning to blossom.

33
Welcome Signs

In the fall of her sophomore year, Ella rode the T to South Station to meet Kimmie, who had taken an Amtrak from Virginia to Boston. Ella didn't like the idea of hauling Kimmie's sleeping bag and overnight suitcase on the subway—too much stuff, and too busy a time of day. She was a bit broke since she refused the allowance that Roz wanted to send, and her only income was a work-study job at the library that paid peanuts. But why not splurge on an Uber for her one and only sister? This was the first time Kimmie had come north to visit except for when the whole family had moved Ella to Harvard the year before. Harvard had kicked Ella's butt, a humble fact she shared with Kimmie just after they hugged and Kimmie had asked how everything was going. Ella knew Kimmie was having a rough junior year at the University of Virginia and had failed a political science class. Ella was actually doing fine according to general standards, just not the ones she had set for herself. She had earned As and Bs for her first two semesters and had joined the robotics club. Still, distinguishing yourself at Harvard was a full-time job, and few really achieved it. It took a lot out of a person to be exceptional among the exceptional.

Ella knew better than to bring up robotics as they chit-chatted in the back of their Uber. Kimmie, who seemed far more interested in the Cambridge nightlife and in sharing her own University of Virginia social exploits, wanted answers to questions about dance parties and social clubs. It was so good to be together!

They dropped Kimmie's things off at Ella's room in Winthrop House, and Ella introduced her to two of her three suite mates. One of Ella's roomies, a French major, sprawled on their common-room couch reading Diderot, looking as sexy and bored as she did on Friday nights in the local clubs. The other was premed and had this tendency to freak out every finals period and live on nothing but peanut butter sandwiches and coffee until she finished her exams. Both of them were hearing, but Ella's third roommate was deaf too. Everyone in the suite was able to sign some ASL: the French major was interested in languages and was happy to learn them, and the premed major had a deaf brother. They also used their voices. It was like a visit with Viv, Roz, and Quinn—sometimes just a mash-up of what worked. Ella made arrangements for meeting up with her roommates later that night.

She and her sister left behind the luggage and walked up the hill toward the square to a ramen place that Ella liked. The line at the counter extended back eight or ten people, and it took a few minutes to find a seat. Cambridge was always crowded, and timing was everything. You didn't dare try to get something quick between classes because you would be late every time.

At a table a few seats away from them, Ella spied a famous person.

"Don't look over your shoulder. I see Brooke Shields's son."*[137]

Ella knew Kimmie would be interested. She semi-pointed with her chopsticks and signed because it was way too loud in the restaurant to talk, and whispering was not an option.

Kimmie turned to see. "Who is Brooke Shields?"[138]

---

* A fictitious person.

"Don't you know any Hollywood history? She is a famous model and actor!"[139]

"OMG!" She slapped her hand over her mouth and faced Ella again. "You know him?"[140]

"We have the same friends."[141] Ella hoped he didn't recognize that they were discussing him. She didn't think he knew much ASL.

"Can you introduce me to him?"[142] Kimmie asked.

"Not now."[143] Ella lowered her head and shoveled in her noodles. He briefly looked their way.

They had taken one of their big freshman seminars together and had met at the library to work on an essay. They had also talked at a party. He had taken some ASL classes in high school. Their interaction was no big deal. Ella didn't want Kimmie to get the wrong idea that they had become great friends or anything.

Over Kimmie's shoulder, she watched him stand and say something to his friend. The friend headed toward the door while he made a beeline for Ella and Kimmie's table.

He approached and signed a greeting.

"Oh, hi!"[144] Ella pretended she was noticing him for the first time. She introduced her sister.

"Do you mind if I take a selfie with you?"[145] Kimmie bounced up from her seat.

Ella winced.

A lot of well-known people or their offspring attended Harvard, but you couldn't make too big a deal about it. Every once in a while, people recognized Ella as Roz's daughter, and she thought it was nice knowing that her mother's reputation intertwined with hers.

He leaned in between Ella and Kimmie and took a photo using Kimmie's phone.

He returned it and asked what classes Ella planned for the next semester. They talked for a few minutes, with Kimmie twisting in her chair and smiling and flinging her pretty dark hair off her shoulders.

"Sis, he likes you!"[146] Kimmie said, and her face lit up with awe when he was gone.

Ella had coveted Kimmie's sisterly approval for so long, she had to reason her way out of taking the compliment for more than it was worth. Too often it had felt like it was Kimmie who knew all the answers and Ella who didn't know up from down. Kimmie seemed less interested in stealing Ella's friendship with a guy (the way she had often liked to borrow Roz's gifts when they were younger) and, instead, shared in Ella's excitement, asking more about the friendship.

"Maybe I should talk *you* up next time I see him!"[147]

"I am already dating someone," Kimmie confessed. "A basketball player. Don't tell Paul and Eliza."[148]

"You mean Mom and Dad."[149]

"Who else?" Kimmie asked. "You should date that guy—you could get yourself in magazines, get fame! Just date him, nothing serious."[150]

"Well, he is nice. But there's J.P."[151]

At least Kimmie refrained from trying to persuade her to swap J.P. for Brooke Shields's son. Yes, the distance between Boston and Washington, DC, caused problems. Yes, J.P. had only come to Harvard twice, and Ella had gone to Gallaudet once, so the only real time they had spent together was the one week that Ella had been in St. Paul over the summer. No, they had not been intimate. Ella was freaked out at the thought of becoming pregnant like Roz. Also, Aunt Viv had talked to her about waiting to have sex until after she was married because that was what God wanted. But J.P. had talked about being together forever, and Ella believed in her heart that it could happen.

Ella didn't even have to ask if Kimmie's basketball player boyfriend was hearing. She knew her sister. Why should hearing be more of an attraction? It was J.P. who had persuaded Ella to listen to Roz and go to Harvard, and it was J.P. who had encouraged Ella to respect her relationship with her birth mother, not for her fame or fortune, but because they shared blood. J.P. spoke deeply and reverently of his late deaf godmother, Dr. Jane Norman, a pioneer in Deaf theater and media, and his life's purpose in honoring her work after her death. He reminded Ella sometimes of Aunt Viv.

"After I graduate from Harvard, I plan to get an MA from Gallaudet. J.P. will stay at Gallaudet for his PhD. So finally, we will be together."[152]

"Paul and Eliza will be thrilled."[153]

"Please don't diss Mom and Dad. Why do you insult our parents? They will be happy to know I will go to Gallaudet. It is an important legacy in their lives."[154]

They carried the raman bowls to the counter. Kimmie hit the restroom to do a hair and makeup check. They walked down the hill through crowded streets to Winthrop House, blending in with the other students making their way through campus after dinner. In the dim light, you might have recognized them as sisters because they shared gestures and had a quick and light way of communicating with each other, but they could have been two individuals from distant countries who just happened to come together in this place.

Ella was reminded of a story her mother loved: Why do deaf birds on a wire stay together, even when the hunter's gun is pointed at them? Why don't they save themselves and scatter?*

The answer perhaps: You have to be deaf to understand.**

---

* Elizabeth Beldon ended her Deaf culture classes at the University of Akron's interpreter training program with a question regarding deaf birds on a wire and the fact that they did not scatter when a hunter aimed a gun at them. She would tell students that they were to find the answer to this question in the Deaf community.

** "You Have to be Deaf to Understand" was written by Willard J. Madsen in 1971. The poem first appeared in the Dee Cee Eyes newsletter and has since been

Epilogue
Signs for Infinity

Quinn flew to the States for Ella's Harvard graduation and didn't meet up with Roz until a few minutes before at her town car next to the outer gates of the Yard. She knocked on the car's dark window, and Roz stepped out onto the street, her dazzling Stella McCartney ensemble catching the light, and the people on the street gaping. She took Quinn's arm, kissed her lightly on the cheek, and waved at the interested spectators around them. Two or three paps recognized the dark cars all in a row as belonging to members of the graduating class's most famous parents. One of the savvy paparazzo palpated the air in front of Roz with a microphone and asked if she had a few minutes to speak about her daughter's accomplishments.

"Of course, of course."

Roz indulged him with a few brief answers to questions about how easy she had found her travel east, and about the adoption and reunion with Ella. But when the reporter pressed her on whether she knew ASL, a language Ella had been touting in her interviews, she darted a quick look toward Quinn. Quinn informed him politely that they had to hurry inside and find their seats.

Quinn speculated from the incident that the answer to the reporter's question was likely no. She was amused that Roz still retained the habit of relying on her as hired help in these situations when a lapse had been exposed despite Quinn not

---

reprinted in publications all over the country. Madsen was an associate professor at Gallaudet University and a graduate of the Kansas School for the Deaf (Madsen, "You Have to be Deaf").

having worked directly for her in a long time. As for their friendship, it had churned along at a distance, maintained through the occasional calls and late-night video chat sessions. Some of the intensity had worn off, and Quinn found it easier to appreciate Roz from an objective distance.

There was such a crush of people in the Quad finding their seats that they got somewhat lost. Quinn tapped the shoulder of an usher, who showed them to a row close to the front. Before they were seated, music began to play, and the people around them stood. Quinn hurried to text Eliza their relative location, and Eliza texted back that she, J.P., Ginger, Aunt Viv, Kimmie, and Paul were nearer the back, close to the library steps. Viv had also brought along Chas, who was in their entourage. Quinn thumbed a response that she and Roz would meet Eliza and the group later, at the second ceremony taking place at Winthrop House that afternoon.

When the processional started, Roz stood on her tiptoes. She asked Quinn if she could see Ella among the people in regalia marching toward the empty rows of seats between the two of them and the stage.

"I think those are the faculty." Quinn pointed to the program the usher had given her and showed Roz where they were in the ceremony.

Roz took the sheet of paper and looked at it briefly before using it to fan herself. Finally, after hundreds of people marched by, Quinn found Ella in the precession of undergraduates. On the back of her mortarboard, she had taped the message "Hi, Moms!"

Quinn felt a rush of excitement.

"Moms?" Roz sounded displeased. "People are not going to get what she means."

The day was sweltering. They melted a little in their good clothes, but Roz stood an extra second or two after the provost on stage invited everyone to sit, scanning for Ella among the undergraduate seats.

There were to be several orations. Ella had told Quinn to expect them. She had entered a contest to deliver one herself, hoping to use ASL to present it, but the faculty who made the decision had instead gone with a wire-haired political science major who delivered a harangue about Harvard's global leadership while a pair of ASL interpreters worked behind him. A young woman wearing graduate robes approached the podium after the undergraduate speech and gave an address in Latin.

Roz removed her phone from her purse and checked her email while Quinn tried to make out the woman's words from the fragments of Latin she knew. Probably less than one hundred people in the crowd of thousands understood what was being said, and those few laughed or applauded at various intervals, sending echoes through the respectfully quiet crowd. Quinn leaned in: something was familiar about the strange speech of the woman on the stage, drawing her to listen without the need to understand. She was close enough to see the orator's face. So much of what the woman was saying expressed itself in the negative space beyond the words. A current of feeling ran through Quinn. She felt pulled into the timelessness of communication, the thread that ran between the past and the present, individual to individual.

When it was all over, the president of Harvard asked the undergraduates to stand in groups to bestow upon them the degrees of bachelor of arts and bachelor of science. There was a tremendous round of applause when he finished, and the sky filled with their mortarboards.

Roz and Quinn waited until the crowd thinned, then hobbled to Roz's blissfully air-conditioned car, Roz removing her stilettos as soon as they reached it. They couldn't move in the traffic of the square, so they waited quietly in the back of their dark car. Roz texted Ella, and a few minutes later, someone knocked on the window. Ella hopped into the back seat, nearly into Quinn's lap. She had unzipped her robe, and it billowed around her like a cape. She kissed Roz on the cheek and put her arms around her.

Ella SimCommed, "What do you think, Mommy?"[155]

She brought so much freshness and excitement into the vehicle, Roz was stunned into silence.

Quinn signed, "Congratulations! Awesome! You worked like mad!"[156]

Roz slapped her hand down.

"Do it in English."

Before she could repeat herself, Ella kissed Quinn on the cheek and breathlessly signed that she had to go. Her house ceremony was due to begin any minute, and she had to get down the hill. She promised to find them again afterward. After she left, Roz asked their driver to take them the short distance to the lawn behind Winthrop House. When she was free of the car, Roz posed for photographs with family members of the other graduates.

Eliza texted Quinn, and they found each other using the big crowd around Roz as a guidepost. Eliza introduced Quinn to Chas, who supported Viv with his arm. Paul, Kimmie, and J.P. hung back. Ginger was there, looking very nervous, unsure if Roz was upset due to her presence.

Paul signed, "Unbelievable!"[157] in Quinn's direction, over Kimmie's head.

He was beaming broader than Quinn had ever seen.

They took seats beside each other in the small group of seats on the lawn. A much smaller group of people had assembled after the big production in the Yard. Paul showed Quinn an ASL-to-English app on his phone while they waited for the second ceremony to start. All Paul had to do was sign into the app, then the English appeared in text on the screen, and when he changed a few of the settings, Siri translated his ASL out loud.*

"Cool, right?"[158]

Quinn nodded in appreciation.

The new technologies for the Deaf community really were amazing. She nudged Roz with her elbow and tried to interest her in the innovation, but now that she was sitting, Roz was holding herself aloof from the rest of the group. She fixed her gaze on the podium in front of them. A few of the speakers were on stage, preparing to begin. J.P. scooted closer to the edge of his chair so that he could see over the woman with a hat in front of him. Kimmie fiddled with the telephoto lens of an expensive-looking camera she got last Christmas. A dean tested the microphone on stage and finally introduced himself and the other officials in the seats behind them. The president of Winthrop House gave a short address. In a surprise to them all, he began describing Ella's childhood—her signing parents and her famous mother. At first, Quinn mistook the little speech as Harvard congratulating itself for accepting a poor deaf student, but when he finished his story, he invited Ella to the stage.

Ella approached the podium and paused for several seconds.

She gave off a kind of light.

She began to sign, an interpreter providing the spoken English, as she introduced a poem she would recite written by her namesake, Ella Mae Lentz, entitled "Eye Music." As she began the actual poem, no interpreter spoke the words she was signing or explained in English what the poem meant. Quinn could see that, as with the Latin oration, many people were confused by what she was doing, but her delivery did not make them restless in the same way the Latin address had. The

* A hypothetical technology utilizing visual artificial intelligence that is hoped to be a reality in the future.

locket Roz had given Ella when she was a baby swung on her neck, glinting in the sunshine. When she finished the poem, she paused again and looked out over the crowd. She made the I-Love-You sign and laid her hand over the locket. She turned her hand toward Roz and her family in the audience and made the sign a second time.

Paul spoke out loud, causing people to stare at him and his skin to flush.

"I love you."

Roz may or may not have understood what Ella was signing, but Quinn could see tears in her friend's eyes. Maybe sometimes it doesn't matter what language you use to convey the words. Of ultimate importance as you gather on a May afternoon to celebrate a new chapter of a life is that the spirit of the truth conveyed will somehow take root in your heart and mind. For after all, the signs of our lives are everywhere if we just open our eyes to look for them.*

* Bauman, *Open Your Eyes: Deaf Studies Talking.*

Authors' Note
The "Arts" to Engage Deep Learning

Why would we choose to employ a fictionalized story blended with research, theory, and historical people and events? We desired an artful way to inspire readers to learn information through a classic, enduring story. Students studying ASL and the Deaf community need to learn a lot of important concepts in a short period of time. We hope this book will reinforce content learned in other classes as well as present new information in an interesting and impactful way.

Dr. Eliot Eisner, a scholar who discussed the arts and education said,

> The arts celebrate multiple perspectives. One of their large lessons is that there are many ways to see and interpret the world....Art is the literacy of the heart.

The book portrays multiple characters' Deaf-World perspectives: deaf people, culturally Deaf people, hearing people who sign, hearing people with no sign language experience, uninitiated hearing people (who may have never met a deaf person or thought about the Deaf community), and characters who appeared for other reasons. We hope you were able to discern different worldviews in the variety of characters you met in the book.

More than anything else, we want to show students and readers a close look at the heart and soul of an American family. This narrative textbook, using arts-based strategies, allows readers to live in the pages of a book with some issues seen in today's Deaf-World. We are glad you joined us on this literary sojourn of the heart.

Never stop looking for signs, and always continue your journey of learning!

Stefanie Amiruzzaman
Patricia Bettis-Eddie
Marsha Moore
Leah Subak
May 2022

Bibliography

Acutrans19. "How to Ensure Accurate Sign Language (ASL) Interpretation." Acutrans.com. January 21, 2020. https://acutrans.com/accurate-asl-sign-language-interpretation.

AG Bell Association. "Cochlear Implants in Children." Accessed April 11, 2022. https://www.agbell.org/Media/Cochlear-Implants-in-Children.

American Sign Language Teachers Association. "Definition of ASL Glossing." Accessed April 20, 2022. https://www.aslta.org/gloss/.

Armstrong, David F., and Michael A. Karchmer. "William C. Stokoe and the Study of Signed Languages." *Sign Language Studies* 9, no. 4, 2009: 389–97. http://www.jstor.org/stable/26190588.

ASHA. "Cochlear Implants." Technical report. March 2003. https://www.asha.org/policy/tr2004-00041/.

ASHA. "Degree of Hearing Loss." Accessed April 20, 2022. https://www.asha.org/public/hearing/degree-of-hearing-loss/.

ASL University/Lifeprint. "INTERESTING." Accessed April 21, 2022. https://lifeprint.com/asl101/pages-signs/i/interesting.htm.

Bahan, Ben. "The Whole Picture: Why Academic ASL Exposure Matters to Sign Language Interpreters." Street Leverage. July 20, 2016. https://streetleverage.com/live_presentations/

whole-picture-academic-asl-exposure-matters-sign-language-interpreters/.

Bahan, Ben, H-Dirksen Bauman, and Facundo Montenegro, directors. *Audism Unveiled.* Dawn Sign Press, 2008. DVD. https://www.dawnsign.com/products/details/audism-unveiled.

Bailes, Cynthia Neese, Carol J. Erting, Lynne C. Erting, and Carlene Thumann-Prezioso. "Language and Literacy Acquisition through Parental Mediation in American Sign Language." *Sign Language Studies* 9, no. 4, 2009: 417–456. https://doi.org/10.1353/sls.0.0022.

Bauman, H-Dirksen L. "Audism: Exploring the Metaphysics of Oppression." *Journal of Deaf Studies and Deaf Education*, vol. 9, issue 2, April 2004, 239–246.

Bauman, H-Dirksen L., ed. *Open Your Eyes: Deaf Studies Talking*. Minneapolis, MN: University of Minnesota Press, 2008.

Bauman, H-Dirksen L., and Joseph Murray, eds. *Deaf Gain: Raising the Stakes for Human Diversity.* Minneapolis: University of Minnesota Press, 2014.

CDC. "Conceptually Accurate Signed English (CASE)." CDC website. June 8, 2020. https://www.cdc.gov/ncbddd/hearingloss/parentsguide/building/case.html.

Dallas Hearing Foundation. "Facts." Accessed April 20, 2022. http://dallashearingfoundation.org/facts/.

DiMarco, Nyle, and Bobby Siebert. " 'Baby hears for the first time' videos aren't inspiration, they hide the reality of deaf lives." LEAD-K Massachusetts. January 28, 2019. http://lead-k.massdeaf.org/2019/02/01/

baby-hears-for-the-first-time-videos-arent-inspirational-they-hide-the-reality-of-deaf-lives/.

Disability Visibility Project. "Stella Young, Inspiration Porn, and the Objectification of Disabled People." October 16, 2014. https://disabilityvisibilityproject.com/2014/10/16/stella-young-inspiration-porn-and-the-objectification-of-disabled-people/.

FDA. "Benefits and Risks of Cochlear Implants." Updated February 9, 2021. https://www.fda.gov/medical-devices/cochlear-implants/benefits-and-risks-cochlear-implants.

Gallaudet University website. Accessed April 13, 2022. https://www.gallaudet.edu/.

Gallaudet University. "Visionary leader - July 2014." Accessed April 22, 2022. https://www.gallaudet.edu/about/history-and-traditions/george-veditz/.

Groce, Nora Ellen. *Everyone Here Spoke Sign Language: Hereditary Deafness on Martha's Vineyard.* Cambridge, MA: Harvard University Press, 1985.

Hall, Wyatte C. "What you don't know can hurt you: The risk of language deprivation by impairing sign language development in deaf children." *Maternal and child health journal* 21, no. 5. 2017: 961–965. https://doi.org/10.1007/s10995-017-2287-y.

Humphries, Tom, Poorna Kushalnagar, Gaurav Mathur, Donna Jo Napoli, Carol Padden, Christian Rathmann, and Scott Smith. "Bilingualism: A Pearl to Overcome Certain Perils of Cochlear Implants." 2014. https://www.ncbi.nlm.nih.gov/pmc/articles/PMC4237221/.

Johnson, Robert, Carol Erting, and Scott Liddell. "Unlocking the Curriculum: Principles for Achieving Access in Deaf

Education. Working paper 89-3." Gallaudet Research Institute. January 1989. https://files.eric.ed.gov/fulltext/ED316978.pdf.

Kelleher, Ann. "Heritage Briefs. Who is a heritage language learner?" Center for Applied Linguistics. 2010. https://www.cal.org/heritage/pdfs/Who-is-a-Heritage-Language-Learner.pdf.

Lane, Harlan. "Do Deaf People Have a Disability?" *Sign Language Studies* 2, No. 4, 2002: 356–379. https://doi.org/10.1353/sls.2002.0019.

Lane, Harlan. *The Mask of Benevolence: Disabling the Deaf Community*. New York: Random House, 1992.

Lane, Harlan, Richard C. Pillard, and Ulf Hedberg. *The People of the Eye: Deaf Ethnicity and Ancestry.* New York: Oxford University Press, 2010.

Lapiak, Jolanta. "Simultaneous communication to use or to avoid." Handspeak.com. Accessed April 20, 2022. https://www.handspeak.com/learn/index.php?id=353.

LEAD-K. "What is Language Deprivation?" December 20, 2016. http://www.lead-k.org/posts/what-is-language-deprivation/.

Leigh, Irene W., Jean F. Andrews, and Raychelle L. Harris. *Deaf Culture: Exploring Deaf Communities in the United States.* San Diego: Plural Publishing, 2018.

Madsen, Willard J. "You Have to be Deaf to Understand." Dee Cee Eyes. 1971. Accessed April 13, 2022. Aquinas College website. https://www.aquinas.edu/sites/default/files/DCPresentationYouHaveToBeDeafToUnderstand.pdf.

Medline Plus. "Cochlear implant." Updated April 1, 2022. https://medlineplus.gov/ency/article/007203.htm.

Mindess, Anna, Thomas K. Holcomb, Daniel Langholtz, and Priscilla Moyers. *Reading Between the Signs: Intercultural Communication for Sign Language Interpreters*, 2nd ed. Boston: Intercultural Press, 2006.

Mitchell, Ross E., Travas A. Young, Bellamie Bachleda, and Michael A. Karchmer. "How Many People Use ASL in the United States? Why Estimates Need Updating." Gallaudet Research Institute. Gallaudet University. https://www.gallaudet.edu/documents/Research-Support-and-International-Affairs/ASL_Users.pdf.

National Association of the Deaf (NAD). "About Us." Accessed April 20, 2022. https://www.nad.org/about-us/.

NAD. "American Sign Language." Accessed April 20, 2022. https://www.nad.org/resources/american-sign-language/.

NAD. "Assistive Listening Systems and Devices." Accessed April 20, 2022. https://www.nad.org/resources/technology/assistive-listening/assistive-listening-systems-and-devices/.

NAD. "Early Intervention Services." Accessed April 20, 2022. https://www.nad.org/resources/early-intervention-for-infants-and-toddlers/information-for-parents/early-intervention-services/.

NAD. "NAD History." Accessed April 20, 2022. https://www.nad.org/about-us/nad-history/.

Newman, Aaron J. "Language Development in Deaf Children: Sign Language and Cochlear Implants." February 23, 2017. https://www.ncilab.ca/documents/Newman_DeafnessLangDevpt_preprint.pdf.

Oyez. "Board of Education of Hendrick Hudson Central School District, Westchester County v. Rowley." 1982. https://www.oyez.org/.

Padden, Carol A., and Tom L. Humphries. *Inside Deaf Culture*. Cambridge, MA: Harvard University Press, 2005.

Pro-Tactile: The DeafBlind Way. Video blog. March 2016. http://www.protactile.org/.

RID. "Supporting Quality in Interpretation." January 30, 2021. https://rid.org/supporting-quality-in-interpretation/.

Seladi-Schulman, Jill. "How People Who Are Deaf Learn to Talk." Healthline. April 2, 2020. https://www.healthline.com/health/can-deaf-people-talk.

SKI-HI. "Stories: SKI-HI Deaf Mentor; Parents, Deaf Mentors, Programs, Professionals." January 21, 2022. https://ski-hi.mystrikingly.com/blog/stories-ski-hi-deaf-mentor.

SKI-HI. "What Is a Deaf Mentor?" Accessed April 6, 2022. https://deaf-mentor.skihi.org/.

Sorenson. "About Us." Accessed April 20, 2022. https://www.sorenson.com/.

Sparkbot. "NERDA." Urban Dictionary. April 18, 2011. https://www.urbandictionary.com/define.php?term=NERDA.

Subak, Leah. "Becoming HEARING: A qualitative study of expert interpreter Deaf-World cultural competence." Unpublished dissertation. Last modified 2014.

Traynor, Robert. "Breaking the Legal Sound Barrier." Hearing Health Matters. July 31, 2019. https://

hearinghealthmatters.org/hearinginternational/2019/breaking-the-legal-sound-barrier/.

University of Texas at Austin, The. "Deaf & Hard of Hearing." Accessed April 13, 2022. https://diversity.utexas.edu/disability/deaf-and-hard-of-hearing/.

U.S. Equal Employment Opportunity Commission. "Religious Discrimination." Accessed April 12, 2022. https://www.eeoc.gov/religious-discrimination.

Wikipedia.com. "Plausible deniability." Updated March 24, 2022. https://en.wikipedia.org/wiki/Plausible_deniability.

Winefield, Richard. *Never the Twain Shall Meet: Bell, Gallaudet, and the Communications Debate*. Washington, DC: Gallaudet University Press, 1987.

Appendix

Gloss #1

OH-I-SEE #YES, ns-PAUL MENTION/STORY PRO-2 (you). SELF-3 (Paul) [INJECT/ADD NAME WHAT] RhQ #DR fs-Stacker.

Glossing conventions used in this glossed translation.

x-x-x = Hyphens between individual glossed signs indicate that one lexical item (sign) is used

[ ] = to house a phrase

ns = name sign

fs = fingerspelled

= lexicalized fingerspelling

RhQ = rhetorical question

/ = sign has multiple meanings

, = pause

. = end of utterance/sentence

Pronouns used in glossing

Singular pronouns	First person – PRO 1 (I, me) Second person – PRO 2 (you) Third person – PRO 3 (he, she, it)
Plural pronouns	First person – PRO 1-pl (we) Second person – PRO 2-pl (you-all) Third person – PRO 3-pl (them)
Possessives Reflexive pronouns Specific nouns	Possessives – POSS (himself) Reflexive pronouns – SELF (themselves) Reflexive pronouns referring to specific people
Numeral incorporation	Various numbers of persons (two-of-us, three-of-us)

Gloss #2

TRUE++. UNDERSTAND++ STUDENTS PRO-3-pl (they) x-LOOK-AT-y (me), [NAME/CALL WHAT] RhQ ns-Charles (C hs forehead to chin).

Glossing conventions used in this glossed translation.

[ ] = to house a phrase
ns = name sign
, = pause in utterance
. = end of utterance/sentence
RhQ = rhetorical question
++ = repetition
(see Pronoun chart above)

Acknowledgements

First and foremost, we need to express our gratitude to project contributors: Cathy Alznauer, Jimmy Beldon Jr., Mrs. Vivian King Brown, Kathy Geething, Dr. Clara Jean Mosley Hall (Warm Heart), Lucas Hamilton, Dr. Randall Hogue, Tina J. Perry, and Carole Stacker. You provided in-depth information about multiple aspects of the plotlines, the CI debate, name signs for the characters, adoption, translations of ASL to English, cultural considerations, glossing, CODA issues, and discussions related to interpreting.

Along with our book contributors, there were many individuals who added to the creation of this project. There were multiple meetings with community members/stakeholders. We applaud the contributors' involvement, feedback, and expertise.

Jim Halischak, Charles "Chuck" Williams and Patricia Cangelosi-Williams, Elisabeth and Pauly Battista, Juliette Regnier, Debbie Hartman Giaimo, Carrie Morgan, Michael Reymann, and Anna Paulson—you provided invaluable feedback as the project was taking shape. Also, thank you to the following people who agreed to have their name appear in the book, bringing their persona/expertise to aid in making the book more authentic: Dr. M.J. Bienvenu, Dr. Laurene Simms, Marla Berkowitz, Sherry Bradley-Koo, James Paul Beldon, Ella Mae Lentz, and Ginger Noble. A huge thank you to two individuals with strong ties to Ohio: Writer Sally Domm of Charleston, SC, who guided our work early on—your advice was invaluable! And Amy Alznauer of Chicago, IL, another writer and friend who assisted the project with her expertise.

A huge thank you to the students who read the pilot book and their professors who guided them through it: Patricia Bettis-Eddie, Cuyahoga County Community College; Kathy Geething, Kent State University; and Kim Bass, the University of Akron. Our Zoom discussion sessions were fun and meaningful, and your feedback was priceless.

Special thanks to:

Professor Kim Bass's students: Emily Anstead, Charity Hoover, Lauren Lyle, Lydia Marek, Camryn Moore, Anthony Raineri, Frankie Srp, Tyerra Whitted, Mikaela Fridline, Nevaeh Kline, Ivana Shah, Callie Terrell, and Savanna Sisson.

Professor Bettis-Eddie's students: Brandon Childers, Micayla O'Keefe, Kenneth Darby, and Josiah Hull.

Professor Geething's students: Tiffany "Brook" Ballert, Kalea Brown, Jill Confreda, Amanda Fullen, Kate Giet, Kailee Griffith, Kailey Helton, Elias Hinkle, Shannon Lagrou, Ainsley MacGillivray, Lizzi Petrey, Kaleigh Pratt, Marissa Sell, Amber Stayer, Sydney VanHove, and Donna Wuerschmidt.

To those who read the book in its various iterations, we thank you for your patience as the book took form: Elisabeth Battista, Andrew Subak, Alex Subak, Paula Keener, Vivian King Brown, Dr. Clara Jean Mosley Hall, and Hollie Fry. Thank you, Ken Subak, for your technical support!

Special thanks to the following professionals. Our writing consultant, Jeanne Dutton—we could not have accomplished this project without you! You brought the story to life! Callie Walker of Proof Corrections by Callie—your contributions were invaluable to the final product! Patrick Douglas Campbell, owner of Hat Trick designs—you took our ideas for the cover and turned them into reality!

The project took a village, and we are so glad we had a deaf, Deaf, hard of hearing, hearing, CODA (child of deaf adult), GODA (grandchild of deaf adult), and SODA (sibling of deaf adult) village!

Bios

Co-Authors

Stefanie Amiruzzaman, PhD

Stefanie (she/her/hers), a white woman with long wavy brown hair, is outside on a bright day. She stands in front of a red brick wall. She smiles at the camera. She wears a blue top with a black jacket.

Stefanie Amiruzzaman, PhD, is an ASL/Deaf studies coordinator and an assistant professor in the Department of Languages and Cultures at West Chester University in eastern Pennsylvania. Dr. Amiruzzaman teaches American Sign Language courses. She holds a PhD in evaluation and measurement, an MEd in Deaf education, and a BA in American Sign Language, all from Kent State University, Ohio. Her previous experience includes teaching several undergraduate levels of ASL and Deaf culture courses at the University of Akron and Kent State University, both in Ohio. Also, Dr. Amiruzzaman taught both undergraduate and graduate level ASL courses at Ball State University, Indiana.

Patricia Bettis-Eddie, MEd

Patte (she/her/hers), an African American woman with long braided hair, is inside in front of evergreen wall decor. She wears two-toned glasses and has a slight smile as she looks to the left of the camera. She wears an off-white top.

Patricia "Patte" Bettis-Eddie, whose credentials include a BA in English and a master of education from Cleveland State

University, recognizes and appreciates the full worth of the Deaf and DeafBlind communities of Cleveland, Ohio. Patte owes much of her DeafBlind interest, training, and skills to her close friend Sherry Raymont, an LSW DeafBlind specialist at the Cleveland Sight Center, where Patte started interpreting in the summer of 1985.

She then began her first "real job" as an educational interpreter for the Beachwood City School District, where she was employed for thirty-one years and from where she retired in 2015.

Later, in 2017, she returned to the Sight Center to intern while also completing an internship at the Helen Keller National Center for DeafBlind Youths and Adults in Port Washington, New York, during the same year.

She is currently employed at Cuyahoga Community College in her second-year lectureship teaching American Sign Language. Patte obviously has no clue what the word "retire" means.

The Deaf and DeafBlind community, with their unique language and culture, continues to inspire and motivate her, as she has added non-contracted "alphabet" braille to her skill set and is determined to develop fluency in contracted "literary" braille.

Patte clearly lives by her quote: "Know what you know and know it well; likewise, know what you don't know and use humility to learn."

Marsha Moore, MA, CDM, ABD

Marsha (she/her/hers), a white woman with longer than shoulder-length light brown hair, is outside with flowers in the background. She smiles at the camera. She wears a black top and tan slacks.

Marsha Moore is a Central Ohio native who was born to two deaf parents. That was a considerable advantage because language acquisition utilizing oral and sign language and total immersion in the Deaf community started on day one. Moore attended AG Bell School for the Deaf for preschool and kindergarten. After that, she was mainstreamed from first grade until she graduated from Upper Arlington High School.

Moore graduated with her BA in business from Muskingum University. Accommodations for classes from first grade to her BA degree studies were only note-taking and tutoring. Moore studied at The Ohio State University, where interpreting services were offered, for an MA in public administration. This was an eye-opening experience where she realized gaps she had missed in class discussions. She graduated with a master's degree in public administration and is currently ABD in the doctorate of strategic leadership degree at Liberty University.

Moore is an adjunct professor at Columbus State Community College and teaches American Sign Language (ASL) and Deaf community and culture classes. She also coordinated social media initiatives for Deaf Services Center, a nonprofit organization for the Deaf, hard of hearing, and DeafBlind communities, and executed monthly electronic newsletters for the communities. Moore coordinated the Kids Connect Mentoring Program, where Deaf and hard of hearing youth ages seven to eighteen were connected with Deaf mentors during the COVID-19 pandemic.

Moore is a Certified Deaf Mentor. She has held offices in professional organizations, including Deaf Women of Ohio (DWO), and has chaired several conferences, including Ohio Association of the Deaf's Ohio DEAFair 2003 and 2005 and DWO's Regional Conference in 2019. She has presented at conferences locally and regionally on various topics, including Deaf culture, communication, and technology initiatives.

Moore resides in Dublin, Ohio, with her husband, John; their four CODA children, Jason, Sara, Megan, and Jack; and two Bernese mountain dogs, Popcorn and Salsa.

A fun fact: Moore was a member of the drill team and a majorette for her high school marching band. Her four children have also followed in her footsteps and marched for their high school band. Her oldest son, Jason, went on to become one of The Ohio State University Marching Band members and is now an alumnus. Moore mentioned this because most Deaf parents do not encourage their hearing or deaf children to participate in musical activities because they cannot hear them.

Leah Subak, PhD, CI & CT, IDI QA

Leah (she/her/hers), a white woman with shoulder-length brown and highlighted hair, is seated in front of greenery. She wears blue glasses and smiles at the camera. She also wears a gray top with a blue scarf.

Leah Subak appreciates the Deaf communities of Akron, Ohio, and Washington, DC, for sharing their language and culture, leading her to a lifetime of learning and joy! Subak is currently employed with Sorenson Communications. Previously, she was affiliated with Kent State University as a faculty member, staff interpreter, and interpreter coordinator. Credentials include: BA in speech/language pathology and audiology, MA from Gallaudet University, and PhD from Kent State University in curriculum and instruction.

Deaf and hard of hearing people were evident throughout her life. There were deaf children in the neighborhood where Subak grew up and at the local church. Deaf education classes for the Akron Public School District were housed in Goodyear Junior High School and East High School where

Subak attended. Working as a parks and recreation counselor in the summers, deaf children who lived in the neighborhood attended the summer program in a nearby city. Then, when she enrolled in college, during her first semester, she took an ASL class. A pilot class for CODA children of Deaf parents was offered at the University of Akron where Subak was able to practice her clinical competence and budding ASL skills. While in college, Subak watched a *60 Minutes* segment about Gallaudet University and vowed to go there. She moved to the Washington, DC, area; went to the campus; found a job; and worked for two years before going into graduate school. Subak believes the experience of being at Gallaudet was one of the richest cultural experiences possible.

Working as an interpreter was just becoming a viable career option. Subak took classes in the interpreting program at Gallaudet but ended up graduating with an MA in Deaf education. Interpreting was a more flexible career with children, and she pivoted to freelance interpreting in order to be available for her four young children, who are now adults.

Certifications held include: IC/TC, CI/CT, NAD, and EIPA. Subak has held offices in professional interpreting organizations, chaired various conferences, and presented at conferences locally, regionally, and nationally. She is a qualified administrator of the Intercultural Development Inventory. Subak along with her husband, Ken, are co-producers of a movie directed by Kent State Professor emeritus and documentary filmmaker Dave Smeltzer titled *I'm So Amazing*, about Angie Orlando, a writer who is DeafBlind. The film is slated to premiere summer of 2022.

Consulting Author

Jeanne "Jen" Dutton, MFA, ABD

Jeanne (she/her/hers), a white woman with shoulder-length brown hair and side-swept bangs, is outside on a bright day. She wears two-toned glasses and looks at the camera. She wears a rose-colored top with black neckline trim.

Jeanne "Jen" Dutton lives in Northeast Ohio with her husband and two children. She holds an MFA in fiction from the University of Alaska, Fairbanks, with a concentration in fiction. This fall she passed her qualifying exams to attain ABD status for a PhD in literacy, research, and social practice at Kent State University. Prior to returning to school, she served as assistant professor of writing and director of developmental writing at Hiram College. Her outside interests include dog walking, horseback riding, cross-country skiing, and yoga. In the mid-2010s she published two novels for teens under the pen name J. T. Dutton. She has contributed to multiple academic and fiction projects either as content editor, ghost writer, or co-author, but experienced special joy in developing this manuscript because of its embrace of the diverse issues of the Deaf community.

Book Contributors

Cathy Alznauer

Cathy (she/her/hers), a white woman with short brown and highlighted hair, is seated in a room with other people. She wears glasses and smiles at the camera. She wears a blue printed top with a black jacket.

Cathy Alznauer, formerly of Ohio, and who currently is residing in the Chicagoland area, grew up near Akron and attended Akron Public Schools with many other deaf friends. Throughout her life, she was involved in church activities, taught noncredit ASL classes, and owned a jewelry store for ten years in Ashland, Ohio, with her husband, which was a big challenge but also a great learning experience. Cathy was a Deaf mentor in several schools in Ashland, Mansfield, and then Columbus, Ohio. Cathy worked at the Alice Cogswell Center for Deaf infants and toddlers at the Ohio School for the Deaf. She then transferred to the elementary school at the Ohio School for the Deaf as a teacher's aide for approximately ten years. Cathy and Michael, her husband, then moved to Chicago to be near their son Mark and his family in 2014. Michael is still working as a self-employed jeweler for a family business in Evanston, Illinois. They are both active and involved in Deaf senior organizations and attend many Deaf workshops, where they still get together with great Deaf people in the Chicagoland area.

They have two hearing sons (CODAs): Dr. Mark Alznauer is an associate professor of philosophy at Northwestern University in Evanston, Illinois, and their daughter-in-law,

Amy, writes children's books and teaches mathematics at Northwestern University. Mark and Amy have two children, John and Meg. Their younger son, Tony Alznauer, works as a senior director at Digital Assistant Management in California, and their daughter-in-law, Kate, is an immigration attorney. Tony and Kate have three children: Rita and twin boys, Peter and Nick. All of the family members are very active. Mike and Cathy are enjoying their golden years, trying to relax and travel to various places.

Jimmy Beldon Jr., MA, CDI

Jimmy (he/him/his), a white man with short blonde hair and a goatee, is inside an auditorium with chairs and a screen behind him. He wears a gray shirt and smiles at the camera.

Jimmy Beldon, CDI, MA, has been a professional involved in the interpreting field on many levels. Beldon received his master's degree in Deaf education with an ASL specialty from Western Maryland College. He taught at St. Catherine University in Minnesota and has extensive experience providing training, workshops, and lectures. Beldon served on the National Conference of Interpreter Trainers (CIT) board as vice president as well as the Registry of Interpreters for the Deaf (RID) as vice president. He is co-owner of Keystone Interpreting Solutions, an interpreter referral business in multiple locations.

Mrs. Vivian King Brown

Viv (she/her/hers), an African American woman with short salt-and-pepper hair, is outside with greenery behind her. She is smiling as she looks to the left of the camera. She wears a white top and a black, gray, and silver pendant necklace.

Mrs. Vivian King Brown lives in Twinsburg, Ohio, and is the first lady emeritus of the Mount Gillion Missionary Baptist Church. She is the mother of two and matriarchal mentor to many. Viv has been widowed for over ten years, since she lost her beloved husband, Reverend Freddie Lee Brown in 2011. Reverend and Mrs. Brown led the Mount Gillion Missionary Baptist Church in Cleveland, Ohio, for thirty-seven years as senior pastor and first lady.

Viv drives a limousine for the House of Peace Funeral Home in Cleveland, Ohio. She continues to influence many by sharing her testimony by service to others through her work; volunteering with the group, Transparent Women affiliated with the Temple of Praise Baptist Church in Cleveland, Ohio; and providing guidance to the many people in her circle. The character of Vivian King Brown, the shero of the book, is based on Mrs. Brown and her servant's heart, spirit, and legacy of love toward others.

Kathy Geething CI & CT, MA

Kathy (she/her/hers), a white woman with short blonde and highlighted hair, is inside with a gray background behind her. She wears black-rimmed glasses and smiles at the camera. She also wears a brightly colored flowered top with a black jacket.

Kathy Geething, has worked as an ASL/English interpreter for twenty-five years, but still feels like a novice learner beginning a bicultural bilingual journey. One of the things she appreciates most about her connection to Deaf culture and community is that it is like living in a kaleidoscope where the transforming and evolving view never ceases to fascinate. Her interpreting degree is from the University of Akron under the tutelage of amazing pioneers in the field of interpreter education: Dr. Karen Turner, Mr. John Bradley, and the late Mrs. Jackie Lawless. They equipped scores of highly skilled interpreters without the benefit of technology or professionally developed curriculum. Their methodology was passion for deaf people and the interpreting field. Thank you! Geething's master's degree is from Kent State University in teaching English as a second language. The knowledge gained about second language acquisition influenced much of her teaching philosophy. She was an ASL teacher at Kent State University before becoming an instructor and practicum coordinator in the ASL/English Interpreting Program at Kent State University for fifteen years. She is now retired from teaching but continues to interpret as an employee of Sorenson Communications. One of the greatest honors of her life has been the privilege of learning from and working alongside members of the Deaf community. She is indebted to them for their patience, support, and trust.

Clara Jean Mosley Hall, PhD (Warm Heart)

Jeanie (she/her/hers), a Black and Indigenous woman with long dark-brown hair and bangs, has a light-blue background behind her. She wears hoop earrings and smiles at the camera. She also wears a white blazer.

Dr. Hall is a professor at Cuyahoga Community College in the Department of American Sign Language. She holds a

BA in business from Delaware State University, an MEd in Deaf education from McDaniel College (formerly known as Western Maryland College), and a PhD from Cleveland State University in urban education.

Dr. Hall has taught American Sign Language and other courses in deafness and interpreting for more than forty years. Her work has been recognized by the Ohio State Senate for her outstanding contribution of service, by Phi Delta Kappa as a Distinguished Educator, by Rochester Institute of Technology's (RIT) Distinguished Teacher Recognition Program, by Cuyahoga Community College as a recipient of the Ralph M. Besse Distinguished Teaching Award, by the League for Innovation in the Community College through receiving the John and Suanne Roueche Excellence Award, and by Who's Who in Black Cleveland. She has published work examining the construct of racelessness among African American Deaf adolescents in the *American Annals of the Deaf.*

Dr. Hall has also written a memoir entitled *Paris in America: A Deaf Nanticoke Shoemaker and His Daughter* published by Gallaudet University Press. It is the story of being raised by her Deaf Native Nanticoke father, a shoemaker, as a single parent in the 1950s in Dover, Delaware. The book is currently being made into a feature-length film by CJ Jones, producer, director, and actor, at Sign World Media.

Dr. Hall has traveled nationally and internationally, speaking and observing various programs and schools for Deaf children and Deaf adults. She established the J. Paris Mosley Scholarship Foundation Fund in the name of her father with the Cleveland Foundation to provide financial support for the higher education of Deaf and hard of hearing students who use some form of sign language to communicate. Being the only child of Deaf parents, she has seen firsthand how obstacles for Deaf people can become opportunities.

Dr. Clara Jean Mosley Hall is married to Dr. Howard Ralph Hall III. They have two outstanding daughters, Karelle Ayita Hall and Ilea Elizabeth Mosley Hall Speight; an amazing son-in-law, Bryan Speight; and a lovely grand-daughter, Ariyah Speight.

Lucas Hamilton, MA, EIPA 4.5

Lucas (he/him/his), a man of color with a black beard and shaved head, is seated inside in front of a multi-designed wall with an oak and a blue diamond pattern. He wears dark-rimmed glasses and smiles at the camera. He also wears a gray shirt and has his arms crossed.

Lucas Hamilton holds the Deaf community near and dear to his heart. He is a special member of the community known as a GODA, grandchild of a deaf adult. Both of his grandparents were Deaf and members of the Akron Deaf community. Lucas attended Kent State University and graduated with his BSE in ASL/English interpreting in 2016. He worked in educational, community, and post-secondary settings for four years before applying to Gallaudet University. He is currently working at Sorenson Communications in Baltimore, Maryland. As the book was going to print, he graduated with a master's degree in linguistics from Gallaudet University in the Spring of 2022.

Randall Hogue, PhD

Randall (he/him/his), a white man with short brown hair, is outside on a bright day with a landscape behind him. He wears a navy-blue polo shirt and smiles at the camera.

Randall Hogue has always been fascinated by languages. He began learning ASL during his teenage years and is now shocked that he's been working as an interpreter for forty years. He graduated with his undergraduate degree in psychology and linguistics from Youngstown State University and went on to earn a master's and PhD in linguistics from Gallaudet University. During his time at Gallaudet, he served as a graduate assistant in the English Department and Linguistics Department. In addition to teaching linguistics courses for Gallaudet, Hogue has taught for a number of colleges and universities, including the University of Mary Washington; the University of Nebraska, Lincoln; and Georgetown University among others. Most recently, he held the position of ASL program coordinator for Kent State University. He has presented at local, regional, national, and international conferences.

Tina J. Perry, MEd, CI & CT, NAD 5, CODA

Tina (she/her/hers), a white woman with chin-length chestnut and highlighted hair, is inside a house. She wears black-rimmed glasses and smiles at the camera. She also wears visible earrings and a dark gray top.

Tina Perry hails from Columbus, Ohio, and upon her recent retirement has now found her new home in Tennessee. She is currently employed with Sorenson Communications. Perry is also a professor emeritus at Columbus State Community College and still teaches in the Interpreting Education Program when needed. Tina's parents were both deaf and from Ohio and used ASL to communicate. She is married and has five children and five grandchildren. Perry is currently developing her podcast page, which includes interviews of interpreters of all different walks. In her spare time, she enjoys working, walking her dogs, and fishing with her husband.

Carole Stacker, AAS, MA, MEd

Carole (she/her/hers), an African American woman with chin-length red hair, is inside, seated at a desk in her office. She wears a red, gray, and white top and smiles at the camera. She also wears silver hoop earrings and a watch on her wrist that sits on top of papers on her desk.

Carole Stacker was born and raised in Cleveland, Ohio. Carole received her AAS at the University of Akron where she was introduced to the Deaf community. After graduating, she was hired in Cleveland Metropolitan Schools as an interpreter for twelve years. Carole attended and graduated from Kent State University where she received an MA in rehabilitation counseling and an MEd in school counseling. Carole taught ASL at Kent State and interned with BVR, where she continued to work with the Deaf community. Carole currently resides in Indianapolis, Indiana, where she works as a school counselor with Indianapolis Public Schools.